LOST IN HIS EYES

LOST IN HIS EYES

Andrew Neiderman

This first world hardcover edition published 2015
in Great Britain and the USA by
SEVERN HOUSE PUBLISHERS LTD of
19 Cedar Road, Sutton, Surrey, England, SM2 5DA.
Trade paperback edition first published 2016
in Great Britain and the USA by
SEVERN HOUSE PUBLISHERS LTD.

British Library Cataloguing in Publication Data

Neiderman, Andrew author.
   Lost in his eyes.
   1. Housewives–California–Fiction. 2. Adultery–
   Fiction. 3. Romantic suspense novels.
   I. Title
   813.5'4-dc23

ISBN-13: 978-0-7278-8542-5 (cased)
ISBN-13: 978-1-84751-644-2 (trade paper)
ISBN-13: 978-1-78010-701-1 (e-book)

To my wife, Diane
'Here's looking at you, kid.'

This is a work of fiction. Names, characters, places and incidents
are either the product of the author's imagination or are used fictitiously.
Except where actual historical events and characters are being described
for the storyline of this novel, all situations in this publication are
fictitious and any resemblance to actual persons, living or dead,
business establishments, events or locales is purely coincidental.

All Severn House titles are printed on acid-free paper.

Severn House Publishers support the Forest Stewardship Council™ [FSC™],
the leading international forest certification organisation.
All our titles that are printed on FSC certified paper carry the FSC logo.

Typeset by Palimpsest Book Production Ltd.,
Falkirk, Stirlingshire, Scotland.
Printed and bound in Great Britain by
TJ International, Padstow, Cornwall.

PROLOGUE

I'm in a deeper silence than I have ever been. Unlike the silence that usually accompanies traditional meditation, I don't hear the monotonous beating of my heart or the soft sound of my own breathing. Often, nearly a half-hour or so will pass, during which I will not have a single thought, envision a single memory or experience a single daydream.

It's a realization that I resisted at first because I didn't want to become conscious of it. I put up a wall woven out of rationalizations, like so many of my girlfriends who wrap blankets of excuses for their unhappiness around themselves to keep from falling into a well of depression. In fact, I have reached the place where I don't have any ambition to find ways to identify the problem and explain it away. I won't see a therapist, a psychologist or psychiatrist, and definitely won't see my doctor about it.

However, I am aware that it spells loneliness with a capital L and reminds me I am shrinking in a corner. Like someone caught in a drug-induced hallucination, who imagines herself only inches tall, I'm often afraid that I might eventually be stepped on, and even that would go unnoticed. I'm not dying as much as I'm drifting out of worldly existence. Eventually, I'll be like a black hole in space, close to invisible.

Our sixteen-year-old daughter, Kelly, is in her room upstairs. Her walls are covered with movie and rock singer posters that look as if they were splashed up there in a hurricane full of the icons teenage girls worship. I think she'd cover the windows with them if I didn't stop her. She wears earphones that are plugged into her iPod so she can listen to music while she's texting a cadre of electronic friends, gossiping in letter combinations that reduce whole sentences to a few symbols on her smartphone. It's the abbreviation of life, emotions and relationships. When I watch her doing it, I think of the radio operator on the *Titanic* sending out an SOS. Her face expresses that sort of desperation. There are not enough lifeboats.

We can go days without saying ten complete sentences to each other.

Right now, my husband, Ronnie, is in his home office on his computer, forwarding political diatribes and jokes to his ditto compatriots who watch the same television talk shows and listen to the same radio talk show hosts parroting each other in a wide echo chamber. Although I can't imagine why, it invigorates him. When he finally does come up for air, he has his chest out and a broad butter smile smeared over his face. He looks as if he has accomplished something important, as if he knows something the rest of the world doesn't know.

Ronnie can project that sort of self-confidence easily. He's six feet two, broad-shouldered, with blue eyes that can blaze like the blue light of a Bunsen burner when he's excited about something. It was what first caught my attention and held it during those days when I was lighting the wicks on my explosive emotions with the frenzy of someone terrified her youth would be full of duds.

Ronnie rants with the kind of regularity that someone constantly threatened by thought constipation would cherish. Any news event can set off a spontaneous speech. He stores his op-ed pages in the back of his mind with the determination of a squirrel storing acorns. I just listen and nod and never offer up a counter-argument. But don't misunderstand me. I take my citizenship seriously. I read and always vote. However, lately I envy women in the late nineteenth and early twentieth centuries who left all the political bickering to men whose cigar smoke billowed out of their mouths like the puffs around Civil War cannons. They left their exclusive men's clubs strutting like victorious generals, their lips stained with tobacco and the flavor of cognac, all thinking they were Masters of the Universe.

Internet chat rooms have become the twenty-first century's men's clubs. Technology democratized them. Anyone can bluster on Wi-Fi. He doesn't have to be some powerful attorney or CEO of some corporation. Sanitation workers circle the electric fire, chanting their slogans and sound bites alongside bank executives. Alone in an office or a den, the new Masters of the Universe can be in rooms that are just as stuffy and create their own clouds of pipe, cigar or cigarette smoke. Ronnie will smoke a cigar occasionally, but, thankfully, no cigarettes. He still thinks seriously about his health, or at least gives it the required lip service, especially because he's in the commercial insurance business and feels required to recite statistics for all insurance enterprises, including health and life.

Tonight, the air has a fresh chill suggesting that winter might be introducing himself to our affluent Orange County California community. We don't have definitive seasons. They're all far more subtle. There has rarely been snow, and if it does get cold enough for ice, it's only a temporary phenomenon. Also, right in the middle of January or February there could be unusually warm days. Legal, card-carrying American immigrants from north-eastern and north-western states laugh at the very idea of it being winter with seventy- and occasionally eighty-degree temperatures. A Santa ringing a bell on Christmas looks far less authentic to children here who are on the brink of losing childhood fantasies at a much younger age than children in other parts of the country. It's as if the entire state has turned into Disneyland, and every child knows it and accepts it because they have all been force-fed cartoons so long that they believe they live on a movie set.

Mommy or Daddy can flip a switch and make it stop raining.

Actually, I socialize with friends who act as if they live within a magical bubble. To a great extent, there's some truth to that. Unlike most of America, we enjoy the best possible medical and dental care. Specialists of all kinds are peppered over the face of our world like a bad case of acne. We shop in immaculate supermarkets and exclusive boutiques where unattractive people are practically banned from becoming service personnel. If he wanted to live as comfortably and as safely as possible in America, Benjamin Braddock should have listened to that one word of advice he was given at his college graduation party: 'Plastics.' That's what this affluent world is to me: plastic.

But like him, I'm beginning to suffer from the ennui of near perfection. I long to be threatened, as illogical and maddening as that might sound. There are parts of me that haven't been challenged for years and consequently have become dull. There are no edges, no cliffs and no deeply threatening potholes on the monotonous road I travel daily.

My home has become a space station. Neither my husband nor my daughter seems to notice that lately, when I leave it, I come rushing back as if I am running low on oxygen out there. Sometimes, I literally gasp when I step back inside and close the door behind me. It takes a while for my heart to stop racing and my palms to stop sweating. My urge to explore is dwindling. It's barely a spark.

However, eventually, especially tonight, the silence in my house gets too deep for me. Television is no companion yet. I'm not old enough to suckle on its glow and bask in someone else's evocative romantic adventures or their jocular family turmoil devoid of any serious consequences. Even nature in public television shows looks contrived, too well organized. I don't have the patience brought on by crippling arthritis or familial desertion. I refuse to turn my house prematurely into an adult residence, even if it means spending so much time alone in a world of silence conversing with myself.

Every clock in the house looks like a spy, ticking and waiting for me to do something or say something unusual so it can sound its alarm. I have the urge to put black sheets over all of them, cover their faces and live in a world without hours and minutes, but I don't do anything like that. I don't need to. I'm an expert in avoiding discovery. I can blend into the puppet world of everyday life so well that I wonder why I haven't been recruited by the CIA.

When the feeling at the base of my stomach grows too irritating, I rise out of my pool of silence with the energy of a killer whale feasting on air. I scoop my ankle-length dark blue sweater coat off the coat hook in the entryway of our five-thousand-square-foot Normandy-style house, with its breathtaking views of mountains and city lights, and then turn and hurry down the dark oak hallway to Ronnie's office doorway.

His shoulders are shaking as if he's in a bumpy old car going over a dirt road. Sometimes, his office is so stuffy that it smells like a school locker room, so I don't actually enter it. He's chuckling over a graphic picture of one of the candidates he opposes locked in a cage with thick bars woven with metal thorns and a floor covered in smiling snakes, pythons ready to crush and swallow up the opposition. He has an opened bottle of beer on the desk. I envision it to be some adult baby bottle with an orange nipple and an orange areola. Men never stop breastfeeding.

'I'm going shopping,' I announce. I wear my sweater coat so he can visually understand what I'm saying as well. He never hears me the first time, so I repeat and he turns around.

'What?'

'I'm going grocery shopping. It's the best time of day to do it. It's not crowded and the shelves have been restocked for the morning.'

'Oh,' he says, as if it has just occurred to him that someone actually brings in the food we eat daily and that someone is me.

There is always the obligatory, 'Do you want help?'

'No, I'm fine. We don't need that much,' I tell him.

He nods and smiles like a little boy who has been given permission to stay out longer and play. He turns right back to the computer and says, 'You gotta see this.'

I don't reply. I'm walking quickly now, retreating through the kitchen and into the garage like some prisoner in a maximum security institution who just realized there was a way out, moving through the convoluted maze to the exit. I get into my late-model black 535 BMW, press the button to open the garage door and press the button to start the engine. Someday, I think, everything in our lives will be reduced to pressing a button, even for women giving birth. Many of my girlfriends have buttons on their bodies only people like me can see. Their husbands, even their children, know which button to press and when. I pause after taking a shower lately and study myself in the full-length bedroom mirror to be certain that I don't have those buttons. Not yet. But I'm not fooling myself. I know they are coming any day now.

There were times when I was tempted to start the engine and not press the other button to open the garage door, but, fortunately, those urges lasted only a few seconds. Buttons are so difficult to ignore, which is why I worry about presidents, premiers, dictators and the like who have their forefingers close to the nuclear launch button.

I back out and close the garage door, leaving my daughter and my husband in their private caves, and drive off, too fast at first and then slower.

Suddenly, like that killer whale rising out of the sea, I can breathe. The radio goes on automatically. It's tuned to an NPR station because the voices are so soothing. Most of the time, I don't even know what's being said. The melodic rhythm of calm talk drifts through me like wave after wave of some cool body lotion, relaxing me. Ronnie hates this station. He says it puts him to sleep. He enjoys going to sleep at night, but he hates taking naps. Either he doesn't want to miss anything or he's afraid he might never wake up. Once I told him that he thinks like Shakespeare, who called sleep 'Death's second self.' He laughed quickly to wash the terror out of his eyes, and said, 'You and your damn liberal arts education.'

Women are supposedly more vulnerable and weaker, but as far as I can tell, men get more frightened at the mere reference to death. If anyone really thinks about it, he or she would readily admit that more young boys are sissies than young girls. It's no comfort for me to know that. To me, it means that, in the end, more responsibility will fall on my shoulders than on Ronnie's. Mothers are always more responsible for their children than fathers, and most end up being more responsible for their own and their husband's parents.

The supermarket is less crowded this time of night. There are so many available parking spaces that, for a moment, I have trouble deciding which one to choose. Choice can be agony. Few would admit it, but I know they're relieved when they see they have only one or two possibilities. Too much freedom can nourish anxiety. You can't help but worry that you'll make a mistake. I watch people when they have choice, especially with parking spots. They keep looking back and wondering if they should have taken this one or that one because it's closer or wider and would provide less chance for their car doors getting nicked. You could wake up in the middle of the night from an anxiety attack over how close you had come to a dent because you had been too lazy to park twenty more feet from the supermarket's entrance.

When I enter the supermarket, I glanced about cautiously, choosing my aisles strategically. I hate to meet women I know in the supermarket this late, especially the wives of husbands who work with Ronnie in the commercial real estate insurance company. Invariably, one of them will say something bitingly true like, 'You're deserted, too, tonight, huh?' I just smile or shrug and say something equally inane like, 'Que sera, sera,' and move on quickly.

Tonight I see none of them. I actually begin to concentrate on the groceries we need. I take the time to read ingredients on cans and packages, and I examine the cuts of chicken and meat more carefully. I want to drag this out. I want to go home feeling tired enough to go right to bed, maybe read a few pages of a new novel, take something to help me sleep, and turn over just as Ronnie says, 'What a night. The country's coming apart.'

Why is that so good? Why does that make him so happy? What has he lost of his manhood during this journey into adulthood that needs to be replaced with this macho disparagement of everyone who dares express a contrary opinion? When did he become unrecognizable? Or was I simply too blind to see or unwilling to see right from the start? It's not impossible. Wasn't it John Lennon who said, 'Living is easy with eyes closed?'

I'm so deep in all this thinking that I don't realize I've collided with someone's grocery cart until he cries out. A box of his cereal tumbles to the floor.

'Oh, I'm so sorry,' I say, kneeling down to pick it up. When I hand it to him, I finally look at him.

His eyes capture me in a way I never thought possible. Whenever I read about such male animal magnetism in my favorite novels, I always smiled to myself, half ridiculing the idea that a man could mesmerize a woman so quickly that she would turn into a fumbling, insecure teenager, struggling to say the right words and not look so foolish.

But that's how I feel right now.

He smiles. He is beyond handsome, his features perfect with a symmetry that recalls Greek statues. Of course, artists can manipulate a face and make it look like the face of what we imagine a god's face would be, but to see someone born to look this way is startling. I am speechless. He is manly but his face looks brushed for a photo shoot like some runway model. In fact, his complexion is so perfect that it seems to glow. I'm not thinking about anything else because my gaze is locked so tightly on his that my eyes can't wander.

He's not smiling continually like some mannequin. His strong, straight lips move but I'm not really listening to what he's saying. My eyes move from his eyes to his lips as I fumble for words, maybe because he is so calm and apparently quite amused. I am there for quite a while, babbling and flirting. It's like that moment you don't want to lose when you step out of a warm bath. I didn't want to let go of the moments I was spending with him. I was luxuriating in the afterglow.

Finally, someone says, 'Excuse me,' and I blink and look at an elderly man trying to get past me with his cart. He pulls back with a look of abject fear on his face, an expression I understand. So many elderly people wear that look habitually, the look that reveals they are more aware of the ticking of the clock now. Some are counting their own heartbeats all through the day like someone counting pennies, trying to determine how many are left to spend in this life. They push right against you at the checkout counter. They are always looking for quick escapes so they'll have more time to wait for death at home. No one wants to die on a checkout line. It would be too ironic, not to mention embarrassing.

And what would happen to the groceries you've chosen? Would they put them back immediately or take them quickly out of sight? Who wants to buy the box of rice touched by someone who just died?

'Oh, sorry,' I say and step aside. He still hesitates. Something more about me is frightening him. I wonder if I had smeared my lipstick like Bette Davis in *What Ever Happened to Baby Jane?* I pull back even farther.

'If you want to go by, go by,' I say sharply.

He moves past me as quickly as he can. He looks as if he thinks I am going to pluck out one of his precious groceries and make him return to an aisle. Maybe he thinks he is in danger of becoming the mythical Sisyphus of grocery stores, doomed to choose his groceries only to have them disappear before he reaches the checkout counter and have to go back down the same aisles for eternity.

Shaking my head almost to get my brain working again, I move on to finish filling my list, occasionally watching for the handsome man whose cart I bumped. I don't see him in any other aisle and assume he has left. I shudder with disappointment and continue shopping.

Everything that normally happens does happen. I pay the bill and, with the wheels squeaking and rumbling over the macadam parking lot, I push the cart of groceries out to my car, loading the bags on to the rear seat and floor as carefully as someone loading fine china. I never put my groceries in the trunk. I like having them ride along with me so I can mumble to the milk and juice, and warn the cereals to do what their labels claim they can do for my health.

After that, I put the cart in the place to leave carts and pause, looking back at the supermarket as if I have forgotten something, but really searching for one more sign of him. There is none and, besides, there is something terribly depressing about a well-lit large store with few people in it. There's a sense of emptiness, of desertion. It looks like a scene in one of those after-the-bomb movies. I push the images out of my mind, get into my car and drive home robotically, looking, I'm sure, like someone who has just been stunned with the news that she will, after all, live.

When I arrive, Kelly is in the kitchen making herself a club sandwich with the same precision she had when she first started doing that for herself at the age of four. She has the sliced turkey pieces exactly matching the size of the sliced Munster cheese and applies the mustard in surgically neat, even strokes so that every drop of it comes off the butter knife. I'm amazed at her concentration, and when I watch her doing this now, I see her as a little girl again, dainty, holding her fingers up to keep from smudging the tips with mustard or mayonnaise.

Did I do that to her, carry on so about neatness and femininity?

Actually, she never eats properly at dinner and is always hungry later, but nothing I can say or do changes that. At least she eats and is not into one of those fad diets other girls her age fall into like stepping into bear traps. She has a firm, mature figure that is better than mine was at her age, but she is terrified of gaining too much weight and falling off her imaginary magazine cover. She's cute enough to be on one, with those crystal-green eyes, button nose and sweet, soft, very sexy Scarlett Johansson mouth. She hates when I refer to her as 'cute'. Babies are cute. Young women are either attractive or beautiful or shut up.

She pauses to help me with the groceries.

'You should have told me you were going shopping. I would have gone along to help,' she says. She says that all the time as if she was a wind-up doll with taped messages to play. In this way, she takes after her father. They're often reading off the same script.

'I thought you had so much homework that you were going to "drown in it,"' I remind her. Like most teenagers her age, she's prone to hyperbole. Everything has to be 'the most' or 'the worst'. I don't think I was like that, but more and more, lately, I have been having trouble remembering myself. It's almost as if I was always the age I am.

'Oh, I did. Got a test in math tomorrow, too! I'm going to become a hunchback,' she says, leaning over the table to illustrate how she had to lean over her computer keys or text-books so long.

Kelly's grades aren't bad, which always amazes me when I see how much time she wastes. They're so good, in fact, that I can't get myself to complain about the nonsense she finds to do. Ronnie goes right to the bottom line, as he does with everything else, if I mention her distractions.

'She's doing well. Why complain?' he replies, and I stop.

Loneliness has all sorts of ways of showing itself. It's perhaps the most inventive feeling of all.

'Anything exciting happen at the supermarket?' she asks, and for a moment I'm too stunned to reply. Had the mother of one of her girlfriends seen me talking to that handsome man? Had she told her daughter who immediately had texted Kelly? Maybe the girl was there as well. It's the age of instant Breaking News, news that can reach us even in the grave.

Thoreau would have committed suicide by now. Walden Pond is not free from text messages.

'Yes,' I say. 'Ground beef is on sale.'

I don't smile. She stares at me and then she shakes her head and returns to her cave where her iPod and head phones, smartphone and computer wait for her. I almost believe they will share her sandwich.

Ronnie is in the living room now. He has satisfied his computer addiction and is shifting through channels. We have something like four hundred or so choices, but he rarely finds anything he thinks he'll enjoy. It's difficult to watch television with him because, like someone with attention deficit disorder, he'll abruptly flip the channel to something else, calling what he started to watch 'crap' or 'boring'. Between him and Kelly, the word 'boring' seems to characterize ninety percent of life. I think they expect to wake up and go to sleep to fireworks. They're both always looking for distractions, action, excitement and noise. I know what they believe: stillness is dangerous. Silence encourages people to start getting philosophical which always leads to being maudlin and depressing. Ugh.

Usually by this time, I would go up to our bedroom and escape in a novel anyway. Books and movies are portals through which we escape from sour reality. They enable us to change our names, our history, our faces and our tomorrows, at least for a few hours. Most people don't realize they are traveling on magic carpets.

Tonight is a little different, however. My eyes drift from the pages and I have flashes of visual memories of the man I bumped into at the supermarket. He won't sink into the sea filled with other seemingly insignificant memories. Instead, he is right in front of me again. I see his lips moving. I recall his eyes and travel over his face, lingering on one or another of his perfect features like someone fingering a precious jewel. It stirs me in ways I have almost forgotten. I even hear myself moan softly.

Later, when Ronnie is in bed beside me, slipping in like an afterthought, and the lights are out, I fold into a fetal position and drift softly into repose unlike any I had for years. The following morning, for the first time in a while, I wake after

Ronnie, instead of before him as usual. I'm not working again yet, so I have no time clocks to punch, no non-domestic responsibilities to fulfill. Ronnie is ready to go down to have his breakfast.

'You must have been tired,' he says from the doorway. He waits to have his diagnosis confirmed.

I am grateful that he has at least noticed a deviation from my normal behavior, but I have no fear that it will rouse some suspicion in him. I can always be tired, but never depressed, distracted and unhappy. I can be in a daze, but never in deep regret. Both he and Kelly have absorbed my share of boredom and depression. If I even dare express a feeling close to it, either one will explode with 'What about me?' 'I'm always working to make ends meet. This job is sucking the life out of me.' Or 'I have to go to a boring class with boring teachers. Even my friends are boring.'

There will be no sharing of their precious ennui and their self-pity. I excuse it by telling myself they are more needy than I am, but that delusion is crumbling more and more every day.

'Yes, a little tired,' I say. I know my lines. I recite them just the way an actress recites her lines daily on the stage, never making it sound as if she's said them so many times that she's bored with them.

He smiles, satisfied he is right.

'Relax. I have it under control,' he tells me, as if we are an ocean liner or a jet plane that is having some mechanical trouble.

I knew Kelly would have gobbled down her breakfast nevertheless and been out of the house before I went downstairs. I remembered her saying something about her going to a high school basketball game with Patricia Del Marco and staying over at her house. She blurts out plans like headline news and moves to something else quickly. If she had to announce World War Three, most wouldn't know or understand it had begun.

When I finally do go down, Ronnie has gone, too. There is a new silence, a more complete emptiness, knowing there is no one else physically in the house. I start to make a fresh pot of coffee and ponder about what I will have for breakfast as if it is a life-or-death decision. Too many of my ordinarily simple decisions in the kitchen have become like this. I could ruminate for ten minutes over whether to have a herbal tea or a tea with caffeine.

Suddenly, my cell phone rings. It is so early in the morning that I worry it is a call reporting something serious has happened to either one of my parents or one of Ronnie's. The four are still alive and well, submerged in their warm-bath retirements out in Palm Springs, even playing foursome golf and going to dinner and shows together. Ronnie has a younger sister, Tami, who fell in love and got married in the middle of her sophomore year at Berkeley. Her husband went into international law and they moved to Paris almost immediately afterward, so for all practical purposes, Ronnie is just as much an only child as I am.

Our parents' friendship is probably the best thing to have come out of my engagement and marriage to Ronnie. It is easy for my parents to sympathize with his parents if they complain about him or vice versa. They joined a new AARP club with the motto, 'Little children, little problems; bigger children . . .' In essence, there is no retirement from parenthood.

'Hello?' I say cautiously.

There is a moment of silence and then I hear the words softly.

'Hi. I think I might take you up on your offer,' he says. When I am silent, he adds, 'To show me around? You remember me, the supermarket last night?'

'Oh, yes, yes, sorry.'

'Is the offer still good?'

'Yes, certainly. Where and when?'

'How about in an hour at the corner of Western and Parker?' he says.

'That's fine.'

'Thanks. Looking forward to it,' he adds.

For a few moments. I stand there in a daze. Obviously, I had told him more about myself in those few minutes at the supermarket than I recall. I am sure I was babbling like some lovesick teenager. I shouldn't keep saying 'teenager'. Many of my so-called contemporary friends babble about their infatuations with this actor or that singer, too. Adolescence doesn't really disappear. It hides behind adult responsibility, poking its head out every time it has the opportunity.

I can't remember what I did immediately afterward, not exactly. I mean, I don't remember showering, fixing my hair, choosing what to wear, putting on lipstick and perfume, and then leaving the house. I don't even remember if I ate anything. If I had done any of that, I had done it quicker than ever.

It was as if I had closed my eyes, as if my car and I were on some sort of remote control. I suppose I resembled someone sleepwalking.

And when I opened my eyes again, I was just pulling into a parking space on Western and Parker where he was waiting for me patiently, as patiently as someone who was confident he had installed himself securely in my psyche and was well assured that I would come.

It was how it began.

And when I think about it now, I realize I would have had it begin no other way and certainly not with a long, titillating courting process, during which we slowly revealed what we already knew was inside us. All that pretending that it was something else is like swimming through currents of lies, self-delusion and hypocrisy.

Besides, there is no real excitement without spontaneity. Planning dulls the senses and the wonder of discovery. The Boy Scouts and Girl Scouts are wrong there.

Being prepared isn't always best.

And while surprise isn't always best, it's so often better.

Otherwise, why have gift wrapping paper?

ONE

It never occurred to me to wonder or guess how he had gotten my cell phone number. I couldn't recall revealing it when I spoke to him in the supermarket. On the other hand, what would have been the point of my offering to show him around if I hadn't given him my number? Of course, there was always the Internet anyway.

During the past five years, I had worked as a paralegal for Sebastian Pullman who practiced commercial law for more than forty years before he sold his practice and retired nearly two years ago at the age of seventy-two. His fifty-eight-year-old wife drove him to it. When we parted, I could see the palpable fear in his eyes. Without his work, his life was going to be golf dates and cruises and charity events, where he would meet the Usual Suspects and have conversations on the same topics, until one day he would stop talking and pop like a soap bubble.

I wasn't sure I wanted to continue that legal work, so I didn't attempt to stay on with the new attorney who had bought his practice and building. I felt like a tightrope walker during those working years because Kelly was left so much on her own. Ronnie didn't fill the gaps as much or as well as I had hoped he would.

However, I knew from the work Sebastian did, the investigations he ran, that anyone could find out anything about anyone else if he was determined to do so. The Internet enabled those capable of navigating through it to have the powers of the best private investigator. We were all amateur Philip Marlowes and Sam Spades. It gave new meaning to the word 'snoop'. Peeping Toms were sunburned from the glow of computer monitors.

Sebastian contracted out his sophisticated business detective work, but I always prepared the reports for him, so I was aware of how successful the professional detectives were with their high-tech assistants infiltrating anyone's personal life. Sebastian loved to discover hidden assets, whether it was a supposedly bankrupt company or a party in a divorce who was trying to avoid sharing the wealth that he or she had accumulated. His weathered face would brighten into the delighted face of a young boy who was given the gift he had hoped he'd receive. To Sebastian, discovering these hidden assets was as good as solving a murder.

The thing is, I didn't wonder at all about anything concerning the man I had met. I didn't question why he was free right now to meet a woman on a weekday in the late morning. I didn't wonder about his family, whether he was married too, where he was born and had lived, and if he lived here now. I didn't think about whether he had a college education, worked nearby or knew Ronnie. None of it seemed to matter. Some bell inside me had been rung, some door unlocked, and as if I had been anticipating that it would happen for some time, I moved without hesitation. Not a second thought, not a cry of conscience put any pause in me.

After I parked and shut off the engine, I waited, naturally quite nervous. I didn't even turn to look at him when he opened the passenger-side door and slipped like a shadow into the car. I was trying to be cool, casual, and look very experienced at this sort of thing. I didn't want to do anything that might cause him to change his mind or his image of who I was. I was trembling a little, just as I trembled when I walked out too far on a diving board and knew there was only one way off.

'This is very nice of you,' he said.

'I don't exactly have a full schedule these days.'

'I hope I'm not simply someone to help fill your time,' he said, and I looked at him directly. I could feel myself slipping into that warm excitement I had felt when I spoke with him the night before. His eyes were just as mesmerizing.

'No, you're definitely more than that,' I said. I might as well have started to undress.

He saw that. The confidence in him was overwhelming.

'Why don't we skip the preliminaries?' he said.

'Preliminaries?'

'What you want and what I want is so clear. Do you mind if we just go to a motel?' he asked.

I had to rake the deepest places in my memory to think of another girl or woman I knew or had known who wouldn't simply ask him to get out, but those I did recall surely felt this same surge of exhilaration. All the danger, all the risk made it more so. When had I last thrown caution out the window this quickly? I felt as if I was ripping off chains. I longed to be naked.

But a motel? Why not his apartment or his hotel? Motels were painted in anonymity, even the ones that weren't national franchises. Unlike hotels that people might frequent with some regularity (many had a favorite hotel in New York or some other city), motels were more like hubs, some unassuming, unremarkable stop between the start and the finish of a journey. They had the essence of temporariness. You left nothing of yourself there. You didn't take time to make friends with the employees, unless you were some sort of regular like a truck driver or salesman, and you didn't have a favorite room. Maybe you would ask for the quietest and one type of bed or the other, but nothing more. Of course, a motel.

Recently, I had stayed at a motel, considering it a stop on my way from a normal life to insanity, a welcome pause during which I might be able to find my way back. I needed nothing but a different bedroom where I could fall asleep to the glow of the television set and enjoy the sense of being free. I paid in cash. From my days with Sebastian, I knew how credit card bills could convict you of some indiscretion or reveal some secret. I lied about going to see an old girl-friend of mine in Palos Verdes, Patty Cutter. I let her know I was using her name occasionally so she could cover for me. Patty thought I was having an affair back then and was titillated that I had used her as my alibi. So many of us live vicariously through others.

'I never believed you could last with one man, Clea,' she said. 'This is probably not your first time.'

'Probably not,' I said. The vagueness reinforced her theory and her pledge to cover for me. The truth was I didn't need to concoct elaborate alibis. Ronnie enjoyed these 'free' nights as well, not that he spent more time with Kelly. I wondered if they even knew I wasn't there for most of the evening. It was odd, I know, to think of a motel as an escape, a refuge, but it was.

However, when he suggested a motel, it took on an entirely new image. Go with a man to a motel? I hadn't gone to a motel for a romantic tryst since my senior year in high school. Ronnie and I skipped all that and went right to his apartment on the second date. I recalled how nervous I was when I did it while still in high school – so nervous, in fact, that I nearly backed out after Sonny Reuben had paid for the room and we had parked in front of the motel room door. I still remembered the number – twenty-one. I was not quite seventeen.

'Do you know that if we're caught, you could get into legal trouble?' I asked Sonny. 'I think this qualifies as statutory rape. It could even be a federal crime since we've gone over the state line.'

Sonny was nearly nineteen, a late entry into kindergarten and actually the oldest boy in the senior class. The idea that he could be held accountable seemed ludicrous to me as well as to him, but I mentioned it anyway. Even then I was thinking like a paralegal.

'It's worth the risk,' he had said and had given me that smile that could melt ice-cube hearts. He had kissed me, too, and stroked my hair lovingly, far more lovingly than anyone would expect a senior high school boy capable of doing. I felt as if in me he had found exquisite beauty, and any boy who can give a girl that feeling is worth his weight in future aggravation. 'Ready?' Sonny had asked.

Heart pumping as fast as the engine Sonny had just shut off, I nodded and we got out.

How sexually sophisticated I had felt then. I knew he had been here with other girls. He didn't have to say it, and I didn't have to hear it from any of my girlfriends. He simply had the experience written into his walk, his cool way of turning his head just slightly with that licentious smile to look at me coming into the classroom or approaching him in the hallway, and, of course, the confidence in his words and his no-hesitation embrace.

I wasn't a virgin, but I hadn't lost it in a motel room. It was done clumsily in the rear of a Chrysler Town Car, one of the vehicles in Jeffrey Morton's father's limousine service. It was clumsy because Jeffrey was six feet three and I was no slouch at five feet ten. A few times we nearly fell off the seat, and when he came, bursting like a water balloon, he did fall off, laughing. I laughed, too, which wasn't the way I had envisioned this life-changing event to establish itself. Like any young girl full of fantasy, with tons of romantic movie and novel love scenes stuffed in her backpack, I was anticipating soft, poetic words of love and a beautiful melody in the background. I wanted to hear him swear that he would never take me for granted and I was nobody's trophy. This was to be real, something to cherish for a lifetime. When he dropped me off afterward, I felt as dazed as anyone who had stumbled into womanhood unsure how she had gotten there and whether or not it was worth the effort and the journey. The disappointment was enough to make me want to swear off sex, become a nun and spend my life stifling my hormones.

But there was nothing specific to only me back then that reinforced all this disappointment. I wasn't 'out there', 'weird', 'different'. I was an A-student, on the cheerleading squad and up with the latest teen fashions. No, for all my contemporaries, sex had become just something else we did. Even though I thought it and believed it, it infuriated me whenever I saw that or heard it said. Tell that to William Holden in *Love is a Many-Splendored Thing*, or Ingrid Bergman in *Casablanca*, or Kevin Costner in *The Bodyguard*, I would rant. Where were the men who felt something as strong, if not stronger than the women, and where were those women now? They were difficult to find in my high school at the time and, I suspected, just about every other one in the country. Well, maybe not in the Bible Belt, but they had other obstacles blocking their feelings which were too often viewed as signs of sin to come.

However, I was determined this would be different from any love affair I had, even when I began with Ronnie. This would be what it was meant to be. I would soar into clouds of ecstasy and it would be more than just another sexual experience to bury in a closet of my memories so deeply that it would take an oil rig to bring them up.

I guess I drove about thirty-five miles east of where we

were to the motel I knew. Coincidentally, he knew it too, but I didn't ask him why. I had passed it by many times since I last had been there, each time tempted to stop and check in, if only for a few hours. I'm not even going to pretend I knew how many miles were on the odometer of my car. I'm not that exact or precise about all this. I just knew how long it would be to get there. It helped to harness the anticipation and control the trembling in my body and in my voice.

I wanted at least to match how sophisticated and how confident he was.

Talk about confidence . . . he already had the room booked, and it wasn't because that was where he was staying, either. He didn't tell me that; he just said he wasn't keeping it as any sort of temporary residence.

'That's an oxymoron anyway,' he said. 'You don't think of a residence as temporary.' He looked at me and smiled. 'Just like an experience can't be temporary. It becomes a part of you, of who you are, don't you think?'

'I try not to think,' I said. I knew I took that line from some movie and hated using it. That was something Ronnie would do. I don't know if I hated anything more than I hated sounding trite.

He laughed.

'You're a terrible failure, then,' he said. 'Anyway, I doubt very much that you hate to think. You probably think about things more than most people you know.'

Why was it a stranger could look at me and immediately see me, but my husband of nearly twenty years could barely see me standing in front of him most of the time? Do we eventually wear each other, put on each other like a pair of old gloves, hardly noticing what we're doing because we've done it so often? I often wondered if soldiers off on some Middle Eastern tour of duty are loved more because they're so far away and seen so infrequently, despite Skype or FaceTime or whatever Internet magic puts husband and wife on a computer screen. Until they find a way to convey touch, it doesn't do more than increase your longing. And passionate love does need longing and anticipation; otherwise, it's too mechanical. You don't want to come home from a date feeling like a prostitute, and I certainly had no intention of feeling that way now.

When he directed me to the parking spot, he got out of the car before I did and came around to open my door and help me out, not like he would an elderly woman, but how he would if he were escorting a debutante to her ball or some other formal gala where eyes were like microscopes looking for imperfections in your dress and behavior. He paused to see if I would hesitate, if I would shake my head and say, 'Sorry, I can't do this. You see, I'm married with a teenage daughter, and although I've fantasized about being with other men, I've never so much as returned a flirting glance or in any other way encouraged any man to pursue me. I'm in my second virginity, you see, the virginity that comes with matrimony.'

I didn't say any of that. I didn't hesitate either. I walked with determination toward the door. He opened it. Apparently, he had unlocked it earlier, maybe thinking that fiddling with a motel key in a door lock would look too low-class or something. This was more like opening the door to his private bedroom. I thought that was a nice touch. It made it all just a little more special, and although I might be writing too much into the gesture, it showed more respect for me. By their very nature, motel assignations could seem cheap. There was hardly an investment, whether it was time or money.

The curtains were tightly closed, barely permitting a thin sliver of daylight, yet there was nothing cheap or gloomy about the room. The covers of the bed had been neatly folded back and there was a single rose on the pillow on the left side. I remember thinking, that's the side I sleep on at home. Once you get married and you establish which side belongs to whom, that's the way it stays forever, even when you travel or go to a resort on vacation. This is considerate, I thought. He has taken into consideration where I'm comfortable in bed. I didn't even wonder how he might have known that. Maybe I just looked like someone who would sleep on the left. I like leaving theaters through the exit on the left.

Ronnie used to put a rose on my pillow occasionally during our early years. Somehow, he would sneak it past me so that I wouldn't discover it until we were ready for bed. He told

me he had seen it done in some movie. I suppose I felt as if
I had stepped into a movie now. My lover pretended he didn't
know how the rose was there.

'Maybe it grows out of pillows,' he suggested. 'Magic
pillows.'

'I put away my fairytales years ago,' I said.

'Pity.'

He didn't say anything else and neither did I.

We both simply started to undress. He was very neat with
his clothes, going to the closet to get hangers for his jacket,
shirt and trousers. He waited for me to hand him my dress
and then he hung that up, too. He sat on a chair by the small
desk and took off his socks while I sat on the bed, unfastened
my bra and slipped off my panties. I put them on the chair in
the corner and then I slipped under the blanket and looked up
at the pinkish white ceiling which had embossed circles,
smaller ones within the ones, giving the illusion of looking
down a tunnel. I was so fascinated with it that I didn't look
at him until I felt him get into the bed.

The sheets felt cool on my skin which was already hot with
anticipation. I pressed my feet against the bottom of the cover
sheet which had been tucked in by someone who made beds
in the military. It was like a straightjacket. In its own way, it
had captured and was holding me, not that I was making any
effort to break free, change my mind, dress and rush out.

I turned to him, and he smiled and leaned over to kiss me
softly on the lips, a kiss that felt as if it was made out of sweet
mist and yet left the warm, salty taste of a sea breeze. I kept
my eyes closed the way a little girl might just before she was
to get a surprise. I waited for him to touch me, but he didn't,
so I opened my eyes. He just lay there looking into my eyes.
All that while, my heart beat faster as the anticipation began
somewhere between my neck and shoulders and slipped down
like a thin layer of warm water over my breasts, the small of
my stomach and down the inside of my thighs to my ankles.

'Just for a while,' he said, 'let's not move. Let's just anticipate.'

It wasn't easy, but it wasn't torture either. It was an exquisite
longing that nudged the erotic part of me that had been sleeping
too long inside my very soul. I could feel its eyes open and

the happiness that was beginning to rage. It was the Rip Van Winkle of my feminine longing finally awoken. I was a teenage girl again, relaxing the inside of my thighs to welcome the tip of that hardened, usually very limp penis that now would be like a key opening all the feelings and behavior we were both warned to avoid by one set of rules and encouraged to get into by another.

After a while, he smiled, as if to say, 'Well done. We can move on now.'

We kissed again, my mouth opening like soft petals, my tongue touching his, warm and wet like I was increasingly becoming between my legs. His hands began to play my body, gently lifting my breasts so he could bring his mouth to my nipples. Every muscle in my body, some seemingly tense forever, relaxed. My softness hardened him faster. I could feel his muscles tightening, his body pause to drive itself into me, almost absorbing me into it, taking charge of every cell, every strand of hair, every bone, all of me welcoming and demanding more. The small of my stomach resonated in a symphony of pleasure that echoed up and down the passages from my head to my feet, turning and twisting through every part of me until I felt lit up, my eyes glowing, my breath salty, my lips wet, my hips moving to fit him carefully and completely inside me. It was trite to say it, so I just thought it: it was as if we were made for each other, as if the spiritual power that mixed and stirred our genes did so with the intention of making us for each other, eventually.

We were part of some celestial plan, which was why everything that had happened and was happening now happened so quickly, with neither of us offering the slightest resistance. We were under divine orders to make Him proud of inventing sex as the ultimate statement of love. He would use us as an example, cite us in footnotes in celestial papers.

I have heard my girlfriends say that making love with their husbands had become as ritualistic and as ordinary as brushing their teeth. Some were clever enough to realize that their husbands made love out of fear. With all the talk about erectile dysfunction, the commercials about the loss of testosterone, men were haunted by the images of limp penises. Every successful act of sexual intercourse reaffirmed their manhood. For many, it could have been with any vagina. The important thing was to reach that climax and, oh, by the way, trigger at least one climax in his wife, if possible. But hey, if she didn't have it, that was her fault. Maybe she was the one who needed hormones and not me.

'Do married people make love or make sex?' Kelly once asked me. She was only fourteen at the time, but one of her girlfriends, Elise Shelly, whose parents were divorced, told her that Elise's mother said people fall in love for ten minutes, get married and follow the dots. She finally figured out that Elise's mother meant they do everything together afterward because that's the way it was supposed to be and not because they wanted to, passionately.

Because children are so honest, Elise told her all this without hesitation, and then Kelly came to me, hoping to get an equally honest response. Should I tell her that's true, at least for me, I wondered, and then have her become cynical about love and marriage? She was too young for that, I thought, and, besides, everyone needed to develop his or her own cynicism. Cynicism was something that had to be born of personal experience. Otherwise, especially in relation to your child, he or she could hate you forever for spoiling tomorrow.

But I couldn't say no, that's not true, and say it with the sort of enthusiasm she was hoping to see. That would be false and she would see it, I thought. Rather, I used the easy escape.

'What's true for Elise's mother is not necessarily true for everyone else,' I said. 'There are things you should learn for yourself. Sometimes the journey is more important than the destination, Kelly. Don't look for shortcuts.'

She knew what I meant. She is a very perceptive girl when she wants to be. She had to open her eyes. For the moment, that answer seemed to suffice. I knew she knew she had gotten a more sophisticated response than Elise had gotten or ever would get. She didn't ask me if it was as true for me as it was for Elise's mother, but I wasn't in a divorce, so maybe it never occurred to her.

Our time making love in the motel seemed to evaporate once it had ended. My orgasms were more like gongs on a grandfather clock, sounding the ecstasy, until, finally, he withdrew and slipped away as gently and carefully as a surgeon closing a wound. I closed my eyes and fell into a warm repose, drifting on the memory of the moments that had just passed.

I awoke at the sound of him dressing.

'Oh,' I said, as if I had missed a cue. I sat up.

'I have to be somewhere,' he said. 'No worries. I have someone picking me up.' Then he smiled. 'Don't even think it. This is not slam bam thank you ma'am.'

'You didn't give me a chance to think it.'

He laughed.

'Take your time. Relax. I'll see you again.'

He came to the bed and kissed me. Then he picked up the rose and put it in my hands.

'That's how I want to remember you when I think of you later,' he said.

I watched him leave and fell back against the pillow. I closed my eyes, feeling happy and complete, and fell asleep again.

When I awoke this time, I felt alone and the room seemed colder. My dress, still hanging in the closet, was a lonely-looking garment that resembled something forgotten by the previous visitor. I sat up and ran my hands through my hair. The curtains were still tightly drawn. I got up and, still naked, parted them to look out at the motel parking lot. My car was practically the only one there. Another car, an SUV, was down toward the far end.

Without any more delay, I dressed, checked myself in the bathroom mirror and then walked out and got into my car. Traffic flew by on the street that ran past the motel, but there was no one outside. It looked like mid-afternoon, but when I glanced at my watch, I saw it was much later. It was nearly five. I had slept longer than I had thought. It amazed me that I wasn't hungry, having missed lunch. I got into my car, backed out and drove out of the motel parking lot. I glanced at the office. There was no one standing in a window or looking out. In fact, it looked deserted, just as deserted as the supermarket had looked the night before. I was in a world where cars flowed like shadows spirited forward by beams of light, cars driven by people who looked built in, mannequins depicting human beings in comas.

The drive home was uneventful. I didn't rush, even though I knew Ronnie would be there by now. I didn't sift through ideas in my mind to come up with stories to explain my absence either. I just pulled into our driveway, opened the garage and drove in. When I entered the kitchen, I heard nothing. Neither Ronnie nor Kelly shouted to let me know they were there, and then I remembered Kelly was going to go to a ball game and staying at a girlfriend's overnight.

I started toward the stairway when Ronnie poked his head out of his office and called to me.

'Guess what?' he said.

'What?'

'We've got the night to ourselves. I made a reservation for us at the Outpost.'

'Oh. Good.'

'You knew Kelly was staying over at the Del Marcos', right?'

'Yes.'

'It's for seven, OK? I just want to catch up on some paperwork here.'

'Fine.'

'We can have a cocktail about six thirty, if you want.'

'I want,' I said.

'Right,' he said and disappeared from sight as if something or someone had pulled him back into his office abruptly. Not a question about where I had been or what I had been doing had apparently even occurred to him. Was that trust, lack of curiosity or simply a symptom of someone too self-absorbed? Did it make any difference? I didn't have to dip into the well of fabrication to bring up a full pail of untruth.

I smiled to myself and walked slowly up the stairway.

I was an adulteress and I didn't feel an iota of guilt. If anything, I felt larger, stronger and more complete than I had felt in a very long time. It was as if I had gotten younger and was back at that time in my life, in any young woman's life, when all of her senses seemed so sharp, her body so vibrant. I was feeling as I had when I was eighteen, sensing more freedom, thrilled by travel, excited about meeting new men and new women, eager to take some chances by staying up later, drinking more and going faster. Caution was quickly dropped into the wake of my lunge forward. My laughter was longer and richer, my eyes were strengthened by new curiosity, and all the chains and limits of the young were cast aside. I felt as if I could burn my candle at both ends and go on and on forever.

I went into the shower. I didn't want to wash the sex off me. I wanted it to linger like some wonderful new perfume, a scent that would circle me and turn the heads of whoever was nearby. Only Ronnie wouldn't notice it, or, if he did, would think it was because of him. How confident he was of my fidelity. I wondered. Did that mean he thought I was incapable of attracting another man or incapable of infidelity, either because I was too devoted to him or because I was too insecure about myself? Was that how most men thought of their Stepford Wives? Certainly, the wives of the men who worked with him struck me as being one or the other. They talked about flirting – some did flirt right in front of the rest of us – but as far as I knew, none had gone anywhere with it.

'Hey, move over,' I heard and turned around to see Ronnie naked, getting into the shower stall with me. We hadn't done this for a long time.

'I'll wash yours if you'll wash mine,' he said.

'I'm already washed.'

He embraced me and kissed me awkwardly. As usual, he was rushing his sex. It made me think he saw it as just another thing on his list of things to check off. I found I wasn't comfortable doing it in the shower. Was I ever? The memory seemed too vague. I backed away. His disappointment was palpable.

'I'll wash you,' I said, and got behind him and embraced him. I brought my hands around, the soap in my right hand, and quickly got him hard. He was moaning and chanting, 'Oh boy. Oh boy.' My motel tryst began to play across the insides of my closed eyelids.

Was this how it would always be now, making love to Ronnie, but really making love to my lover? Did it matter?

How many married couples realize they're not making love to each other anymore? Wives simply don't have what they had to arouse their husbands or vice versa, and so they rely on fantasy or, if they're lucky as in my case, a recent, very exciting extramarital experience they can load into their sex like a magic bullet and use to hit some bullseye of fulfillment. I've even heard the idiotic argument, maybe not so idiotic for some, that it's good to have affairs. They strengthen your marriage. I didn't think that was why I had done it, but how well the devil rationalizes sin.

Ronnie moaned, leaned back and came in the shower. When he came, I held on to the stem as if I was aiming a garden hose, his body seemingly crumpling in my arms afterward. I stepped out quickly to dry myself. He began to sing.

How odd, I thought. *I feel more like a prostitute with my husband than I did with my lover in a motel.*

I made a mental note to ask my closer girlfriends if they ever felt used. I imagined one or two of them saying, 'Of course, silly, but I always get paid one way or another.'

I sat at my vanity table and gazed at myself in the oval mirror. Every woman wants a magic mirror; not one that tells her she's the prettiest of them all necessarily, but one that reflects back an image of what she would like to see. In this mirror, she can cure all wrinkles and imperfections. The ravages of time melt away quickly. It's more than just the makeup. It's what makes us all Cinderellas. We can be potential princesses, models, movie stars, until the clock strikes twelve. *Just sit here long enough to hypnotize yourself*, I thought.

There I am, truly eighteen again. I'm a man killer, so hot I can melt them and turn them into clay easily molded. Through the corner of my eye, I watched Ronnie dress, choosing what he thought was his sexiest shirt and then slipping into his abbreviated briefs, flexing his muscles or what was left of them as he stood before his mirror, and then nodding at himself as if the image in the mirror was really and truly someone else, someone to please. He put on his jeans and slipped into his blue boat shoes.

'Ready?' he asked.

Throughout our marriage, it was always like that. When he was done with any preparations, he'd assume I would be as well or I would rush to be.

'Almost,' I said.

He grimaced that old boy's grin that said, 'Women,' and he walked out, whistling the theme from *The Bridge on the River Kwai* as if he was in some war movie as he bounced down the stairs. He had been invigorated, recast to play a new role. The set was changed as well as the lighting. He had a different mission than he had this afternoon. He was the James Bond of all James Bonds.

Who lives in fantasy more, I wondered, Ronnie or me? No one's to blame for it. In fact, we should be grateful. That's what the highest species can do: imagine. Without it, we'd have only rain when it rained and not a romantic walk in the rain without feeling a drop. We'd be overwhelmed by age and never believe anyone envied us. We'd be at the mercy of facts.

I rose slowly.

What if the image I saw of myself in the mirror didn't leave when I left?

What if she remained there, waiting for my return, and when I did return, she mouthed, 'Are you all right?'

'No,' I'd probably say, 'but I'm getting better.'

TWO

R onnie's Usual Suspects were at the Outpost. Some were married men who had gathered at the bar after work and were taking just a little longer to get home, as if going home was like going to the dentist. If you just could put it off a little longer, it wouldn't be as painful.

I took particular note tonight of how they looked at me. I don't know if it was my imagination or wishful thinking, but it seemed that all the men at the bar turned our way and viewed me with raw male lust and longing. It occurred to me that men like Ronnie's friends or men in general, when they saw a woman who stirred their virility, reached back as far as they could to find that youthful magic they had once had in their smiles and eyes. They were pleading. *Take me to my fantasy. Get me out of this rut.*

I kept my smile very Mona Lisa and my eyes down. None of these men presented anything of interest to me, but it occurred to me that I might very well still have that glow I saw in myself before we had left, a glow I knew had come from where I had been and what I had done.

I wondered why Ronnie didn't realize that my being the only woman at this section of the bar made me uncomfortable. After the initial smiles and hellos, he and his friends closed in on each other like one large hairy fist and left me twirling my Cosmopolitan in its glass and waiting like a trained puppy. Their laughter was as grating as fingernails on a chalkboard, and if any of them threw me a bone in the form of 'What do you think of that, Clea?' I would toss back a plastic, camera-ready smile and shake my head as if to say, 'Oh don't ask me. It's way beyond me. It's male stuff.'

Ronnie would glance at me each time, as if he had just recalled I was with him. Finally, nearly ten minutes past our reservation, the boys began to come apart, disintegrate quickly, as if whatever glue had held them together had thinned out, causing them to leave like shadows fleeing the light, each one tossing back a glance at me, a weak smile left over from their private jokes and chorus of laughs.

'How about those guys?' Ronnie asked me. 'Phil's thinking of getting married again. You'd think a three-time loser would learn something from the experiences. I don't know if he can keep his alimony straight.'

'Don't worry. I'm sure his ex-wives do all that for him,' I mumbled.

'I'm sure they do,' Ronnie said with a smirk.

Was there ever a man who, after his divorce was final, believed his ex-wife deserved anything more than a copy of the documents? To them, the papers were keys removing handcuffs and unlinking chains. Did they wake up years later and think maybe they had lost something? Or was it part of the male psyche never to admit a mistake? Or face the fact that he failed to satisfy his wife sexually?

I had a theory that when most men stopped working with their hands, using their muscles either as farmers or factory employees, they began to fear losing their manhood. If a man didn't love football, basketball, boxing, hockey, baseball or NASCAR, he was suspect. If profanity or pornography deeply offended him, he was suspect. If he favored same-sex marriage, he was suspect. In fact, there were so many suspects out there now, you had to hover closer to the urinal to protect your goods. Ronnie often said things like that. It occurred to me then that men were, on average, more paranoid than women. In fact, men were looking at themselves in mirrors more these days, worrying that something feminine had invaded their bodies or that maybe, deep inside, they had gay tendencies.

We went to our table. Our waiter rushed to pull out the chair for me. Ronnie looked as if the young man had sacrificed himself for him. He nodded at him and sat almost before I did. I felt that I had been delivered to dinner, the wife package just shipped in by UPS.

The Outpost was a middle-range restaurant, two or three computer mouse clicks above a Denny's. I never ate anything here that I didn't believe I could make far better, but as some of my girlfriends who do cook and prepare their family dinners

always say, 'We go out for a break, not for a better dinner.'
That's the logic behind coming to a place like the Outpost. If
we went to Les Agarves, which is twice the cost, but about
as gourmet as we can get without actually being in France,
that would qualify as a special evening out. Ronnie will do it
on an anniversary or on a birthday, but I know his true opinion
of it is that it's not worth it. I've come to believe his taste buds
can't reach gourmet level so he can't appreciate the difference.
For him, then, it makes little sense.

But it's not only the food that is exquisite; it's the ambience
and the service. You feel you're special, even if only for
one night, one dinner. Ronnie likes to make it seem that only
women want this. Sometimes I wonder if that's not true. It's
certainly true when it comes to his friends or most of the
husbands of my girlfriends. It's almost as if there's something
unmanly about elegance. They'd rather associate themselves
with Clint Eastwood than Cary Grant or George Clooney.
Eastwood can be tough, virile and dangerous, and be grimy
at the same time, except, of course, in a movie like *The Bridges
of Madison County*, but men don't talk about that film.

It's too hard to be Cary Grant or George Clooney, to have
your hair always well trimmed, to care about the clothes you're
wearing and not fight wearing a tie or cufflinks. And then
there's all that sophistication, that smooth handling of women
and that air of intellect. That's too much brain juice, and,
besides, you're not supposed to think too deeply when you're
with a woman. You simply glide on your smile or the alcohol.
The only thing more obvious in its intent is a shark.

As I looked across the table at Ronnie and watched how
he studied this uncomplicated menu, I wondered if the simple
answer to all bad marriages is that one outgrows the other.
Maybe people shouldn't marry until they're in their fifties.
By then, the two people are well formed and can see clearly
if they have anything or enough in common to sustain a
commitment.

What about children? someone would surely ask.

Perhaps we should get into Brave New World faster than
we are. Create children in laboratories, raise them in Israeli
kibbutz-style complexes and get all that stress out of our lives.

'What are you in such deep thought about?' Ronnie suddenly asked.

I didn't realize he had stopped analyzing the menu, a menu that hadn't changed for years and a menu he had seen dozens of times.

'I can't decide between the spinach or baby lettuce salad,' I replied. I really wanted to see if Ronnie would believe that such a decision would put me into deep thought, even though it very well could.

'Baby lettuce,' he said, pointing his right forefinger at me as if he's punching in the choice on an invisible candy machine. 'That salad has figs in it and you love figs.'

I was actually taken aback.

'You remember that I like figs in my salad?'

'Hell, yeah. Didn't you ask me to bring some home on the way back from work last week and I forgot? I thought you might stab me in my sleep that night.'

'I considered it,' I said, and he laughed and looked around for the waiter.

'Hey,' he called. He shrugged and raised his hands as if the waiter should have known telepathically when we were ready. Of course, he hurried over to our table just the way he had to pull out my chair for me.

Actually, he looked as if he wasn't long out of high school. I wasn't even sure he shaved yet. He had that orange-yellow hair and peach fuzz on his jawbone and cheeks. It was pretty obvious to me that he had just begun working here and was desperately trying to make a good impression. He was the type who would be proving his maturity all his life. He wouldn't appreciate that until he was over sixty.

'What do you think of the pork chop?' Ronnie asked him.

'It's very good. Nice size, meaty.'

'Um. Clea?'

I ordered what I've always ordered here, a shrimp salad. Ronnie smirked. It wasn't exciting enough for him. He didn't realize that I hadn't ordered a salad first because I was having a salad as an entrée, so the whole question of spinach or baby lettuce had been irrelevant.

'I'll have the chop, but it better be good,' he warned, putting on his best Mafia hitman face.

'Anything first?'

'Naw, that's it. Oh, wait a minute.' He looked at the drink he'd brought from the bar. 'Another vodka and soda. Grey Goose. Clea?'

'A glass of Cakebread Chardonnay,' I said.

The waiter took our menus and Ronnie sat forward.

'I have a surprise tonight,' he said. He held his wide, childish grin.

'What?' I asked with control. Too often his surprises were a new lawnmower or computer printer.

'I'm going to be the office manager. Promoted. I get a nice raise, too.'

'That's great, Ronnie. You should have told me before we left the house, or at least we should have toasted it when we first came in and were at the bar.'

'I didn't want to tell those losers anything. Jealousy drips from their lips.'

'I meant just you and me.'

'Yeah, well, that's what we're going to do now,' he said. He reached for my hand. 'You look really good tonight, Clea. Did you change your hair or something?'

'No.'

I wasn't shocked by the question. I had often bought new clothes, new earrings, and changed my hair from time to time, but he didn't notice when I did. Kelly always did, and then he realized something was different and woke like someone in a daze on an escalator who is coming to the bottom or the top and had better get with it.

'Well, whatever you're doing, keep doing it,' he said.

I smiled at the irony. If he only knew.

'So?' he said.

'So what, Ronnie?'

'This promotion. How about it?'

'I said we should celebrate.'

I guess I wasn't enthusiastic enough. He looked like a little boy who was told he didn't do well enough at school to get the teacher's accolades.

'You know this is a very tough market right now, but I've done real well for the company. You know the saying: when the going gets tough, the tough get going. That's me. I've been that way since kindergarten.'

I found myself staring at him and trying to remember if he ever said anything original. How many women look at their husband one day and wonder what in hell it was that made them want to be with him for a lifetime? Didn't they realize what it meant to spend day in and day out with the same man, hear the same phrases, see the same expressions and realize the same emotions?

Was I being unfair?

Wasn't there a time when he was fun to be with and inter-esting in an exciting enough way to keep my attention? I couldn't go on explaining this dread I often felt by blaming it only on him. I had my eyes wide open when I said, 'I do.' I oohed and aahed over the engagement ring. I was excited about the honeymoon in Capri. Like his, my heart was young and gay once, too. I was ready to see everything through four eyes and hear everything through four ears. I was willing to compromise my opinions and diminish my ego if it was necessary. In short, I would invest myself in him until death did us part.

Perhaps he often thought the same things about me, but was never obvious about it. Why couldn't it be that I was very different now from the girl he had first dated and it wasn't entirely his fault? I was hard in places where I had been soft. I was too cynical and certainly too critical now. I was sure that, at least once a day, he probably looked at me with disappointment and had his second thoughts, too.

Or maybe it wasn't anyone's fault; it just *was*.

'You know, you should go back to work,' he suddenly said, nodding as he said it, as if some invisible wise man had whispered it in his ear.

'What? Why do you say that?'

'You're too smart and energetic to simply care for the house and Kelly and me. She's on her own now most of the time anyway, Clea. We're almost extraneous in her life these days, just like most parents are for their teenagers.'

'Are we?' I thought about it. Was I like that when I was her age? Did my parents suddenly become too old, too square or just too oblivious to anything I liked or wanted to do?

My father is and has always been, even in my mind at age five, an Eisenhower Republican. I wouldn't say he was sexually repressed, but he wouldn't have any problem understanding why Victorians wanted skirts on piano legs. Sex talk made him uncomfortable, but my theory is he was just overly shy. He lucked out meeting and having my mother fall in love with him. She had no problem taking on ninety percent of the responsibility for managing our family life and, in particular, my growing up, while he devoted ninety percent of his time to his brokerage firm. As far back as I could remember, he was out of the house before I opened my eyes in the morning.

The waiter brought our drinks. I sipped my wine. Ronnie drank his vodka and soda and wiped his lips with the back of his hand.

'Use your napkin, Ronnie,' I said.

'What? Oh. Just a habit.'

'*Attack your habits. Embrace your dreams* – remember?'

It was a plaque he had on his office wall at work.

'Yeah, yeah.'

'I'm not as convinced about Kelly's ability to be an independent agent, Ronnie. She looks older than she is, just like most girls her age.' I thought of an expression he'd appreciate. 'Remember, don't judge a book by its cover.'

'Whatever,' he said. That was his fail-safe word when he knew he might very well be wrong.

'Another thing. If I return to work, we're going to have to have the maid back,' I warned.

'Bottom line is, it's worth it,' he said with a surprising sense of conviction. He held his palms up and bounced the right one in the air first. 'Weigh the pros and then the cons. Analyze and then act with confidence. More often than not, confidence carries the day,' he concluded, slapping his hands together.

Ronnie and his business techniques, I thought and nearly laughed. He was like most businessmen. He thought the rules that applied to everyday commerce could easily be applied to everyday relationships. A marriage was more like a merger. He was always the CEO and CFO, however. We were back to that famous 'bottom line' of his.

The waiter brought our meals. He stood back while Ronnie sliced his chop, studied it like a meat inspector, tasted it and then nodded. The young waiter looked as if he had been spared the electric chair. He asked if we needed anything else.

'Not at the moment,' Ronnie said, 'but stand by.'

He left like someone who knew he had not yet quite gotten away from something dangerous or tragic. I ate slowly, gazing around. There was no other couple here whom we knew. Ronnie couldn't lean over and start a conversation with someone and make me feel invisible. Tonight, though, he didn't want that either. I rarely saw him so focused on me.

'I was going to order a bottle of champagne,' he said between bites, 'but I remember that you didn't like the choice here last time.'

'It's below average,' I said.

'Champagne's champagne.'

'Actually, no, Ronnie. Real champagne has to come from France. The so-called champagne here is sparkling wine.'

'Cheaper.'

'And tastes like it. I think the hardest lesson for we Americans to learn is you get what you pay for. We're bombarded so often with deals and bargains on television and the Internet that we get to believe it's possible to have something of value for small change.'

'Aren't you an American, Clea?'

'I said *we*.'

'I never liked champagne or caviar or any of that ritzy stuff.'

'You want to have a ritzy car,' I reminded him. 'You keep talking about having that Jaguar convertible.'

'Cars are different. Cars make you look and feel good. We wear our cars here,' he offered. 'We don't just drive them.'

'That's very clever, Ronnie.'

I guess he *is* capable of coming up with something original from time to time, I thought.

He stopped chewing and smiled.

'That's what I like about you, Clea,' he said. 'You appreciate

being surprised. You always did. You'd have this bright look
in your eyes – the look kids have on Christmas morning. I've
got to work on getting that look from you more . . . What?'
he said when I just looked at him with a half-smile on my
face.

'Nothing. You do surprise me sometimes.'

He looked like a little boy who had just been patted on his
head.

My mood actually improved. After my main course, I
ordered a dessert and coffee, something I rarely did. Ronnie
had a Black Opal after-dinner drink and recited the changes
he was going to make at the office now that he could. I really
tried to be interested, but someone caught my eye at the bar.
I held my breath for a moment and waited for him to turn.

He nodded, his smile like twinkling crystal.

How did he know we were here? Was he stalking me now,
watching our house, following me? Did I mind?

When we rose to leave, I was nervous about going past the
bar, but when we did, I saw he was gone. After we stepped
outside, I looked around the parking lot, but I didn't see him
anywhere.

Ronnie was talking about plans for our new money. Maybe
it was time for us to consider a modest condo on the beach,
something we could enjoy on weekends and when he took his
vacation in the summer. He had his eye on one in Newport.

'You need a new car soon, too. Your lease is nearly up. And
despite what we've saved for Kelly's college tuition, I'd like
there to be a little more,' he added. 'Inflation is just around the
corner and who suffers that more than the middle class?' he
said.

Despite all his faults, he was still thinking family. Maybe
that was what attracted me to him the most.

'I suppose you're right,' I said.

'Sure, I'm right. With this added income and the potential
if you went back to work, we could do even more, Clea,' he
said. 'And a lot more for Kelly now, too.'

'She doesn't exactly lack anything.'

'You know what I mean,' he said. 'She wants her own
car. Many of her girlfriends have their own. It's not a sin to

want more. I wanted my own car when I was her age, and
so did you.'

'Did I?'

'Your parents told me how you nagged them,' he said,
smiling like someone who shared a special secret.

'OK. I'll think about it,' I promised.

'Maybe the lawyer who bought Sebastian's practice needs
help,' he suggested. 'As I recall, he wanted you to stay on. I
hear he's doing well. He might want to add on staff.'

'Maybe he does,' I said.

'I could find out for you.'

'No. I can find out things like that for myself.'

'Whatever,' he said.

When we were home and into the bedroom, Ronnie came
up behind me while I was brushing my teeth.

'I know something better than champagne when it comes
to celebrating anyway,' he said.

His look of lust took me by surprise. Twice in one night?
I finished brushing my teeth. He was waiting for me in bed,
that broad boyish smile on his face as if we were about to do
it for the first time.

'You really do come up with surprises,' I said.

'No, it's you who surprised me. You look great. I'm sorry
I don't tell you that more often.'

He reached up for me.

Again, I wondered how I would make love to him. Would I
make love to my lover rather than to him? If I did, would that
be another instance of adultery? I thought if I kept my eyes
open, I would be forced to think only of Ronnie, but when I
looked into his eyes, his face seemed to dissolve into my lover's
face. Even when I closed my eyes, I saw only him.

Ronnie was shocked at my aggressiveness. I fought to stay
on top and I held his hands down. I had other hands over my
breasts, other hands moving down over my hips, and other
hands pressed against my buttocks, moving me. I could hear
Ronnie's moans and cries, but they seemed far off, down at
the end of some tunnel. He was inside me and squirmed to
get into a better position, but I leaned back and held his legs
until he finally surrendered and lay back.

Every time I came, I cried out. When I did open my eyes again, I saw him looking up at me with a shocked but pleased expression.

'What did you eat tonight?' he asked, as I slipped off him and fell back beside him, waiting for my heart to relax and my body to stop feeling as if I were sinking in the mattress.

'Shrimp salad,' I replied, as if that was really his question.

'Warn me next time. Maybe I'll order the same thing.'

I looked at him.

'Be careful what you wish for. You might get it,' I said, and he laughed.

'What a night. What a day!'

He got up, and I turned over and pressed my cheek to the pillow.

I was positive. *He was in that bar*, I thought. And then another thought occurred, and I got up and went to the window that faced the street. I didn't recognize the car parked across from our house, but because of the streetlights I could make out the driver sitting there – only a dark shadow, but silhouetted enough to for me to recognize that it was him.

Did he expect me to come out?

I remained in the window, naked, looking down at him. Apparently, that was all he wanted. He started his engine, his lights went on, and he pulled away, disappearing around the corner.

'What's out there?' Ronnie asked.

'Nothing,' I said. 'I was looking at the stars.'

He stood smiling at me. I returned to the bed.

'Something's different about you, Clea,' he said, getting into bed. 'But I'm not complaining.'

'Good,' I said.

Tonight I was unafraid of sleep. My dreams were lined up like rush-hour traffic, waiting impatiently to move forward, each one more anxious than the one previous to take me away, take me to a place where people didn't have to dream anymore because it was all there.

THREE

'Where were you yesterday?' Rosalie Okun asked me as soon as I lifted the receiver the following morning. Ronnie and Kelly were already gone.

'Hello to you, too, Rosalie.'

'I called late morning and then in the mid-afternoon, about three thirty, I think.'

'I didn't see any messages.'

'I was moving around and didn't leave any. I know how long it takes you to return a call left on your answering machine, and you've never given me your cell phone number,' she added petulantly.

'I hate using my cell phone,' I said. 'I'm like one of those AARP people who use it only for nine-one-one emergency calls.'

I heard her sigh deeply. I smiled, enjoying how frustrating I could be, especially to my so-called girlfriends. Yet they all continued to offer me their friendship out of what I was certain they thought was an act of charity. Or maybe they couldn't stand knowing how easily I could do without them. Ironically, self-respect is often sacrificed in the name of ego. I knew I wouldn't call someone like me twice in one day, especially if that someone refused to give me her mobile number.

'So? Did you go to the Fashion Mall in Newport Beach without me?' she asked, which was her way of asking where I was.

'No, I didn't go to the mall. I just went after a string of errands I had been avoiding. The good old American wife's procrastination.'

'All day?'

'What is it they say about time when you're having fun?'

'Since when are errands fun?' she asked. There was a long pause. 'You sound strange.'

'Do I?'

She was silent again for a moment, and I didn't speak as I wondered if I did sound different.

'What about today? I'll pick you up,' she said. 'The new spring fashions are out. We can have a good time at the mall.'

Normally, I jumped at distractions. I wasn't simply coming up with an easy excuse when I mentioned procrastination. There were all sorts of minor and not-so-minor chores I really had been putting off, including taking clothes to the dry cleaner, catching up with some of the routine housework, getting some essentials from the drug store, working with the gardener to change some plants, and scheduling routine car maintenance for my BMW that had indicated it needed to be done nearly ten days ago.

I had no legitimate excuse for not doing any of this. Thankfully, I was well. I had no job at the moment, and there was nothing else more important cramming my attention. No one had to explain to me that my lack of enthusiasm was characteristic of deepening depression either. I had read enough about it and the symptomatic behavior which usually centered around obsessive eating or drinking as well as sleeping too much.

But as the song says, *Along came Jones* and – voila! – my depression, although not completely gone, had dissipated considerably.

Was I insane? I didn't even know his full name. All I remember was Lancaster. Was that his given name or his surname? Of course, I thought about Burt Lancaster and especially the great kissing scene in *From Here to Eternity*. Why is it that scenes like that in the movies really can never be duplicated in real life? Is it simply because there is so much imperfection in real life? The sand on the beach is irritating, the ocean waves are too salty and, as everyone knows, the sun causes skin cancer. None of that happens or bothers anyone in the movies. Of course, they move about with music in the background, too. Where's our music in real life?

'I wish I could go today, Rosalie, but I have a dental appointment that I've already put off once and you know how they get. They tell you they're booked solid for nearly two months, but someone else canceled and they called yesterday.'

'Oh,' she said, her voice dripping with disappointment and dropping the sound of the O as though it was falling into a deep well. 'Maybe tomorrow?'

Was she as lonely and as lost as I was? Didn't she have any previous appointments, responsibilities? What does she think of when she wakes up in the morning? Does she ever ask herself what she has done with her life?

That was one reason for my problems, I thought: my friends. They're all so insignificant, replaceable. Each was a mirror image of the other. I'm drowning in the mediocrity. Ronnie was actually right to push me toward returning to work. At least I would be exposed to more interesting people, events and conflicts. It wasn't difficult to raise the level over what I had now. Toby Ludlow was in a crisis because her French poodle's kidneys were failing. I loved dogs, too, but she was actually seeing a therapist. Brondi Spector was shopping plastic surgeons because her face lift had dropped after only a year and a half. Ari Deleon was convinced her beautician was causing her hair to fall out and was thinking of a lawsuit. It went on and on until it droned into a blur. I had gotten so I couldn't tolerate the weekly lunch, and the thing of it was, none of them would understand why.

Maybe I should join the army. All I might need is a new cause.

'Let me call you,' I told her. 'I have to check a few things about tomorrow. I'll call you if I'm free.'

'You're going to be at the weekly lunch Thursday, aren't you?' she asked, this time with more panic because my reply pretty much confirmed I wouldn't call her.

'At the moment, I don't see why not,' I said.

'At the moment? You're too busy. You should still have that maid.'

'Actually, Ronnie suggested I might want to go back to work.'

Silence. I was the only one in our group who had worked outside the home after marriage. Sookie Furnis toyed with the idea of selling woman's clothes in Nordstrom so she'd be up on all the fashions and get discounts. Not that she needed any. Her husband owned a prestigious Mercedes dealership. I think she was simply teasing herself with the idea.

'You? Get a job? Didn't he just get a promotion?'

I wasn't surprised she knew already. Mack Okun worked with Ronnie.

'It's not a matter of money,' I said. 'Well, maybe it is. Ronnie wants things faster than I do, but I want them, too. We'll see. I haven't decided yet.'

Suddenly, all restraint was thrown off. The floodgate opened.

'I wasn't going to tell you this, Clea, but all of us are a little worried about you. Lately, you have seemed different, more withdrawn. Is everything all right with your marriage? You know I'm only asking because I'm very fond of you, fonder than I am of any of the others.'

'Well, I'm sure that's the only reason you'd ask. I'm as happy with my marriage as the rest of you are with yours,' I replied. She didn't get the sarcasm.

'All I can say is think twice before you commit to something that might diminish you.'

How utterly stupid or ironic, I thought. She thinks going to work would diminish one of us.

'I appreciate the advice. I'll call you,' I said. 'Bye, bye, Blackbird,' which was what I called her. She did have beautiful ebony hair and a Middle Eastern complexion, with rich olive skin and naturally perfect full lips. Lately, she had gained a little too much weight, but she was confident her personal trainer would get her back in shape for her Caribbean cruise. How relieved I was when Ronnie refused to go. He hated being confined on a ship, despite what it had to offer.

She laughed, said goodbye and hung up.

I started to work on my list. As long as I keep moving, I thought, I'll be all right. Everything will be all right. I had a lot more energy in my step as I made me way out and got into the car. This time I was sure to get the garage door up fast. I backed out, paused to close it and then backed on to the road. For a moment, I just sat there, not shifting into drive.

The car I had seen last night from my bedroom window was parked on the other side of the street.

But there was no one in it.

I looked at our front entrance and over our grounds. I saw no one. Why would he leave his car out here? Where was he? I debated turning off the engine and getting out to look around. I was sure I would feel silly doing it. If he wants to see me, he has to show himself, I thought. Why was he doing this anyway? Had he been spying on me through a window? I waited a few more moments and then I drove off. I kept looking in the rearview mirror, anticipating him following me, but I didn't see him.

I did run down my list of chores, but at about midday I was close to what had been Sebastian Pullman's offices. I paused, thought about Ronnie's suggestion and went in. I had met the attorney who had bought out Sebastian's practice. His name was Carlton Saunders. He was in his early forties and had built a good reputation for his trial work. To service Sebastian's clients and continue to build his practice, Carlton had taken on two junior partners, Gerald Wilson and Bob Sayer. Brondi Spector's husband was Carlton's CPA, so I got the updates at our regular Thursday lunch. It always began with 'I thought you'd be interested, having worked there.' I was confident that Brondi's husband Garson would not like her talking about one of his clients. I never showed any real interest in knowing about the firm, but that didn't dissuade her.

I was curious as to how Carlton had refurbished the offices. Sebastian was quite conservative in his politics and his style. The furniture when I had worked there was the same furniture he had when he had begun the practice. Leather chairs were well worn, curtains somewhat faded, and the prints framed on the walls were country scenes remarkable only in their mediocrity and dullness. My office space had been furnished with an IKEA discounted desk, tables and chairs. The only thing Sebastian modernized was his computer technology. He often commented that all new law graduates needed now was a desk, a chair and a PC or Apple iPad, but he didn't make it sound like progress. He made it sound like giant backward steps, stripping the practice of law of all of its style, etiquette and morality, if there was ever any.

Actually, I had a great deal of respect for Sebastian. I thought he was the last of a class of men who really cared about the values of their profession more than the money they could earn. Maybe it was naive to think it, but surely there was a time when someone would want to be a doctor or a lawyer because he or she really wanted to help people, make the world safer.

On the other hand, Carlton Saunders was one of those aggressive, hungry men who went after clients and cases to build his net worth. Although he was good at what he did, image was still more important than substance. I could see that immediately when I entered the lobby, richly decorated with expensive-looking new leather sofas and chairs, rich mahogany tables, real oil paintings of dramatic seascapes and landscapes on new dark-cherry paneled walls. There was a chandelier where Sebastian only had a simple light fixture at the center of the ceiling, but there were also fancy, modern standing lamps at the sides of the sofas and chairs. One wall had shelves of law books, obviously there to impress would-be clients that they were in an upscale, well-educated, hard-working firm.

Sebastian Pullman's receptionist, Marion Godletter, had been with him for more than twenty-five years. She was a mother and grandmother with seven grandchildren. She never attempted to look younger, never touched up her ash-gray hair or improved on her makeup, which was really just some lipstick and a smidgen of rouge. She was more like a mother to me than another employee, never failing to ask how Ronnie and Kelly were doing and commenting on my hair and clothes. She was the sort who stored a virtual drugstore in her desk so she could offer cold and headache medicine the way a mother might.

By contrast, Carlton's receptionist looked as if she had just graduated from high school. She was a striking redhead with Kelly-green eyes and an obviously Miss America figure broadcast in a tight-fitting light blue knit dress. She flashed a well-practiced smile at me the moment I entered. I felt as if I had wandered on to a movie set of an attorney's office. Any moment someone would shout, 'Cut. Print that.'

'May I help you?' she asked. I was impressed that she used *may* and not *can*.

'I'm Clea Howard. I was wondering if Mr Saunders might have a moment.'

'Regarding?'

'My past employment here when it was Sebastian Pullman's law offices.'

She stared a moment.

'He knows who I am,' I added.

'Oh. One moment, please.'

Instead of calling Carlton on some intercom, she turned and typed my name and request on a computer. I was sure it appeared instantly on a screen at Carlton's desk.

'You may take a seat,' she told me.

'Thank you,' I said and sat on the sofa. I sorted through some of the magazines, but before I could get into any, Carlton Saunders stepped out.

Carlton was just under six feet tall, with firm, full shoulders molded by hours in some gym either at his own home or at a private club. His gray pinstripe suit was obviously tailored. He had a tanning-bed perfect complexion that emphasized his intelligent blue eyes, heightened sharply by his light brown hair. When I had first met him, I immediately imagined he came out of central casting when an actor to play a successful trial attorney was sought, which was why I had that movie-set feeling right now. Some people are born for the parts they will play in life, I thought. Carlton was one of them.

'Clea, how nice to see you.' He flashed a look at his receptionist and then turned back to me. 'Come on in.'

I followed him into what had been Sebastian's office. It looked larger and there were bigger, more expensive works of art, trophies for golf victories and framed letters signed by important political figures and clients. I noted the plush caramel-colored rug and the light blue curtains. Sebastian had dull coffee-white curtains that looked as if they might crumble in your fingers.

'Did you expand this somehow?' I asked.

He laughed.

'Yes. I carved out that walk-in closet and punched through the wall between this office and what had been yours. We've taken the office space on the second floor for my junior partners. There's a stairway just outside this door,' he added, nodding at a door at the rear, 'but you can approach it also from the lobby. I wasn't going to keep this building, but I decided to have some fun with it instead of selling. It's practically an historical site anyway. So? Have a seat,' he said quickly, nodding at the soft black leather chair in front of his desk. 'What's up?'

He sat behind his much larger and less organized-looking dark-walnut desk, and I sat, too.

'I was thinking of going back to work and thought first of you.'

'Really?' He nodded as the concept settled in like a piece of chocolate into boiling milk.

'Yes. I find I have too much time on my hands now that our daughter is teenage self-destructive, and my husband is more of a workaholic than ever. There's just so much you can occupy yourself with, and little of it is any sort of intellectual challenge.'

He laughed.

'My grandmother used to tell me that idle hands are the devil's workshop.'

I held my smile and he quickly lost his.

'You're not making friends with the devil now, are you?'

'Not since I left working in a law office,' I countered.

He laughed, but not like someone who enjoyed being satirized.

'Sebastian claimed you were the spine of his successful practice. He thought you'd make a good lawyer yourself and was disappointed that you didn't go on.'

'As am I,' I said.

'It's not too late. These days, many people pick up new professions late in life. Well, how can I help you?'

'I just thought I'd leave my name with you just in case you have a need for a paralegal.'

'I appreciate that; appreciate your thinking of me first.' He nodded again, thoughtful. 'Maybe I can get you going part-time here and see what develops.'

'I'd like that,' I said. 'Actually, I think I might prefer part-time.'

'I have a new case coming up. It's a bit complicated because it involves three different business entities. Lots of footwork needed.'

'I'm your man,' I said.

He smiled. 'One thing I'll never accuse you of, Clea, is being a man.'

I shrugged. 'It's still a man's world. All of us women make little compromises so that our men can feel more significant. It's practically become the American way.'

He stared at me a moment, his eyes narrowing with suspicion.

'Anything in particular motivating you to get out of the house these days?'

'You're really a lawyer's lawyer, Carlton,' I replied, and he laughed.

'OK,' he said, holding up his hands. 'I have your number. I'll call you in a day or so and outline what I think you can do and when.'

'Thank you.'

'However, I think it's a fair guess to say you must be desperate to get work,' he said.

'Oh? How do you know that?'

'You didn't even ask me about salary.'

'I just assumed—'

'Not a rule you break in court,' he said, coming around his desk. 'No assumptions. I know what Sebastian paid you. I'll add ten percent since I reduced the office space you'd be using by at least that.'

'I never needed much space.'

'If you become full-time, we'll talk about it again,' he added and held out his hand.

I took it, but we didn't shake. We simply made some contact. It seemed to be enough for him as well. He walked me to the door. His receptionist looked up, surprised, when I stepped out. I was sure she was wondering what could have transpired in so short a time. I smiled back at her.

When I stepped back out on the street, I paused. Normally, I wouldn't make a decision like this without first discussing it with Ronnie, even though he had suggested it. Half the suggestions he made were half-hearted, stuffing to fill a gap or get a problem out of his face, I thought. I envisioned them being put in stockings on a fireplace on Christmas Eve, little notes full of little suggestions.

Come to think of it, though, what decisions did most of the wives I knew make on their own? Clothes? Hair and nails?

Maybe what was for dinner? None of them made any dramatic changes in their homes without first consulting their husbands. It didn't sound as if it offered them any true self-respect, but the women I knew who led very independent lives had marriages that reminded me of the line 'We shared coffee,' as an answer to the question 'What was your married life like?' They resembled the German Confederation, the Deutsche Bund, a loose association of Central European states, more than they resembled the United States. Eventually, they broke completely loose.

Was that where I was heading?

As soon as I stepped into the house, the phone began to ring. It jerked me out of my deep thoughts. I don't know why, but I felt violated. More and more, the phone was turning into something annoying. At night, we still received those damn calls from fundraising agencies, political and others, appeals for firemen and policemen. No one wanted them not to be protected, but I wondered how much of a percentage the fundraisers took.

I almost didn't answer it. This was my time to be alone with my thoughts. I had a lot to decide, but then I thought it might be Kelly or something might be wrong with Ronnie. I wondered why I didn't think of anything else first. I wasn't a Chicken Little. I never cried, 'The sky is falling,' but disasters always did flash first in my mind. Maybe it was that damn Breaking News they flashed on television at the smallest opportunity. We were being trained to expect another attack on another World Trade Center.

I lifted the receiver after the fourth ring, just before it would go to message.

'Hey,' Ronnie said. 'You're home.'

'That's where the phone is.'

'I tried your cell, but it went right to answering service.'

'I just walked in. I had errands today. I forgot my cell phone,' I added, seeing it on the counter.

'Yeah, well, guess what? Management gave me a celebratory gift. They're paying for a group of us to have box seats at the Staple Center for the Lakers game tonight. You mind if I go out with the boys?'

'I haven't before when it wasn't a special gift, Ronnie. Why would I now?'

'Just checking. We're actually on our way, grabbing something to eat first in downtown LA,' he confessed in the tone of an errant schoolboy who had been taught that George Washington didn't lie.

'Really? That's like someone calling from the way down after he had already jumped off the ledge of a twenty-story building to ask if he could,' I said.

'What?'

'Just a joke. Enjoy yourself,' I said.

'You're the greatest, Clea,' he said, going into his best Jackie Gleason imitation from *The Honeymooners*, a show so historic it was relegated to something like TV Land or Shopping Network DVD sales.

I thought about telling him I had followed his suggestion and decided to go back to work and was actually going to do so, at least part-time, but I sensed that he was talking to me with his buddies in the car and wanted to get off quickly. I was sure he was already taking quite a bit of teasing for calling me at all and making it sound as if he needed my approval or permission. That was just the way it was, even though the other married men in the car probably had made the same sort of phone call, just privately.

'Bye,' I said. 'Have a good time.'

I hung up and began to put away everything I had bought. Then I went to hang up the clothes I had retrieved from the drycleaners, but the sound of my cell phone ringing and vibrating on the kitchen counter brought me back. Holding the clothes in my right hand, I answered.

'Clea,' I said.

'Are you all right?' he asked.

'Yes. Why wouldn't I be?'

'What brought you to a lawyer's office?'

'Are you stalking me?'

'Of course,' he replied.

I laughed. 'Not to worry. I'm not starting a divorce because of you. Not yet. Right now, I'm thinking of returning to work.'

'Really? Was that your idea?'

'Actually, my husband suggested it.'

'He's worried you're bored or he likes the idea of more income?'

'A little of both.'

'Any chance I might see you tonight?'

'Actually, a good chance. What did you have in mind?'

'There's an Italian restaurant just outside of Fullerton. You know it,' he said. 'Gianni's.'

'Yes, I know it, although I haven't been there in some time.'

'I'll be at the bar at seven thirty,' he said.

'OK.'

It was as if he had tapped into our house phone and heard that Ronnie was going to be occupied tonight, and knew just when to call me.

But I was glad he had.

I started for the stairway again. Looking out the bedroom window after hanging up the dry-cleaned clothes, I saw that the sky was quite overcast, but somehow, for me, the sun was shining.

'Gianni's, seven thirty,' I whispered.

I was beginning to feel as if I was riding a rollercoaster, and every time I went down, I started up to a higher peak.

Hold on, I thought. This is going to be a very fast and thrilling ride.

FOUR

In probably ninety-nine percent of American households where there is at least one teenager, the teenager at least occasionally lies to the parents about where he or she is going and whom he or she is meeting. It has almost become a rite of passage. The first time they do it successfully, they feel a sense of accomplishment, not guilt. On the surface, it surely looks as though the lies don't harm anyone. In fact, in their way of thinking they are doing their parents a big favor. They are alleviating their worry and concern. Later on, if the parents discover the untruth, they are reminded about their own fabrications when they were that age. They are told that lies wouldn't have been necessary if they had only been more reasonable. Often the blame is successfully shifted to them.

Lying to Kelly, as strange as it might sound, made me feel younger. I was trying to get away with something and, of course, there was no doubt as to whether or not she would approve of what I was about to do if she knew the truth, so that same twisted logic could be employed. If I didn't lie to her, she would be emotionally wounded, very seriously disturbed. The impact could easily affect her for the rest of her life and not only change her personality but have a detrimental influence on her own relationships. If her mother could do something like this, she would never trust her husband or even herself. She would hold her breath before she uttered a single commitment. In the end, she would age cynically, and all this just because I didn't lie. There was no way I was going to let that happen. I was doing this all for her. How's that for rationalization?

She was home before me and up in her room. I had stopped to do two more things before coming home: the drugstore to pick up more toothpaste and the Kwik Stop shop to pick up a quart of milk. I heard her coming down the stairs almost as soon as I ended my call from Lancaster.

'Who called?' she asked. She had heard the house phone.

'Your father.'

'He's supposed to help me with a paper I'm doing for business class. He promised to be my interview. I hope he remembers.'

'In all the excitement, he must have forgotten,' I said.

'What excitement?'

'You don't know? Of course, you don't know. You weren't home last night or this morning,' I said, more to myself than to her.

'What?' she asked, impatient with my detective work.

'Your father was given a promotion with a significant salary increase.'

'Really? Wow. Now he would be even better for the interview.'

'Except he was also given a surprise gift today – box seat tickets to a Laker's ball game. Which is where he is tonight,' I added.

'Oh.' She thought a moment and then shrugged. 'I guess one more day won't matter.'

'You didn't leave it for the last minute, did you?'

'Almost,' she said, with that cutesy little smile of hers that bent rules and got her things Ronnie would normally never get her. 'I work better under pressure.'

'You'll do well in business or politics,' I said. 'You have the right answers. All the time.'

She shrugged again. She obviously never thought deeply about something she did so naturally, as naturally as breathing: avoiding reality until it was absolutely necessary to face it. Was it just her or her entire generation? Had they all become Scarlett O'Haras, deciding they would worry about it tomorrow?

'So what's for dinner?'

'Why don't you order a pizza? I'm going out.'

'You're going out, too? Without Dad?' she asked, her eyes widening like the eyes of a cartoon character.

'We've been known to do it, Kelly.'

'Where? With who?'

'With whom? Or don't object pronouns matter anymore?'

'You mean they once did?'

'During the Middle Ages in America. I'm meeting an old

girlfriend for dinner. Reconnecting. I have to shower and change,' I said, heading quickly for the stairs.

'Do I know her?'

'No,' I said. 'She was before your time.'

'And you're reconnecting after so long?'

'It's been known to happen, Kelly. It will happen to you, I'm sure,' I said. And then I wondered. Would it? Would she end up in the place I was when she was my age? Would she peel off friends like peeling an orange and discard them? Is everything in this world temporary now? Was it always?

She still looked confused. I was tired of the fabricating. It was actually easier most of the time simply to tell the truth.

'Invite one of your friends over to share the pizza,' I told her.

She brightened.

'I should tell you one more thing,' I said, turning again on the stairway.

'What?'

'I'm going to go back to work for an attorney, part-time at first, but it could develop into a full-time job.'

'Wow. Ch-ch-changes,' she sang, and then smiled and said, 'David Bowie.'

'Yes, I know,' I said and continued up, smiling to myself. I knew that was a David Bowie song and I did feel like a teenager again.

Maybe because of that, I went at my nails and makeup more intensely. I couldn't recall when I had spent more time on myself with more interest and care. It took me nearly twenty minutes to decide on what to wear. I was undecided until I moved a few garments and saw the black dress I had bought nearly a year and a half ago for what was to be a special anniversary dinner. Ronnie thought it would please me to have two other couples with us to celebrate. As often happens when we go out to dinner with other couples, the men talked to the men and the women talked to the women. We might as well have been at separate tables. It certainly hadn't had the ring of something special, like an anniversary.

The dress was a form-fitted column style. It had a boat neck and a deep scooped back. I had bought my nearly knee-high black webber glazed nappa boots just to match the dress. I thought I looked great in it back then, but even better now. My DVD exercise program had delivered on tightening my rear and my thighs. I never gained weight on my stomach or waist, something that constantly amazed Ronnie who was always fighting the bulge. He told me I should be checked for tapeworm. I think he was hoping it was true so he could justify his own failure to keep his figure.

I decided not to wear any jewelry beside my watch and a pair of matching black opal ball earrings. I was happy now that I had kept my hair appointment last week and had the stylistic cut. I almost had canceled it because I hadn't felt the need to look pretty for some time. I was settling on a 'this will do for now' attitude, not only about my hair and my makeup, but my clothes, and even the way I was taking care of the house and shopping for food. One might even say I was down for the count just before I was rescued.

When I looked at myself in the mirror this time, I felt a ripple of excitement reminiscent of my youth and my first serious dates. I was a competitor again, for I always believed that all women competed for all men. It was part of our DNA, with origins clearly established during the caveman days. Were we really that far from them? Sexual aggressiveness was simply more subtle, but if they could ply us with alcohol or drugs, they would, and then drag us back into some cave. The goal of the pursuit hadn't changed. Of course not; why should it?

I laughed at myself being so giddy. One would think I was going to my first prom or something. I scooped up my black silk cape with wide tubular sleeves and hurried out of the bedroom, practically bouncing down the stairs. When Kelly stepped out of the living room and saw me, her jaw collapsed, just as Ronnie's did when he wanted to exaggerate his surprise.

'Wow,' she remarked.

I paused at the foot of the stairs.

'What?'

'I haven't seen you look this good for some time, Mom. This must be some very cherished old girlfriend.'

For a moment I felt discovered, but my rationalization sprouted instantly.

'Don't you know how we women are when we reconnect or go to class reunions?'

She shook her head.

'We try to outdo one another and look so good that the others think, "What happened to me? What did she do right and what did I do wrong?" It helps our ego.'

She smiled and shrugged, unable, I'm sure, to imagine this sort of a future for herself. In her mind, just like it had been in mine, she was young forever.

'Waverly's coming over,' she said.

'Try not to make too much of a mess.'

I started for the garage.

'Does Dad know you're going out?' she asked, following me.

I paused at the door.

'No. This happened after he called and he was on his way, but I'm sure I'll be home before he will.'

'Oh,' she said. 'Aren't you going to tell me where you're going? You always make me do that.'

'You can reach me on my cell phone, Kelly,' I replied. I knew immediately that it wasn't the sort of answer I would have tolerated. 'I'm going to Gianni's in Fullerton.'

'So far?'

'It's midway for her and for me.'

Her face was still crinkled with confusion and even – did I imagine it? – suspicion.

She stood there watching me leave. When I got into my car, I sat for a moment, thinking about her. There has always been this belief that a mother has more of a unique connection to her children because they were part of her body. She can sense things about them that their fathers or siblings can't. If that were so, why couldn't it be true in reverse? How well did Kelly read me? Was she old enough to understand whatever signals she was receiving? Did it frighten her? Did it make her more curious or didn't she care?

I was suddenly hit with waves of guilt. My friends, even some relatives and my own mother often accused me of not being selfish enough. The charge was that I was guilty of sacrificing my own wishes and desires for the wishes and desires of my husband and daughter. Their needs always came first. However, no matter what was said to me about it, I didn't change. Frankly, when it came to friends and relatives, even my own mother, I thought I was selfish enough; it was they who were *too* selfish. Many of my friends had broken or fragile marriages because of this attitude, and most had much bigger and more serious problems with their children than Ronnie and I had with Kelly. I always thought that a marriage should be a team effort, and team efforts by their very nature meant that individual desires had to undergo some compromise. Of course, the complaint about me that my girlfriends wave in my face was that I didn't demand enough compromise from Ronnie.

I hated putting the brakes on my new energy and excitement, but Kelly's face and the tone of her questions just now were doing exactly that. I had never wavered from the belief that my first obligation was to my daughter and her welfare. Now that I thought about it all, it amazed me that this consideration hadn't arisen until now. If I had thought about it, I wouldn't have been so excited and enthusiastic about going out tonight. I would have downplayed it so as not to raise any suspicions.

No matter how well we did as a family, how successful Ronnie was and what we could provide for Kelly, I always had the sense that she was fragile. I hadn't intended that she would be an only child, and I did consider some of the medical procedures to increase the possibilities of my becoming pregnant again, but I was terrified of the chance of anything odd occurring and causing me to give birth to a mentally or physically challenged child. I'd much rather leave it up to what would happen naturally. Nothing did. Both of us were tested for potency. Ronnie's results weren't terrible, but they weren't what they should be. I knew how devastating it would be to him to have that pointed up, so I settled – we settled – on leaving it be. If Kelly was going to be an only child, that would be it. Get used to it.

What this did, however, was make me even more unselfish than I had been. What was I doing now? Was I finally overcoming that? Were my needs demanding to be addressed, no matter what the potential risk? Was it my time? Did all adulterers go through a similar self-analysis or didn't they give it a second thought? It was certainly easier not to think about it. Could I do that? Could I avoid imagining Kelly's reaction when or if she found out?

Because of the traffic, it took a good thirty more minutes than I had anticipated to get to the restaurant. I chastised myself for taking too long to prepare. Ronnie would have been moaning and groaning, crying that we would be late. I arrived nearly twenty minutes late.

Gianni's was one of those Italian restaurants that really reminded you of an Italian restaurant in a small Italian village. The pinkish stone building itself was modeled on the traditional architecture, with its small balcony, mostly for show, cantilevered eaves and arcaded portico.

I had forgotten how much I had enjoyed it when we were here, usually on the way home from somewhere. For one thing, it was small, so it gave you the impression it was truly a family-run operation with a Mamma Mia in the kitchen, creating sauces and recipes handed down through the generations. The walls in the restaurant didn't have fancy pictures in fancy frames. They had actual family photographs that were in frames meant to hang on house walls, not restaurant walls. The tables had cotton tablecloths, so it didn't look like some pizzeria in a mall. There were candles lit in small glasses by now, but what hit you immediately on entering were the aromas of garlic and peppers, meatballs and onions. All the pasta was truly homemade.

It was in the bar that the owners had done the most to appeal to a wider clientele. It was almost as long and as wide as the restaurant area. Here, there were a half-dozen smaller tables without any tablecloths, cloth or paper. The walls were a dark-maple paneling with posters of Italian opera stars and famous Italian movies like Fellini's *La Dolce Vita* and Sophia Loren in *Marriage Italian Style.*

The bar itself had the look of something handmade by an Old World craftsman. There was great care in the columns and raised panels of dark oak. A dozen or so red-cushioned stools with backs were nearly filled. I paused. The men and women sitting there all seemed to turn on cue toward me. He wasn't one of them and he wasn't sitting at any table. Oh no, I thought. He didn't think I was coming because I was so late. Or maybe he's just as late as I am. He could have hit the same slow traffic. I decided to take a seat at one of the small tables.

The bar waitress, a girl who didn't look much older than Kelly, came over immediately, as if it was an unwritten rule never to leave an unescorted woman unattended in this bar for more than twenty seconds. I thought she approached me the way someone might approach a celebrity – tentative, her eyes full of excitement and interest. Everything about her demeanor underwent a metamorphosing as she stepped up to the table. Her posture improved and she quickly brushed off the front of her white blouse. She was wearing a light pink, mid-calf skirt, and her light brown hair was cut closely in a boyish style, but there was nothing boyish about her full figure. When she walked, she was followed by an entourage of male eyes.

I couldn't help thinking that Kelly could have a part-time job in a place like this someday, maybe helping to earn money for her college education, and could walk up to a woman like me alone at a table and be thinking, when she saw her wedding ring, that she might be having an affair. Ronnie and I were not regulars at this restaurant. No one knew us. This would be an ideal place to meet my secret lover. But both this girl and Kelly would try to be sophisticated about it and do nothing to make me or any other married woman feel uncomfortable, even discovered.

Ever since I had met Lancaster, it was easier to envision myself in romantic scenarios. I was getting so that I could even hear that movie background music. We'd be on that beach, kissing, with the waves rushing over us. Soon, I thought, I'll become like Ronnie and hum the themes of famous films. For me, beside *From Here to Eternity*, it might be *Picnic* or *An Affair to Remember.* I used to be so intolerant of the way my girlfriends fantasized and here I was doing it. There was that David Bowie again, singing *ch-ch-changes.*

'Good evening,' she said. 'What would you like?'

She set down a napkin.

'I'd like a glass of chardonnay. Do you have Cakebread?'

'No. We have Beringer.'

'OK, fine.'

'Do you want me to bring a bar menu?'

'No, thank you. I'm waiting for someone,' I said. 'We'll probably go to the dining room.'

I thought she almost curtsied before turning to the bar. Most of the customers were back to talking among themselves, but one woman held her gaze on me, a weak smile on her face. I didn't smile back. *Make no friends here*, I told myself. *Come and go like some unremarkable shadow.*

There was music. Pavarotti. Unlike most restaurants, it wasn't simply a subtle background sound; it was clear and loud enough to appreciate. I closed my eyes for a moment. The beautiful music made me feel more philosophical. How did I get here? Was this as destined to happen as any incubating disease that was there at birth?

When your marriage is young and you're building a home, having children, solidifying friendships and developing careers, you don't seem to have time to pause and build on fantasies. It takes someone with far less familial glue to separate him or herself from his or her spouse and children, and give free rein to the lust. He or she has to be dissatisfied not only with his or her partner, but with him or herself. He or she wasn't what he or she had dreamed to be. In fact, either woke up one morning and began to blame the marriage itself as if the institution was naturally a trap. They should have waited, but when people say that, what do they mean? Do they mean wait until the wanderlust dies in you? Until you're less selfish? Wait until you believe you're lucky to get whom you have? Does any of that ever happen?

The waitress brought my drink. She stood there for a moment, waiting for me to take a sip and approve of it.

'It's fine,' I said.

'I love your dress,' she said.

'Thank you.'

'Did you get it around here?'

'No. Actually, I got it in Los Angeles. Beverly Hills,' I said.

Her eyes widened and she nodded as if I had confirmed a suspicion she had about me.

'I knew you weren't from here.'

'How do you know that?'

She shrugged. 'You look like someone from Beverly Hills,' she said, but it didn't sound pretentious or derogatory. It sounded like mere fact.

'Do I?'

She nodded. 'Do you want anything else? I can bring a dish of peanuts.'

'No, I'm fine,' I said.

She nodded and returned to her other customers. I watched her hold conversations with others and smiled to myself. She couldn't be more than twenty-one, I thought, a young twenty-one, but most her age were young for their ages. Ronnie was always complaining about that. Whenever the company hired any young people, he complained that they were immature and as impatient as teenagers when it came to getting promotions or getting to their vacations.

'I hate to think of the future of this country when we're gone,' he would say, and I would think, *But what about the future you and your contemporaries are creating now?*

I looked to the doorway when I heard someone entering, but it was two couples arriving for dinner. They were followed by two more and then a single couple and another couple with a teenage boy. I glanced at my watch. It was nearly eight. If he had been detained, he couldn't be much longer. I had just about finished my wine, but I wasn't going to order another without him. The aromas of various shrimp, eggplant and chicken dishes had turned my stomach into a grinder, too.

The young waitress returned.

'Did you want another glass of wine?'

'No. Thank you.'

I turned to the doorway again. Someone was leaving – an early-bird couple. Two men entered and came to the bar.

'Maybe you should give me the check,' I said. 'In case I have to leave quickly.'

'Your friend's really late?'

'Something might have happened,' I offered.

'Didn't he try to call you?' she asked, assuming it was a man.

I didn't correct her. I didn't want to add an iota of fact. However, I should have realized, in this day and age of cell phones, old excuses lost air and fell flat.

'He doesn't have a cell phone,' I said. That was about as far as I wanted to go with information, but I also realized that my being vague and secretive made my being here seem more illicit. Afterward, she would probably elaborate and invent her own fantasy. It wasn't unlike a game my girlfriends and I played occasionally during our Thursday lunches when we saw a stranger enter the restaurant and sit at a table alone. It could never be anything innocent.

'No cell phone?' She looked incredulous.

'He's old-fashioned. He still writes letters and mails them.'

She nodded, barely listening now. He sounded boring and had to be old. She wrote out my check and put it on the table. 'You should think about having something to eat anyway. We serve in the bar, and the food here is fantastic.'

'I know,' I said. 'I've been here.'

Actually, the prospect of eating alone was terrifying. She waited a moment, flashed another smile and returned to the bar. I looked at my watch. It was ten after eight. Now I was feeling rather foolish, all dressed-up and eager. All I could think of was getting out and never returning. I dug into my purse, came up with some money that would also suffice as a good tip and placed it on the check. After taking one more glance at the door, I nodded at the young waitress and rose.

'Night,' she said, hurrying over. 'I hope it's nothing serious.'

'Probably isn't,' I said. It was a dumb thing to say. This was serious already as far as I was concerned. Like anyone angry about being stood up, I told myself I would accept only a fatal accident as an excuse and walked out. I paused just outside the door. Two more cars entered the parking lot, but both had couples in them. Slowly, my head down, I made my way to my car.

I got in and just sat there, imagining Ronnie at the game, screaming at the refs, slapping high-fives when the home team scored, he and his friends magically shedding years and becoming high school seniors again. Ronnie's marriage, his fatherhood, his job would be like some distant fabrication, almost a nightmare. A mortgage, saving for your kid's college education? Who had put such ideas in his head? He was back in the days debating whether to ask Tami Woods or Kirstin Dance out next weekend. Both had been giving him signals, promises of a hot date – no teasing, no hesitation, just raw lust.

I conjured up Kelly next.

She was sitting in the living room with her girlfriend, slopping down pieces of pizza and maybe sneaking a glass of wine or a beer. They were both talking fast to get out their thoughts and desires ahead of each other. Music, boys and taunting sex filled their heads. They were at the point of confessing secret thoughts, each swearing to protect the sanctity of the other's revelations. It would be a satisfying evening, both for her and for Ronnie. They would go to sleep wrapped in warm contentment. All was right and safe in the world.

I would lie there with my eyes wide open, staring into the darkness, waiting for sleep like a regular bus line's passenger standing dumbly at the pickup station, not aware that the bus company had gone bankrupt.

I hated myself like this. I pounded at the images and drove them away just in time. The passenger-side door opened and he slipped in like an afterthought, cloaked in the shadows drawn by the way the parking lot lights carved out the darkness.

'Where were you?' I asked.

'I was here. Waited fifteen minutes and left, but then I thought I would wind back and spotted you coming out of the restaurant.'

'You waited fifteen minutes and left? What was this, a college class?' I remembered it was an unwritten rule that if your professor was fifteen minutes late, you could leave. 'Why didn't you wait longer?'

'To be honest, I had the feeling you didn't want to be here tonight, that you were having second thoughts.'

'What gave you that feeling? I didn't say anything.'

'I'm a supersensitive guy. I can feel things others are about to feel.'

'You're going to give me a complex. You keep telling me

how easy I am to read, like you're the NSA tapping into my thoughts as well as my telephones.'

He shrugged.

'When you get close to someone, you're able to anticipate more. You can do that with your husband, can't you?'

'That's no challenge.'

He laughed.

'Well, you can see now that I came and you're feelings were incorrect.'

'Perhaps you came reluctantly?' he suggested.

'Look at how I'm dressed, the care I took with my hair and my makeup. Does that suggest reluctance?'

'Maybe I left because I wanted to give you the chance to change your mind, catch your breath. What's happened between us has been fast and furious.'

'If I wanted to change my mind, I wouldn't need anyone to give me a chance to do it. I'd just do it.'

He laughed again. 'Spirited.'

'When I can be, yes.'

He stopped smiling. 'Look, these things happen in spurts sometimes. It's like riding a rollercoaster. Eventually, you want or need to get off.'

'Is that what you want? Is that why you're saying these things now?'

'I want what you want,' he replied. 'It's all right for me to be someone's little episode, but people don't always realize there could be a price to pay later.'

I was silent. Nothing he was saying hadn't occurred to me. It was just different to have it clearly pointed out. I was more like Kelly, or she was more like me, than I wanted to admit. I, too, believed that, like most things in our lives, we could ignore them comfortably until we couldn't.

Another couple arrived, and when they got out of the car, they immediately sought each other's hand, reaching like two swimmers in the ocean desperate to be safe. They didn't look any younger or older than Ronnie and me. We didn't hold hands very often anymore. Sometimes, I wondered if we even looked married. If I didn't say anything, he would shoot out ahead of me and stand waiting for me at the car. I used to complain, and he always apologized and swore he wouldn't do it again, but he did, and I gave up, just like I had given up with many other troubling things between us.

'Are you hungry? Do you want to go back in there?'

'No, not there,' I said.

As stupid as it might sound, I didn't want to face that young girl again. I didn't want to appear desperate or needy, especially to someone who reminded me of my own daughter. I had no doubt now that she would realize I was with someone other than my husband. My wedding ring seemed to burn into my finger, glowing in the dark.

'I understand,' he said. I looked at him. 'I know what you need.'

'Do you?'

'When we were kids, we would make love in places where it was possible we'd be discovered. It added to the excitement. The challenge became who would take the most risk. One couple made love in the school, right around the corner from the principal's office and got away with it. They got the prize.'

'Which was?'

'Just admiration.' He turned and nodded at the backseat of my car. 'Looks big enough.'

'You're kidding. This is like being in high school.'

'Isn't that part of what you want?' he asked. 'A return to high school?'

He stepped out before I replied, opened the rear door and got into the back seat. Another couple left the restaurant. They were laughing as they walked by my car. Whatever they were talking about captured all their attention. They never looked my way. I thought for a moment. I could see him in my rear-view mirror, but I couldn't make out his face that well in the shadows. Was he smiling?

'This is madness,' I said, recalling the night I had lost my virginity in Jeffrey Morton's father's limousine, but I got out and, before anyone could see me, opened the rear door on my side and got in. He had loosened and lowered his pants already.

'This isn't going to be very comfortable,' I said.

'Leave it to me. I'm a contortionist,' he replied.

'Well, I'm not.'

'You will be,' he said with confidence.

I wanted to resist, I really did, but that was like looking back at an exit off the freeway you had missed. There was nothing you could do but ride on. The best you could do at that point was sit back and enjoy it.

Which was exactly what I intended to do.

FIVE

He was definitely a contortionist. Somehow, despite the restricted space, he was gentle and loving. We didn't grope each other like teenagers in the back of my car. He kissed my breasts, the small of my stomach, and pressed his lips farther and farther up the inside of my thighs. I tried to contain my moans of pleasure, but at one point it was impossible. Every woman wishes her lover would go slower, think about pleasing her at least as much as he thought about pleasing himself. Unless it's rape, it's not a selfish act, or at least should never be. I almost wished I could have Ronnie standing by, watching us to learn.

'See?' I would say afterward. 'This is how it should be done.'

Every few moments, I reminded myself that I was in a car in a restaurant parking lot. There were parking lot lights, the glow of which invaded our small dark space. It should have made me more hesitant, reluctant, but he was right about it being more exciting because we were practically out in the open, and I was conscious of the danger of exposure. Throughout it all, I heard people passing by, some closer to my car than others. I held my breath, anticipating either a scream of outrage or hysterical laughter accompanied by some wisecrack or other if they happened to look in and see us. None of that happened.

Actually, we found a very comfortable position. I was on top, and when I gazed down at him with the glow of the light washed across his face, I saw his smile, not a smile of arrogance, but a genuine smile of amusement and pleasure. I moved gently, working him inside me, fast and then slow, occasionally stopping completely to see the expression on his face and feel him urge me to go on.

'You like to be in control,' he said.

I didn't answer. It was obvious. He laughed when I increased speed and demanded more and more from him, until I was exploding like the firecrackers and fireworks in *Summertime* with Katharine Hepburn and Rossano Brazzi. Just as I had been thinking while I was waiting for him in the restaurant, we all want to be in the movies. I guess I shouldn't be so critical of Ronnie and his playful excursions into one film or another, imitating this actor or that and humming theme music.

When it was over, I lay there on my left side, curled in the fetal position. I felt his hand on my hair, stroking it lovingly, but in a way that was more parental than erotic and sexual. In fact, I kept my eyes closed and resurrected my childhood. I felt the way I did when my mother comforted me. That was what he was doing now, I thought. He was comforting me. I should have been annoyed by it, but I softened and felt as if my body was oozing off of my bones. It was the contentment of an eight- or nine-year-old and not the afterglow of a mature woman who had just made very passionate love.

'Still hungry?'

'Not any more,' I said. He laughed. I turned and looked up at him. His face was still cloaked in shadows. 'Tell me about yourself.'

'Don't you know enough about me?'

'You must be kidding.'

He looked away.

'I'm whoever and whatever you'd like me to be.'

'Stop avoiding it. Reveal yourself.'

'OK. As you probably imagined, I'm independently wealthy – some of it inheritance and some of it just good investment strategies. You know from what I have already told you that I travel a great deal, see wonderful places, startling scenery, and meet interesting people, which is something you've always wanted to do, I'm sure. Like you, I have eclectic tastes in music, art and literature. I've been to the world's greatest museums – the Hermitage in St Petersburg, the Louvre in Paris, and the Prado in Madrid to name a few. I've seen operas in the world's most beautiful opera houses, musicals in the West End in London, plays off and on Broadway. I've met many authors and artists. I don't concentrate on just one type of anything. One minute I'm listening to Frank Sinatra, and the next I'm moving to Lady Gaga. Do I fulfill your expectations of me?'

'So you have eclectic tastes, even in people?'

'I can get along with anyone.'

'Tolerate anyone, you mean.'

He laughed. 'You're so cynical, but when you think about it, the result is the same. And I'm not that unlike you.'

I sat up and brushed back my hair and then thought of something.

'So are we trains passing in the night?'

'Eventually, we all are trains passing in the night to each other, aren't we? It just takes longer for some to pass us. You've said something like that to me.'

'Have I?'

'I think you put it in a quote. *It's better to have love and lost than never to have loved at all.*'

'You don't forget a single thing I say, do you?'

'Aren't you flattered?'

'Beside Nixon who taped himself in the Oval Office, who wants his or her every word to be remembered? We all say things we wish we hadn't.'

'*The moving finger writes; and, having writ, moves on . . .*'

'You quote all my favorite lines. So, how long will you be here?'

'Until you tire of me,' he said. 'Until you turn away when you see me, yawn when I speak, and have your eyes open when we're making love because you're looking or thinking about something else.'

'Nothing or no one demands you be elsewhere before that happens?'

'No. Envy me?'

'Who wouldn't?'

'Oh, there are old home bodies, even your age or less, who couldn't care less about traveling and shedding responsibilities. You know that. Not everyone has that hunger, that thirst and desire to experience and consume from the wonderful smorgasbord waiting out there. Besides, a moving target is harder to hit, so I keep moving.'

I laughed. 'Who's trying to hit you?'

'The list would take the rest of the night.'

I thought about it. Was his mystery getting too deep, losing its novelty, its romance? Do I want to continue asking questions and getting answers? For now, I couldn't help it.

'Were you ever married?'

'What do you think?'

'No. You don't look or sound as if you have ever had any responsibilities for anyone other than yourself. What about family?'

'I create new family everywhere I go.'

'So what are you, beside an independently wealthy man – a poet, a musician, an artist? You have to be something, have some interests.'

'I'm all three.'

'You want to remain my mystery man.'

'Isn't that the way you'd rather it be? You don't really want me to start giving you those sorts of personal details. You'll start thinking about them and corrupt the purity we have between us. Once you learn all those details about someone, you begin to consider the influences of religion, status, peers, geography – the whole enchilada.'

'As I said before, you seem to know a great deal about me – even how I think and what I believe. And don't give me any romantic gibberish.'

'Is that so difficult to do? No offense,' he added quickly.

'Am I really that obvious?'

'No more or less than most people.'

'You sound very arrogant when you say that.'

'Confident. I always wonder where the line is drawn, don't you? Everyone hopes their children will have self-confidence, but no one wants them to be arrogant. When do you know there's enough and stop pouring the compliments into them, stop boosting their egos? You're certainly confident about yourself in many ways, aren't you?'

'Yes and no.'

'Everyone has that little insecurity. You can't be perfect, but you do a good job of balancing the two.'

'You're not perfect?'

'I'll be as perfect as you want me to be.'

'Everything to please me? Even that?'

'Can't you tell from the way I make love? Most men make love to a woman as if she, too, has only one orgasm. Very inconsiderate.'

'You'll get no argument there. I have half a mind to introduce you to my husband.'

'In little ways, you have. I feel like I know him already, know what you want me to know about him.'

'Have I?'

'When you're with someone as long as you have been with your husband, you can't help but bring something of him along with you. Some of it is influence; some of it is . . . stains. Even people who get divorced, after long marriages especially, can't wash them away.'

'Tennyson's *Ulysses*? *I am part of all that I have met*?'

'*Yet all experience is an arch where through gleams that untraveled world.* Yes,' he said. 'Something like that.'

I sat back. More people came out of the restaurant. I watched them walking slowly, talking, some couples still holding hands, some pausing to kiss. It wasn't a chilly night by any means, but the couples I saw seemed to huddle as if to protect themselves from sharp winds coming from places hidden inside them.

We all walk with some fear or another, I thought. Or maybe I was just projecting my own feelings and fears.

'What?' he asked.

'Nothing. I didn't say anything.'

'Your silences speak volumes.'

'Volumes not everyone can hear, even those you thought could or should be heard.'

We were both silent for what Shakespeare called a pregnant moment.

'Look, I realize what you have now is not enough for you. I don't mean me; I mean what you had before we met.'

'I'd be a liar to deny it, not that I'm anyone's little Heidi. Little lies are unfortunately what keeps most marriages together these days. I'm just exhausted from the effort to come up with new ones, I guess.'

'Is that why you're toying with going back to work? Because if it is, it won't be enough. That won't do it.'

'Thanks for the encouragement.'

He laughed. 'I'm going to go,' he said.

'Slam bam thank you ma'am?'

'Hardly.' He leaned over to kiss me. Then he backed away and exited the car smoothly, closing the door so softly that I didn't know it had even been opened.

I watched him walk off into the darkness, a shadow going home. After another minute or so, I got out and got behind the wheel. When I started the engine and backed out, I saw the young waitress leaving the bar and restaurant. She stopped instantly when she saw me driving out of the lot. She wore a smile of incredulity and then looked as if she was laughing before she walked faster to her car. I pulled out sharply and sped away, embarrassed, but a little angry at myself for telling her so much, too.

It wasn't until I was pulling into my driveway that I realized I really was hungry. When I entered the house, I listened for a few moments and imagined that Kelly and her friend had gone upstairs to her room. The living room was cleaner than I had expected – no empty pizza box, dirty glasses or plates left on the coffee table. Even the kitchen looked passable for a military KP inspection. I opened the refrigerator, saw the remaining pieces of their pizza and shoved them into the microwave. I poured myself a glass of cranberry juice and then went at the pizza, standing up and leaning against the kitchen counter. I gobbled it down – wolfed it actually – and hurriedly got rid of the evidence. Maybe a minute later, I heard Kelly and her friend Waverly coming down the stairs.

I stepped out to say hi so they wouldn't be frightened at the sound of someone in the house.

'You're home already?' Kelly asked.

'Hi, Mrs Howard,' Waverly said. Waverly was a good three or so inches taller than Kelly, slim, with a model's figure. However, there was just nothing remarkable about her face to make her photogenic, and her straggly hairdo did nothing to help.

'Hi. Yes. My friend had another appointment. She's at a convention,' I said.

'Oh. Where does she live now?'

'Cleveland,' I replied. If you were going to lie about a city, that seemed to be a good choice. There was nothing that excited Kelly about Cleveland.

'I have an uncle in Cleveland,' Waverly said. 'My mother's youngest brother, Uncle Lloyd. But we've never been there.'

'Amazing,' Kelly said dryly. 'I'll put it on my Facebook page.' She could be so biting sometimes – a chip off the old block, if I could call myself an old block.

Waverly giggled and then looked closely at me. I hadn't checked myself in the mirror after I had entered the house. It suddenly occurred to me that I was probably nowhere near as put-together as I had been when I had left. Instinctively, I ran my fingers through my hair and brushed down my dress. I saw the look of surprise and confusion on Kelly's face. Before she could ask another question, the doorbell rang.

'That's probably my mother,' Waverly said. 'It's nice seeing you again, Mrs Howard.'

'You, too, Waverly,' I replied and smiled at them both before heading quickly to the stairs. I wasn't in the mood to have a small-talk conversation with Waverly's mother, who was a dentist. Whenever I confronted women, especially married women, who had achieved professional careers and managed a family at the same time, I couldn't help but feel inadequate because I hadn't continued with my own education and had instead settled on being a paralegal, and not for that long either.

Kelly followed Waverly to the front door as I ascended and went to my bedroom. When I looked at myself in the full-length mirror, I saw just how disheveled my hair was. There was still something of a flush in my face. Almost always, whenever I made love, I followed it with a shower if I could. It wasn't that I felt particularly dirty or I was afraid the scent of love was lingering. The warm water on my shoulders and my back helped me relax and recall the moments I had enjoyed.

When I stepped out of the bathroom with a towel wrapped around my hair and wearing my robe, I found Kelly sitting on Ronnie's and my bed waiting for me.

'Hey,' I said. 'Something wrong?'

'You ate my pizza,' she said with an accusatory tone. I suddenly felt like a witness on the stand in a courtroom. 'I was going to warm it up and finish it.'

'I didn't think you'd mind. You rarely eat leftovers. Sorry.'

'But why did you eat pizza leftovers if you went to dinner?'

Was this a Perry Mason moment?

'I didn't eat much. Hardly anything, actually. The food was disappointing. And,' I added, the ideas coming quickly, 'my friend was at minimum thirty pounds heavier than she had been when we knew each other. You know the effect very heavy people, especially women, have on my appetite.'

'What does your friend do? Is she married? Does she have children?'

I went to my vanity table and sat. Then I unraveled my towel.

'She works for an advertising company that specializes in prescription drug marketing. I was never so bored. She couldn't talk about anything else. No, she's not married and she has no children. It was like nothing we once had in common survived the years,' I added.

I was actually quite taken with my ability to fabricate. I didn't think a successful novelist or playwright could be more self-satisfied at the moment. Before she could ask another question, I began to blow-dry my hair, but she didn't leave. She waited a few moments and then raised her voice over the sound.

'Why did you take another shower and wash your hair again?'

'I hadn't before I left,' I said.

'Your hair looked great, though, and since when do you go out without showering first?'

'I was in a rush. What difference does it make?'

She shrugged. I thought that might be it, but I was wrong. She had other suspicions.

'Daddy called,' she told me, dropping it into our conversation just the way a good trial lawyer might try to surprise a witness.

I shut off the hairdryer.

'When?'

'Half-time at the game. He said they were winning. He sounded very surprised about your going out. I told him why you didn't call him, but he still sounded very surprised.'

'A man believes he can be spontaneous, but when his wife is, he's surprised. It's in their DNA.'

'I told him you said you were going back to work for sure. He was surprised about that, too.'

I spun around.

'I didn't get a chance to have much of a conversation with him. He was on his way to the game and you know how men can be when they're with each other. They never want to appear hen-pecked. Get off the line quickly before they start getting mocked is their modus operandi.'

'Sometimes you sound like you hate men,' she said and started out, pausing in the doorway. 'And don't tell me it's in our DNA,' she added.

Before I could respond, she was gone. I turned and looked at myself in the mirror. Was that how I was really coming off? Was I hardening, tearing the scabs off old wounds, my memories of disappointing romances from junior high until now? Was I taking out my frustrations on my daughter, poisoning her well, shaping her into a cynic?

If anything, I should have appeared happier when I came home. Didn't I have an exciting and satisfying tryst? Maybe it was having to lie about where I was and whom I met that took away from my feelings of warmth and satisfaction. Rather than blame myself, I blamed the situation that required me to lie. I wanted more freedom. I certainly didn't want to be cross-examined and made to feel guilty, especially by my teenage daughter.

I didn't know why I hadn't thought of it before I came home, but now, when Ronnie returned, I'd have to come up with the same fiction. He'd be more detailed with his questions. Who was this old friend? Why hadn't I mentioned her before? When did I know I was going out to dinner? And why didn't I tell him about my seriously pursuing work again? The classic evaluation made by anyone observing all this surely would be that I was digging myself in deeper by expanding on my lies, but what choice did I have?

I went to bed with my new novel. Kelly looked in just before she went to bed.

'Denver Scott asked me out this Friday for pizza and a movie,' she said.

'Thank God for pizza.'

'He's not the richest kid in the school.'

'I was just joking. I didn't go to fancier restaurants until I graduated high school,' I said. 'Even when your father and I started dating, we didn't go to particularly expensive restaurants. He wasn't fond of spending money on gourmet food, and ambience wasn't important to him, even then. Actually, most men aren't very interested in restaurants at that age. Food's just a path to something else.'

She raised her eyebrows.

'You never told me that stuff about Daddy and other young guys.'

'To be fair, most girls are that way at that age, too. Even the ones used to better things.'

'You're talking funny.'

'Am I?'

'Yes.'

It was my turn to shrug.

'You want me to think of you as more of an adult now, so that's what I'm doing.'

'I suppose,' she said. I smiled at her indecision about whether or not she should be pleased by what I had just said. I recalled the same feeling on the same road traveled. You do want your parents to see you as more mature, more capable of understanding. You don't want to hear real life watered down. And yet, when that happens, you realize what you're leaving behind – the innocence, the freedom that comes with no real responsibilities, and all the make-believe that gave you comfort.

She was staring at me intently now. I could see the question marks in her eyes.

'What is it now, Kelly?'

'What made you fall in love with Daddy?' she asked. She stood there with her eyelids narrowing. I hated when she had that intense look – Ronnie's look – after she – or he – had asked a question that had more of an underpinning than you'd first think. The way she asked the question made it sound as if she believed I had regretted falling in love and certainly regretted marrying. Thankfully, I didn't have to get married. I didn't get pregnant for nearly two years afterward.

'I don't know that anything makes you fall in love,' I said. Good spin, I thought. Politics is seeping through the cracks in the middle-class family dome that had been dropped over our lives, and I didn't just think of it as Ronnie's infatuation with the echo chamber talk shows. We lobby each other in little ways constantly.

'There had to be something different about him, something that won you over, right?'

I lay the novel down. I really wasn't prepared for such a deep conversation at that moment, but I also realized I couldn't give her some short, trite response. I wasn't going to talk about bells ringing either, however. Somehow, hypocrisy had taken on a more offensive odor than ever. Maybe because I was swimming in it.

'Most of the women I know seem to have fallen into their marriages.'

'What do you mean?' she asked, stepping farther into the bedroom. 'How do you fall into a marriage?'

'It's as if they were navigating through various relationships and just stepped into the one that turned into a marriage. I sometimes get the impression it was like they were asking themselves, "What else is there for me to do at this point in my life?" Funny thing is they're not ugly, even comely women. They were obviously very attractive, but the usual pressures were poking and pressing them. You know . . . *What are this guy's prospects? If they're good, shouldn't I say yes? How many more years will I be searching for Mr Right? When will I stop thinking it's all like it is in the movies?* You can grow into love, I suppose. I've even heard one or two say their husbands fit them. Like they were trying on shoes or something.'

'What about passion?' she asked.

'It has to be there for most, I imagine, even if for only a little while. Although there are some women who not only look like they never experienced it and certainly don't now, they look like they don't believe it exists for anyone, period.'

'What about you?'

'Absolutely needed passion.'

'You couldn't keep your hands off each other?' she asked, nodding, urging me to affirm it.

'Something like that,' I said, smiling. 'I used to be afraid my parents could see your father's fingerprints on me.'

'Really?'

'It sounds silly, I know,' I said. Then I quickly stopped smiling. 'You don't feel that way about this boy, do you?'

'No. I haven't felt that way about any boy yet.'

'There's no rush, Kelly. You've got plenty of time.'

'That's what every adult always says . . . and then there's Amy Benson,' she added, her face filling with a dark shadow. Amy Benson was a girl in her class who had been killed in a car accident last year. The girl driving, Teresa Matthews, had been speeding and lost control on a curve. Kelly could have been in that car. For months afterward, both Ronnie and I grilled her on wherever she went and with whom, as if being her age was her fault.

'You can't base your life on things like that. They happen, but thankfully it's the exception, not the rule.'

'Whatever,' she said. I had come to hate that word.

I reached for my book, but she wasn't finished.

'Did you ever feel you made a mistake?'

'Mistake?'

'Marrying Daddy?'

'You wouldn't be human if you didn't think about it. You probably think about it whenever you're with someone – even this Denver Scott.'

'I don't want my parents to be human,' she said.

I was about to laugh, but stopped myself. She was right. I hadn't wanted my parents to be human either. As a child especially, you see them as larger than life, always perfect, always right in the end, no matter what the argument. That was a good illusion. It helped you to feel secure, protected. As soon as you began to see their failings and weaknesses, you were far more aware of your own, and with that came the realization that you could fail, be hurt very badly, even die. My parents seemed to know that instinctively. They did their best to hide any financial problems or health problems. They never wanted me to worry about anything.

I looked at Kelly more closely. How much of my disappointment in Ronnie these days was she aware of? How much of his disappointment in me? What about the disappointment in myself? How well did she pick up on my reactions, my smirks, shaking my head, mumbling to myself? Or maybe she saw me staring into space many times, but didn't approach me to ask if I was all right? Why shouldn't she be sensitive to a woman's feelings, even at her age? She was half me, wasn't she?

'I didn't want my parents to be human either, Kelly. I can't blame you for that, but you're far from a child now. It's all right to grow up.'

She gave me one of Ronnie's 'Duh, I know that' smirks.

'Are you going back to work because we need the money or because you're bored?'

'Your father would tell you we always need the money. He loves doing that scene from *Key Largo* when Lionel Barrymore asks the mobster Rocco, played by Edward G. Robinson, what he wants, and Bogart says he wants more.'

'Don't remind me,' she said. If she had girlfriends over, she fled when Ronnie started to do his actor and movie imitations. Actually, it was one of the things about him that I found delightful. I could see how proud he was of his accuracy, especially when it came to recalling famous lines from famous old movies. It brought to mind one of the positive things I would say about him now.

'He's cute when he does that, Kelly. Your father can be very personable, which is what makes him successful in business.'

'Right,' she said. She yawned.

'Go on, go to sleep,' I said. I held out my arms and she hugged me.

'Love you,' I said.

'Love you back. And sorry you didn't have a nice time tonight,' she added. I watched her walk off.

I lay back and looked up at the ceiling. Lancaster was so right. I was reluctant tonight, and mainly because of Kelly. I had to end this, I thought. There was such a world of danger here. *Stop before it comes tumbling down on all of you*, I told myself.

Could I? Was it all beyond my control now? I felt like someone who had been shot into space. There was no way to turn back, no way even to change direction.

I put my book aside and put out the lights. Ronnie would be home late, for sure, and whenever he was, he was usually very considerate, practically floating in and out of the bathroom and slipping softy into bed. If I woke up, I didn't speak because he was usually still running on high-octane fuel and would talk and talk, which would really wake me up.

If I had continued speaking about love and marriage with Kelly, I would have mentioned what years of being with one person really means. You get used to each other's little peculiarities and habits. Maybe this was why we had so many similar thoughts simultaneously. We could anticipate so much about each other.

And yet what did it really mean that, after all these years, Ronnie didn't have an inkling about my affair? Was it his indifference to me or my ability to disguise and hide the truth from him? Rarely did I ever show interest in any other man. I even hesitated to point out a good-looking actor. It was as if I thought I might open up some floodgate and all my doubts and complaints would come pouring out in the open.

I had told Lancaster that many marriages depended on little lies, a little dishonesty – some marriages more than others. For those marriages, cold truth was debilitating and broke them down too quickly. Perhaps we were always one of those marriages. Maybe I shouldn't have sounded so condescending and ridiculed the little lies everyone seems to need in order to remain viable, above water. Yes, every marriage needs some subterfuge, some mystery, and when the two of you get so familiar with everything about each other, the romance suffers. By definition, love diminishes, I suppose.

What about Ronnie? I saw the way he looked at other women, but I also saw that shyness, almost a fear in him when it came to doing much more than just look. If another woman returned his gaze and smiled at him, his face would flush like someone who was struggling to breathe. If he has done anything extramarital, he would have to be one helluva good liar, I thought. I really did believe he felt I was quite enough for him. Did his friends tease him about that? Would he even say such a thing to them?

Was I being naive? My own behavior now made me question everything about his. Here I was, practically congratulating myself on how well I was hiding my affair, when it could be me who was the cuckolded spouse. What an irony that would be! Actually, if he was having an affair, that would explain why he was so oblivious to mine. But he was still seeking out sex with me, while I wasn't the initiator with him. That has to mean something, doesn't it? Or was he that good at keeping his extramarital relationships hidden? Maybe I'm too arrogant for my own good, I thought. What if I did discover his betrayal? Would I even mention it, considering what I was doing?

These thoughts kept me up longer than I had anticipated. I heard him enter the house, put out the lights and start up the stairway. Better to fake sleep, I thought. He surprised me, however, by being a little noisier than usual. Accidentally, or perhaps deliberately, he walked into the small bench at the foot of our bed.

'Sorry,' I heard him say. I didn't move or respond. He went into the bathroom and didn't close the door as softly as he usually did.

When he came out, he bounced on the bed instead of slipping softly under the blanket.

'OK,' I said, turning. 'What is it?'

'Oh, you're awake?'

'Either that or I'm talking in my sleep. I'd have to be in a coma not to be awakened.'

'Sorry,' he said.

'It smells like a brewery in here.'

'I washed my face and brushed my teeth. You're just supersensitive.'

Lancaster's excuse. How ironic.

'That must be it.'

'How come you didn't say you were going out when I called?'

'She called after.'

'Who's she?'

'Flora Anthony. She was on my dorm floor. We did a geology project together.'

'I don't remember her.'

'She's easy to forget, which is what I'll return to doing.'

'Why did you go out with her, then?'

'I thought it would be better than eating alone. It turned out to be almost the same thing.'

'I thought you would eat with Kelly.'

'She had a girlfriend over. I was hoping to talk about something else besides girls who are doing too many selfies and the pros and cons of body piercing.'

'What's a selfie?'

'Taking pictures of yourself and emailing them all over the universe. You should be the one having dinner with Kelly so you can learn to speak teenager.'

'Sorry, but you've never minded my going to a game with the guys and since—'

'I'm not blaming anything on you, Ronnie. I hope you had a good time.'

'Yeah, we did. It was a great game. So you want to go back to work for sure? I'm not pressuring you to do it. That wasn't my intention. I merely suggested that—'

'Can we talk about this tomorrow? I was in the middle of this dream where I was waterskiing in Nice, on that European trip we never took.'

He laughed.

'OK, goodnight,' he said and turned over.

I'm getting very good at this deception thing, I thought.

Is that something I want to be good at?

Wasn't I much more transparent these past years? How many times do we change in a lifetime? I wondered. Am I anything like the woman I was just before I met Ronnie and immediately afterward? Did a serious relationship and the marriage that followed take me off the path I had been following and expose me to feelings and thoughts I never had

even imagined? If your surroundings, the people you love
and who love you, and everything else you're exposed to and
experience shape and influence you before you were married,
why can't all that be true afterward?

After all, you make so many compromises. You find yourself
laughing at things you might never have laughed at previously.
Your opinions about so many things change, and not because
your husband dominates you so much as because you seek
a smoother, less complicated direction to take or accept.
Specifically, your thoughts about sex, about what you would
do, change. You might eat foods you never really liked, go
to places you'd rather avoid, and tolerate friends you wouldn't
spend five minutes with before you were married. You would
do this all in the name of love and marriage, and then, after
you've had children, you do it mostly for them, so the world
they are growing up in isn't full of static. I knew many
women who wouldn't hesitate to fight with their husbands
in front of their children, but it wasn't something I was
comfortable doing.

It wasn't that Ronnie took advantage of all this. I could see
that he simply and probably naively assumed so much about
me, about us. Right now, it didn't occur to him that I wouldn't
agree with his political thoughts, or that I would dislike to
make something he enjoyed eating. It was as if he believed
that I would always trim and cut around my thoughts and
feelings so they would slip in comfortably beside his own. He
was confident that my surrender or compromise was part of
that famous female DNA I tossed around so lightly when I
spoke to Kelly.

Was that faith or arrogance and selfishness? Should I dislike
him for wanting us to ride on smooth waters, or should I rock
the boat and condemn him for not seeing me as more of an
individual? Many of the women I knew did that, some so vigor-
ously that they defeated their own marriages. I gave up my
maiden name when we were married, but did I give up something
so essential to my identity that I lost all connection with the
woman I had been? Did I have to join some female talk group
to get the answers?

I glanced at Ronnie who had already fallen asleep. Kelly's

questions had stirred some old fears. He was different, too. He still had that edge in business, but he had lost something vital when he grew comfortable and confident about me. When we were dating, as when all couples first date, there was a vivid, hovering fear that something will be said or done that will abruptly end it. Maybe that was good.

Maybe I was seeing Lancaster, this forbidden man, hearing him and admiring him because he embodied that danger, that edge, and somehow, in some way, I hoped and expected it would bring it all back to Ronnie. As Lancaster had said, he wouldn't be here forever and he had yet to propose that I go off with him.

Was I dreaming? Rationalizing? Justifying my sins so I could go on?

I turned over and closed my eyes so I could imagine Lancaster walking into our bedroom softly and slipping under the blanket beside me. His embrace, feeling his muscular body, being nudged and teased by his erection aroused me. I held my breath. Could Ronnie, even in his sleep, sense my sexual energy?

I heard his heavy, regular breathing. We slept beside each other, but we had taken the sleep train in different directions, which somehow, miraculously, brought us to the same station every morning.

I curled comfortably, safely, and bathed in my fantasy, even moaning a little about the pleasure.

Ronnie never heard or sensed it, probably because he was already buried in his own.

SIX

I was up ahead of him, ahead of both of them, in the morning. I needed a cup of coffee and went down for it with the intensity of an addict. Although I hadn't drunk very much the night before while waiting for Lancaster, I felt like I had a hangover, as if my brain had turned to cement. I didn't descend so much as slowly sink down the stairway, taking a deep breath and then holding the air in, as if bubbles would emanate from my lips and nostrils otherwise. After I managed the coffee, I floated on to the chair at the kitchen table and hovered over my steaming cup, clasping it like a Neanderthal cherishing the first sparks of a new fire. The caffeine would burn in my blood and open curtains, raise shades and unlock doors.

Kelly came down first. She, too, looked as if she was walking in her sleep, traveling down the road to some wonderland of her own making. Her eyelids opened and closed like the lid on our mailbox, accepting the incoming messages of light and shapes so she wouldn't walk into anything. Her ears were still clogged with the voices and sounds of last night's dreams. I could tell she didn't even realize I was sitting at the table.

'Were you texting late last night again, Kelly?'

'What? Oh. I didn't see you there, Mom. How long have you been up?'

'Way longer than you. I just got up.'

'Very funny.'

She poured herself a cup of coffee and took a health bar out of the refrigerator.

'Are you remembering to take your vitamins?' I asked.

'What vitamins?' she replied and then laughed. 'Yeah, sometimes. Mrs Norton, the school nurse, says we don't need them if we eat a balanced diet.'

'I haven't heard that since I don't know when. Who eats a balanced diet?'

'Mrs Norton,' she replied and slid into a chair across from me like a soccer goalie retreating to the safety of her zone.

'You should have some juice, too, Kelly. I'm going to make some scrambled eggs for your father and me.'

She put her finger in her open mouth.

'Thanks for stirring my appetite,' I said, and she laughed.

'Actually, I *was* up texting. Art Williams texted me last night,' she said after taking a long sip of her coffee and a bite of her bar.

I stared at her blankly. I don't know how many names she tossed across the table when we ate or at me when I was driving her somewhere, but she always expected I would somehow remember who everyone she mentioned was. She could be halfway through a story before I had a chance to ask about whom exactly she was talking. From the expression on my face at the moment, she could see I had no idea who she was talking about this time either.

'Art Williams? His father is a homicide detective, remember?'

'Vaguely. So?'

'He said he thought he saw you at Gianni's.'

'What?'

'What a coincidence, huh? He and his father picked up his mother from her flight at LAX and stopped at Gianni's to eat on the way home. Turns out it's a favorite of his father's.'

I continued to just stare at her.

'He said he wasn't sure it was you, so he didn't come over to say hello. He said you were in the bar at a table alone. Were you?'

I sat back, finished my coffee and stood.

'I'm going to make some scrambled eggs for your father and myself. Last chance. Do you want any?'

'No. Hello. I never have a big appetite in the morning, Mom. Why were you in the bar?'

'I was waiting for my friend. She was late, so rather than sit alone at a table in the restaurant, I sat at a table in the bar.'

She looked astonished.

'The last woman executed for that was in something like 1428, Kelly.'

'Your friend was late and she had to leave early?'

I spun round. 'What's with the questions, Kelly?'

She shrugged. 'I don't know. It was a long way to go for so short a time. Weren't you upset?'

'I doubt that I'll give it any more thought for the rest of my life,' I replied. 'And I intend to live for a long time.'

'Did you end up eating in the bar?'

I took out the eggs.

'I mean, that's what I told Art. I told him that was probably why they didn't see you in the restaurant itself. He said you were gone by the time they left.'

I didn't reply. I started to make the scrambled eggs. Ronnie was coming down the stairs.

'Art Williams is one of those people who tell you every little detail of what they're doing, even what they're thinking. Facebook was made for him especially. He's always on describing what he's eating or something. Sometimes, it's plain gross – like he found a piece of something he ate yesterday between his teeth.'

'Don't turn on your computer.'

'Yeah, right,' she said, as if I had told her not to drink water.

'Morning, girls. You two look wide awake,' he said, going for the coffee.

'Looks deceive,' I replied. He laughed.

'Who won?' Kelly asked him.

'Lakers by ten, but it was a close game almost all the way.'

'Oh. Congratulations, Dad. Mom told me last night about your promotion.'

'Thanks.' He sat beside her and kissed her. He held his face only inches from hers. She pulled back and grimaced.

'Ugh. You smell like cigarettes.'

'Didn't shower yet and was around a lot of it.'

'Second-hand smoke kills,' Kelly said. 'You always tell me that and quote insurance statistics.'

Ronnie looked to me to come up with something to save him from hypocrisy, but I was silent, even though I usually did. I wasn't feeling particularly charitable this morning. Kelly's questioning had changed my mood. I hated feeling defensive and guilty.

Ronnie poured himself some coffee, ignoring her. It occurred to me that both of us do that quite a bit – ignore our daughter, her questions, her comments. It's like dodging bullets sometimes. She seems to take it in her stride. I get the feeling it's something the parents of most of her friends do as well. Sometimes, we ignore each other to survive, I thought, especially when it comes to teenage sons and daughters.

'Don't forget I'm interviewing you for my paper on business,' Kelly told him. 'Tonight.'

'I'll make sure I don't forget. I'll have your mother remind me.'

The two looked up at me. Usually, I had a good comeback for Ronnie's lame jokes, but I wasn't in the mood this morning.

'Eggs are almost ready,' I said.

'Mom's upset because her date last night was a disaster,' Kelly told him.

'Yes, I had that impression,' he said, looking at me.

'Art Williams saw her in the restaurant.'

'Who?'

'A boy in my class, Dad. His parents were returning from the airport and stopped there to eat.'

Ronnie turned to me, looking as if he had just remembered who I was.

'I never asked you where you went,' he said.

'She went to Gianni's in Fullerton,' Kelly told him. I thought she was acting like an informer. Was that on purpose?

'Gianni's. Why go that far?'

'Do you want to tell him or should I, Kelly?' I asked, holding up the spatula. She giggled. 'It was midway,' I said.

'Food good? I think it was good when we were there last, wasn't it?'

'I wasn't impressed this time. Maybe it was the company. Some people can spoil your appetite, ruin your taste buds and turn your digestion on its head.'

'She was very fat.'

'Who?' Ronnie asked her.

'Mom's friend. But maybe it was also because you ate in the bar.'

'Ate in the bar?' Ronnie asked.

'Don't keep asking me to regurgitate the experience,' I quipped. He shrugged and sipped coffee.

I started to serve the scrambled eggs. Kelly shot up out of her seat.

'Got to go,' she said. 'Denver's picking me up this morning.'

'Denver?' Ronnie asked.

'Her date for Friday,' I said.

'Have we met him?'

'Twice, Daddy,' Kelly said. 'Neither of you ever pay much attention to my friends when they're here.'

Ronnie looked at me, again expecting some defense, but I was tired of playing the lame blame game.

'She's right,' I said. 'We don't, but it's not so surprising. The girls wear the same clothes, say the same things, giggle in the same key, and the boys are always waiting for some sign of disapproval because of their poor grooming or lack of hygiene.'

'Thanks, Mom.'

I ate some of my eggs.

'OK. We'll try harder,' Ronnie said. It was almost as if a button was pushed and his pat answer came spilling out of his mouth. 'For starters, what's his father do?'

'Robs banks,' she replied. 'You always ask that about any of my friends, Daddy. I don't hang out with anyone because of what his or her father does.'

'Don't be a wise ass,' Ronnie called after her. 'And who names their kid after cities?'

He looked at me, but before I could defend her, the phone rang. I looked at it for another ring and then picked it up hesitantly.

'Hello.'

'Am I calling you too early?' Carlton Saunders asked.

'Oh. No. I'm having breakfast.'

'Good. As it turns out, I'd like you to start on this case today, if that's possible. The court calendar was updated. As I said, there's lots of footwork involved, documents to go through and—'

'I'll be there in an hour,' I said.

'OK. Good,' he said. 'I'm expecting a call that might get

me to court sooner rather than later, but I'll leave instructions for you in case I leave before you arrive.'

'Fine.'

'Welcome again to the fight,' he said.

'*This time I know our side will win,*' I replied, and he laughed.

'Who are you quoting *Casablanca* to?' Ronnie asked as soon as I hung up. It was a line he used, too. Maybe he had rubbed off on me far more than I knew.

'Carlton Saunders. He wants me to start today. It's only part-time,' I added quickly.

'Wow. I wish all the employees working with and under me would make decisions as quickly and firmly as you do,' he said, but it didn't sound like a compliment.

I sat and continued eating. I could feel his gaze on me.

'So what made you finally decide to go back to work? I mean, you weren't that keen on it when I suggested it, were you?'

'The sound of silence,' I replied. He grimaced.

'Silence. Oh. You mean, when both Kelly and I are gone and you're home alone with . . . with whatever there is to do here?'

'Yes, that and the conversations I have with my so-called friends,' I added. I wanted to continue and add, 'and the conversations I have with you, too, lately,' but I just ate instead.

'Well, I thought you might enjoy having more to do,' he continued. 'I mean, I'm going to have more to do with this promotion so—'

'So it works out well,' I said.

'Yeah, that's what I mean. Is he paying you enough?'

'Ten percent more than Mr Pullman paid me.'

'Doesn't sound like enough.'

'It's enough for now. I think I can negotiate for myself, Ronnie.'

'Sure, sure.' He thought a moment, then smiled and said, 'Great eggs.' He ate a little faster. As soon as he finished, I was cleaning up. We both had to get out of the house quicker than usual now. He returned to the bedroom to shower and finish dressing for work.

He stopped in the kitchen on his way out.

'Good luck,' he said, giving me a fatherly kiss on the cheek. 'I'm sure you'll do fine. It's like getting back on a bike after you've fallen off.'

'I didn't fall off, Ronnie.'

'Yeah, I know,' he said with that vague look he sometimes captured on his face. I knew he always wondered why I didn't seek new employment when Sebastian retired. 'We'll have to get that maid, huh?'

'Let's wait and see,' I said. 'I'm not sure how much work Carlton really has for me yet.'

'Whatever,' he said. He gave me another quick kiss and headed into the garage, whistling 'The Battle Hymn of the Republic'.

I moved quickly once they had both left. Not long ago, I had divided my closet into what I called my professional work clothes, everyday clothes and evening clothes. That chore had filled one of those gaping holes that formed in my daily life. I chose the black pants suit I had worn the last day I worked for Sebastian. Some women didn't dress much differently for work to how they did for going out to socialize. I couldn't imagine Carlton's receptionist doing much more to enhance her beauty when she went on a date. She was already set for Camera One on a movie set when she took her place behind the receptionist's desk every morning. Was it an old-fashioned idea for a woman to dress down, use less makeup, not be as concerned about her hair and her nails when she went to work for someone else?

It wasn't all that long ago when a woman in the workplace was vulnerable, knew that every time she stood up, walked across a room or addressed one of her male counterparts, she was being judged first for her looks and second for what she was contributing to the job at hand. The concept of sexual discrimination and harassment in the workplace wasn't that old. Was it even possible to think only of the job and not be concerned at all about any of this? Certainly, a woman should feel quite safe working for a lawyer. If anyone knew the dangers of crossing the line, it was a lawyer. Or so one would think.

None of this had been on my mind for some time now. Had

that made my life more comfortable or less interesting? Here I was, rushing out to start again, but did I really want to do it? Was I running after something or running away from something? I had a feeling that was a question more than one woman and man asked themselves daily.

Lancaster had made me think more deeply about it. His comment about it lingered like some bad aftertaste. There was hesitation in my steps as I descended the stairway to leave. Some of that was surely anxiety. Could I do what Ronnie had tritely said and get back on the bike? Did I still have the intellectual concentration to perform efficiently? Did I have enough interest in it? So many of Sebastian's cases, if not most, had been dry wells of excitement, full of balance sheets, resolutions, minutes of dreary meetings. I had to read through, searching for a way to parse agreements, looking for some small hole through which to drive home an accusation and a financial position. It was certainly not the stuff of *Boston Legal* or *The Devil's Advocate*. Most of the time, the only drama was in the choice for lunch.

Why didn't I simply decide to return to college? The degree could put me in real control of my life. Was I afraid that if I had more education and a more prestigious college degree than Ronnie, I would swamp him, diminish him and make this marriage even less than it was? Or was I just plain lazy? I wondered what my father would think. I knew it annoyed him that I hadn't continued my education; unlike so many daughters, however, my pleasing him first and foremost wasn't at the top of my list of life goals.

My cell phone went off as soon as I got into my car.

'This is Clea,' I said.

'You're going to work for that lawyer now, aren't you?'

'What, do you have my phone tapped?'

'Thanks for confirming my suspicion.'

'You must be or have been a detective or some sort of CIA agent.'

He laughed. 'We all have a little CIA in us. Look, you don't want to do this,' he said. 'You're just looking for ways to avoid me now.'

'Just like a man, believing it's all about you.'

'No, this is solely about you and what's good for you.'

'So you're not a writer or an artist or a musician after all. You're a psychiatrist?'

'Joke about it if you want to, but I give you two, three days at the most, before you stop, look out the window – if there is a window in whatever space he gives you to work in – and wonder what the hell you did to put yourself back there. You'll see chains around your ankles. You're too beautiful to be relegated to a desk job. You're even too beautiful to be a trial attorney. No one would listen to anything you said. They'd all just be looking at you. Very pretty women have a hard time in the business world. Or even becoming teachers. Maybe especially becoming teachers. Ever see *Blackboard Jungle*?'

'You know what? You are beginning to sound like a male chauvinist pig.'

'I'm not talking about all women, just very attractive women, which means I'm talking about you.'

'I'd like to hear some note of confidence in my intelligence, too. I have worked successfully, you know.'

'Oh, you can do it. Easily. You're just not going to like doing it now. It's not the solution you seek. I know what you're after. A breath of fresh air. It would be better if you lowered all the windows and took a nice fast ride on the freeway, letting the wind blow through your hair. I bet you have it pinned up severely, hoping you'll be noticed for your achievements and not your looks?'

I did.

'How do you know that? You are stalking me, aren't you?'

'Not half as much as you're stalking yourself,' he said.

'I'm hanging up. I have to go,' I said.

'Look for me. I'll be there when you look hard enough,' he said.

The line went dead and I started the engine.

Hearing his words had put a tremble in my body. I was holding on to the steering wheel for dear life. It was just anxiety, I told myself. It had nothing to do with what he had said. I knew what I was doing was not the pursuit of any goal except the one related to filling my time. He was right about that. I was not going to fool myself into believing I was once again pursuing a career and, by definition, looking to add more meaning to my life. I didn't expect I would decide to return to college.

I couldn't imagine that my work for Carlton would be any more exciting than my work for Sebastian had been. In fact, from what he had told me on the phone, I was anticipating some similar, very dry, financial legal dispute that would require me to read through some company's board minutes, hundreds of emails, and sift through partner agreements and contracts in preparation for a deposition. Twice when I reached intersections, I almost turned back, but I kept telling myself this would be good medicine, and just like good medicine might taste bad or have some side effects, this might as well, but in the end it would do me good.

I parked in the office lot and started for the entrance.

I thought I saw Lancaster on the far right corner, leaning against a telephone pole. When I looked again, he was gone. Without further hesitation, I hurried in. Carlton's receptionist wasn't giving me that saccharine smile this time. Maybe I was only a paralegal, but I was a more important employee. I'd be giving her things to do, too.

'Good morning, Mrs Howard,' she said, as if I had been coming to work here for weeks, if not months. She rose. 'Mr Saunders asked me to show you to your office. He had to leave for the courthouse about ten minutes ago.'

'Thank you,' I said.

She started around the desk and indicated the door on the far left. It was the same way I had entered my office when Sebastian had his practice here, but the door had been changed and the hallway had been shortened. When she opened the door of what used to be my office, I saw what Carlton meant when he said it had been reduced in size. Someone could actually become claustrophobic in it. It looked more like a cell on death row. Even the two big windows had been diminished. They resembled portholes on a cargo ship.

There was a neat pile of documents and folders on the right-hand side of the small desk. The phone was on the left, with the computer taking up the rest of the space. Book shelves were on the right-hand wall and a framed print of *Christina's World* on the left.

'Mr Saunders found that picture in a closet and thought it might be something you'd like.'

'It was always in here,' I said, looking at it. I had often stared at it and wondered about the woman in the picture and how much like her I often felt. 'I do like it. I like it very much.'

'It's interesting,' she said with little enthusiasm, probably to snap me out of my reverie. It annoyed me. *She* annoyed me.

'I'm sorry, but we were never properly introduced,' I said.

'Oh. I'm Jackie Goodman.' She giggled. 'Dumb of me not to have introduced myself right away.'

I nodded, mainly because I agreed. It was dumb of her, but social graces and etiquette were long relegated to rest homes. She had a name plate on her desk, but I hadn't acknowledged it. I wasn't going to make it that easy for her. Was that mean of me? Condescending? Perhaps, I should be more congenial, I thought. As Grandma used to say, you get more with honey than you do with vinegar.

Get past the nervousness, Clea, I told myself.

'Thank you, Jackie.'

'Mr Saunders' junior partners will stop by this morning to say hello. The coffee pot is in the same place it's always been. There's milk and stuff in the refrigerator. I put a bottle of water on your desk about twenty minutes ago, but if you want a colder one—'

'No, that's fine. Thank you.'

'There's a sheet here with Mr Saunders' directions – what he's looking for in that mess,' she said, nodding at the pile of folders containing financial data. 'There's a big fight over what assets were prenuptial. I don't know how it was for you when you used to work here, but seeing all these nasty divorces so frequently fills me with terror every time my new boyfriend starts to sound like he's going to propose or something.'

'Yes, you might have to spend some time at the Betty Ford Clinic first after having worked here.'

'What?' She held her smile. It was obvious she didn't know what the Betty Ford Clinic was. I went around the desk.

'I had this desk,' I said, recognizing some of the scratches in the surface.

'It was in the storage room. I don't think any other desk would fit in here well.'

'No,' I said, gazing around and nodding. 'None would.'

'I usually go to Sol's Luncheonette for lunch at noon. I meet some girlfriends who work at the insurance agency. You're welcome to join us.'

'What insurance agency?'

'Balkin and Morris,' she said.

'My husband works there. He was just made office manager.'

'Oh, that's great.'

'I don't think it would be politic for me to mingle with his employees.'

'Politic?'

'They'll feel constricted.' She looked at me dumbly. I thought I was speaking to an exchange student and had to translate English. 'Afraid to say anything for fear I might go tell my husband.'

'Oh. Gee, I'm sorry. I'd hate to see you have lunch alone, especially your first day.'

'I'm fine. I might meet my husband, in fact,' I said, even though neither Ronnie nor I had suggested it.

'Well, call me if you need anything. You just hit—'

'Zero. I know. Things haven't changed that much since I was here.'

'I suppose not. Good luck,' she said and left. I stared after her a moment as the silence clamped down like a mousetrap. Had I traded one world of loneliness for another? Was Lancaster right?

I pushed those thoughts off the screen in my head and dug into the work. In minutes, it was as if I had never left it, as if all the time in between was a dream. I was on the computer, occasionally finding better sites to utilize, but for the most part, to use Ronnie's metaphor again, I was someone who had simply gotten back on the bike.

I never liked the way time went by when I worked for Sebastian. It wasn't that it dragged; it was completely the opposite. I would look up and discover that I had been swimming for hours and had never lifted my head up long enough to realize it. If anything, it contradicted the expression, *Time flies when you're having fun.* Time just evaporated when I did this dry pursuit of bank accounts, property records and brokerage statements.

In the beginning, Sebastian's excitement in making discoveries infected me and I felt the same joy when I unmasked financial deceptions, but after a while that lost its exhilaration. It was almost expected, anticipated. The numbers turned me into a cynical accountant. Honesty existed only on a blank page. The moment there were entries, deceit reared its ugly head. Satan was probably responsible for the printed word and definitely for numbers.

Less than two hours later, my phone rang.

'You have a phone call already,' Jackie said. 'It's your husband,' she added, lowering her voice as if she was warning me.

'Thank you.' I waited to hear her click off. 'Ronnie?'

'What's it like?'

'I haven't been here two hours.' He didn't say anything. 'So far there's nothing different for me to do, if that's what you mean.'

'I remember you weren't excited about that job.'

'No,' I said, a little impressed that he remembered and had given it some thought. 'We'll see.'

'I'd meet you for lunch, but I have an important business lunch with some national executives.'

'That's OK. Oh,' I said, realizing what day of the week it was. 'Thanks for reminding me. I have to cancel my appearance at the hen house.'

'What?'

'My Thursday lunch with the girls.'

'Oh.' He laughed. 'Well, maybe tomorrow we can have lunch.'

'Don't worry about it, Ronnie. I'm not big on lunch. People eat too much, drink too much and then give thirty or forty percent less for the rest of their workday.'

'Party pooper,' he said. Then he added, 'You're probably right. See you later.'

'Later,' I said and hung up. Then I called Rosalie Okun and

gave her the news in the form of a bulletin: 'Clea Howard has gone back to paralegal work.'

'I had a feeling,' she said. 'Are you sure you want to do that again?'

'Paralegal work?'

'Whatever. I couldn't even begin to imagine myself doing something like that.'

'We're all fruit, Rosalie, but some of us are apples and some of us are oranges. Some are even bananas.'

'What?'

'Gotta go,' I said. 'Give my best to the others. And don't spend your whole lunch talking about me. Give someone else a chance.'

Before she could utter another word, I hung up and turned back to the work. Both junior partners, Gerald Wilson and Bob Sayer, stopped by to welcome me to the firm. Neither looked more than thirty, but I was sure both would be bright and ambitious if Carlton had hired them. Neither was big on small talk; maybe because I wasn't either, after the preliminary questions were asked and answered. They had the look of adjournment on their faces moments after they had stepped in to say hello.

Just before noon, Jackie came in to tell me the office phone would be on answering service for the next hour. That was something new. Sebastian had insisted there should always be a human voice from opening to closing. As I recalled, he wasn't fond of technology and wrote as much as he could in longhand.

'Sure about lunch?' she asked. 'You're more than welcome to join us.'

'Thank you. I'm sure.'

I was thinking I might buy myself an apple or a health bar and call it my lunch. I wasn't very hungry. I folded the files and put them aside, but just as I rose to leave, he appeared in the doorway.

'Someone should put up a *Gone to lunch* sign or at least something like *Gone fishing*,' he said.

'What were you doing? Watching to see them all leave?'

'Just watching for you and, yes, I saw them all leave.'

'I really am all you think about while you're here?'

'As I said, you're the sole reason I'm still here.'

He held up a paper bag.

'What's that?'

'Lunch. I've got apples, oranges and some of those health bars you said you liked.'

I smiled and sat back. 'When did I tell you that?'

'When you were babbling a little in the motel. We talked about our food shopping, how we met. Don't you remember?'

'No. Yes,' I said, even though I really didn't.

'You want to have it here or go somewhere for a bigger lunch?' He looked around.

'Yes, you're right. It's claustrophobic. Let's go to my car,' I said.

'That's not claustrophobic?'

'I know a place where we can park and have something of a view.'

'Great,' he said and he stepped back for me to go out first.

Surely, I thought, there is something magical about someone who was on the same wavelength as you were, feeling the way you felt when you felt it.

Anticipating correctly was the best love song any girl could want.

It meant you cared enough to think hard about someone else beside yourself.

And I'm sorry, but you could count on your fingers how many like that you knew your whole life.

SEVEN

We were on a hill that overlooked the 60 Freeway. Homes on perfectly subdivided lots in an upscale gated community, all built in the same Spanish style and all in a bright yellow or orange shade, looked stamped on the well-combed and shaped acreage, developed by some entrepreneurs who probably lived in houses three times the value on the coast. However, this was a slice of the American dream, both for the homeowners and the businessmen. It looked secure and immaculate. There would be no graffiti, no loud and intrusive music. One could almost accept that the air around the homes was strained and sifted for impurities. Their refuse was placed in clean bins outside their homes on Tuesdays and Fridays. They were good environmentalists and would be sure to put their recyclables out on Wednesdays.

Was most of life compartmentalized like this?

'You stare at those houses like some American Indian planning on attacking a wagon train,' he said.

'I was just thinking about all the rules and regulations we pick up like lice during our lives. When you're a child, there are so many no-nos. Then you become more mature and you get the false impression, live under the illusion, that restrictions diminish. For a while you forget all the new ones. You can drive, but now there are all those traffic regulations. You can stay out later, but there are rules about alcohol and drugs and curfews. You are suddenly aware of other things like jay walking, littering, defacing property, cutting in front of people in lines, obeying the rules your bank imposes and your college imposes. Then, of course, once you're really on your own, earning your own keep, there are the pages and pages of IRS codes. You have all that beside the Ten Commandments and spools of new edicts related to civil and criminal law.'

'So?'

'And then you get married, save up enough money to have

a mortgage and a house in a place like that,' I said, nodding at the development, 'and are handed a booklet of CC and Rs, the covenants, conditions and restrictions associated with your homeowners' association. It never stops. Even after your dead. Did you know there is a mileage restriction relating to how far you have to be taken to have your ashes dumped at sea?'

'You forgot the rules your own body imposes on you, like when to eat and drink, what to eat and drink, and when to seek sexual intercourse. And sleep. I always forget sleep.'

'Thanks for reminding me.'

He smiled. 'You're just very tired, Clea. You've returned to work to see if you can energize yourself that way, but, as you know, I'm not optimistic about it. You need that breeze in your hair. We should take a holiday. Change isn't something you do for a few hours once in a while.'

'Take a holiday?'

'Find a reason to spend time on your own; only you won't be on your own. There must be one place you'd like to go. It doesn't have to be far away. There's a lot of static around you here. You need a chance to pause, take some deep breaths, so you can think better about the things you're doing and the things you want.'

'Maybe,' I said. I was silent for a few moments. To the west, a fighter jet on a training mission was leaving a trail of thin cotton-white exhaust. It looked as if the plane was tearing a seam in the blue sky.

'People who say "maybe" reveal fear and indecision. My motto is to avoid all maybes.'

'I don't think I was ever arrogant enough to assign myself a motto,' I replied, and he laughed. 'I've got to get back to work.' I paused after I started the engine. 'So you're really independently wealthy?'

'More people than you'd expect are.'

'I never knew what that meant – *independently*.'

'I'm dependent upon no one to enjoy my money. There are no rules I have to follow except for insider trading. I invest what I want when I want. Actually, I employ a business manager to do the nitty-gritty.'

'That's always been my husband's dream.'

'Welcome to idyllic capitalism.'

'Do you have it all socked away overseas or something?'

'Something. Talking about money is boring,' he said. 'If you have money, you make money. It's as simple as that.'

'Unless you don't have it to start with.'

'I said, "If you have it." Why pick on money? You might not have health to start with? Or opportunities, or even parents.'

'Are you an orphan, too?'

'We're all orphans in one way or another.'

'You do work for the CIA,' I said, 'or at least were trained by them.'

He laughed. 'Look at it this way. I don't lie. I just avoid the truth whenever possible.'

It was my turn to smile. I started away.

'Being independently wealthy and not having to do anything much is dangerous. Remember? Idle hands are the devil's workshop,' I warned. 'I was recently reminded of that, and by a lawyer, too.'

'My hands aren't idle, especially when they're filled with you.'

I looked at him and gave him what Ronnie called my cold grin. He said it could send chills down his spine.

'You always have the answers that will please, especially me. Maybe you're the devil's work after all.'

'Maybe we all are. But let's stop it. Questions, analyzing, all of it. Just get out there and feel something, Clea. Come back from wherever you've gone.'

I said nothing.

He was so right.

I let him off on a corner and parked.

Twenty minutes after I returned to drain the swamp of data, Carlton stopped by.

'How's it going?'

'Seems like old times,' I sang. He smiled.

'I'll have something more interesting soon. I might take on a criminal defense. I've been toying with it. A friend of mine who is in criminal law has been pushing me to give him a hand with his workload.'

'Oh? What sort of case?'

'Murder,' he said casually. 'It's complicated for the defense.'

'How so?'

'Wife killed her husband. Claims she was brainwashed into it by her lover. She was like a puppet, psychologically manipulated. The lover looks totally innocent, but my friend has done some preliminary investigating of the man and has discovered that this client is one of three.'

'Three?'

'Two previous women who had affairs with him ended up killing their husbands.'

'How can one man have so much power over women?'

'You're asking me that? I had the impression you were one of those women who believed men in general have too much power over women.'

'You mean because we get paid less for the same work and have our reproductive rights challenged and eliminated? Or just the way we're intimidated in everyday life?'

'I had a feeling you would know how to respond. Anyway, I have to seek out this psychologically powerful man and get some advice from him. Don't tell my wife,' he joked. 'I'll know more by the end of the day.'

'Why would any other lawyer drop that at your feet? I don't mean to imply you're incapable of anything. It seems like something that even a seasoned criminal attorney would find difficult, though it has a fascinating side to it.'

'My friend's very busy and knew I was a psych major before deciding to make a sharp right turn and go into law. We went to undergraduate school together. Stop in with what you've found so far on the current matter,' he added, nodding at the paper piled in front of me.

'Will do.'

I sat back and thought for a moment. Why was it that criminal law did have a more exciting and enticing ring to it? Physical or psychological evil was always more attractive than white-collar crime. Who wouldn't want to know more about the so-called manipulator? Look who's more interesting in Shakespeare's *Othello* – Iago, the conniver, the plotter, the killer. And what woman in *Macbeth* is more interesting than Lady Macbeth who drove her husband to kill the king?

It was a fascinating idea for a defense. Othello kills his wife who adores him, but in the end we feel sorry for him because of how he was manipulated. We even feel pity for Macbeth. Nothing has changed that much in the human psyche. The jury in the case Carlton is thinking of taking could be led to some consideration of reducing the charges, some mitigating argument.

In comparison, the evil in these bland documents was color-less and trivial, I thought. The biggest sin here was that a husband hid some assets from his wife. Blah, blah. Of course, Lancaster was right. I couldn't last long in this world again if this was all there was to do.

But as I continued evaluating the assets of the man being sued for divorce, I paused and thought that what really makes this so cold for me is that I don't know the people, the person-alities, the lives of these people who had once been deeply enough in love to vow in a court or in a church that they would spend their lives together.

I thought about my own marriage – the wedding, that night before and that morning. I tried to recall the early moments of doubt. Were there any? It was a little more than eighteen years ago. We had been going together for more than eight months. Most of the time our dates were hot and passionate. Days seemed to collapse into more and more hours we would spend together. I was his first call in the morning. His was the last voice I heard before going to sleep. We had circled each other like two fencers in the beginning and then, perhaps too quickly, had gotten to the point where my friends claimed I was attached to Ronnie's hip. Most of them were complaining because they hadn't yet found anyone they had cared to hold hands with too long, much less devote most of their waking hours toward pleasing and enjoying.

Our wedding day was picture-perfect, with my dress, his tux, the crowd of friends and relatives at church; the profes-sionally arranged reception, with the great food, the cake, the flowers, the toasts and dancing. Even now, looking at the photographs and especially at myself in them, I didn't see even the slightest doubt or hesitation. I was everyone's ideal bride, glowing, hopeful, jingling bells of love, drawing out the oohs and aahs and especially the envy of my bridesmaids and girlfriends. How pretty I was and how handsome Ronnie looked. Even Sherlock Holmes couldn't detect a single doubt, a single threat, an iota of anything ominous.

Was everything in life an illusion?

I looked at the paperwork again. Harry Carl Gordon was trying to hide assets from the woman he once thought would be his reason to be. Once, he would have risked his life to keep her safe and protected. When did they have their last passionate kiss? When did they last say something sweet and loving to each other? When did he last draw her close to him, put his arm around her and kiss her cheek. When did he last say, 'I love you'?

Did either of them even think about that now? Or, when such a memory surfaced, did they both press it back down into the darkness of the past, the land of amnesia where all sad and dreadful thoughts and images were buried in tombs we hoped would keep them sealed even beyond death itself, to the end of time?

I made my last notation, folded the papers, closed the file and got up to go to Carlton's office.

He looked up, surprised. 'Question?'

'No. I'm done. Here's my summary,' I told him and handed it to him. He perused it quickly.

'You've traced about eight hundred thousand out of the country?'

'That holding company, that loan, the Grand Cayman Islands, all tell me that supposed loan he made is cover for socking away money, and if you'll notice, it wasn't that long ago that he had done it. His wife hadn't yet sued for divorce, but he knew it was coming, I bet.'

Carlton smiled. 'This is terrific. Nice work. I'll move this ahead a lot quicker now.' He pushed back from his desk. 'I will probably have something new for you in less than a week. I had a consultation about another divorce.'

'I'm curious about *this* divorce,' I said, nodding at the file I had handed him.

'Oh?'

'How long were they married?'

'Twenty-four years. They have a daughter at Bennington in her freshman year.'

'Vermont?'

'Yes. Maybe she wanted to get as far away as she could,' he said, smiling.

'And there's a seventeen-year-old. I saw the trusts in place for both of their children,' I said, nodding at the file.

'Yes. His mother tells me he's been accepted at USC, early admission. Apparently, he's a football star in high school.'

'How deeply we can wound our own children,' I muttered, more to myself, but he perked up.

'Feel no fear about it. I spoke to these two kids. I think they wrote off both their parents years ago. Kids sense things sooner than we expect. They're even good at hiding how much they know from us. I'm sure you remember things when you were a child.'

'Yes.' Of course, I thought about Kelly and me immediately, especially the way she had been cross-examining me.

'Anything else?' he asked, because I was so into my thoughts.

'Oh. Well, it's not there in those financial documents, but why is she asking for a divorce?'

'Number one reason,' he replied. 'Adultery. Although you probably know that California is a no-fault state. She doesn't have to prove he's done something wrong – i.e. adultery. However, we are suing for misappropriation. You don't have the paperwork, but we can prove he spent money on this girlfriend and I'm looking for half of those funds plus interest as well. He's not putting up much of a defense, which is why I wanted to be sure we uncovered all the assets.'

'Except for the money funneled into Grand Cayman, he didn't try that hard to hide the rest. Maybe there was a time he believed he could smooth things over or keep her from divorcing him,' I suggested.

He stared at me with the look of someone spinning suspicious thoughts.

'I've asked many women if their husband's cheating on them was the real reason they were seeking divorce. You'd be surprised to learn how many tolerated it, but found more serious

– at least to them, more serious – reasons that trumped it. I also had the sense that they weren't angels either.'

'Now there's an oxymoron if I ever heard one,' I said. It seemed to come right out of Lancaster's mouth, into my ears and then through mine.

'Pardon?'

'Angels suing angels.'

He laughed.

'Welcome back, Clea. I have a feeling I'm going to hire you full-time faster than I imagined.'

'Yes,' I said, but not with confidence. He lifted his eyebrows. 'I might be gone for a few days.'

He nodded. 'No problem. As I said, it might be a week before I've got some things together to get you started again.'

'Do you seriously think you might take on that criminal case?'

'Fascinates you, huh? I had that impression when I described it to you. To be honest, it fascinates me, too. Any background in psychology?'

'Are you kidding? I'm married eighteen years and I have a teenage daughter.'

He laughed.

'No, just the usual undergraduate Introduction to Psychology,' I said.

'I'll let you know when you return,' he replied.

I turned and left his office. Jackie looked up from her desk quickly.

'See you tomorrow?'

'Not tomorrow,' I said. She looked worried. 'Nothing's wrong. I just finished this assignment. Call it a hiatus.'

'High what?

'A caesural pause,' I replied and spelled *caesural* for her. Let her go to a dictionary or to Wikipedia, I thought, walking out into the dwindling late-afternoon sunshine that was turning the tops of the mountains in the distance into lit birthday cakes.

Lancaster was leaning against my car, looking his confident, arrogant self. At first I said nothing. I got into the car and he came around and stood there, looking in at me. I rolled down the window.

'What?'

'Call me in the morning,' I said. 'I have to do some pre-planning, but I agree. I need a change of scenery,' I added and drove off, leaving him standing there and watching me disappear around a turn, his face full of 'I knew she would.'

EIGHT

'You finished the first assignment already?' Ronnie asked, the astonishment on his face metamorphosing him into a fourteen-year-old boy full of wonder. In the early days of our relationship and marriage, I found this quality attractive. There was an innocence I could embrace. Over time, that somehow became annoying, even suspiciously contrived.

I think you stop trusting your husband or your lover when you realize he has practically memorized each and every one of your reactions to anything and everything. He's like a taxicab driver who knows every turn, every bump in the road, and knows when to slow down and when to speed up. Surprise diminishes and diminishes until it's almost non-existent. You know he knows how you will react and plans for it. You no longer believe in what you see in his face and hear in his words. He's drifted away under the camouflage woven out of your own reactions and words.

'It wasn't brain surgery,' I said, trying not to sound egotistical. 'The documents were easy to evaluate. There weren't that many. When you've done it as many times as I have . . .'

The little boy in him evaporated in an instant as he maneuvered into his business mind.

'You could have dragged it out and made more money. You're being paid by the hour since you're just part-time, right? I mean, that's what lawyers do anyway. I'm sure he wouldn't complain. He'd just pass on the costs to the client,' he whined. At least, to me, it seemed like whining.

I was going to say I don't like to cheat anyone. I almost said it wasn't in my DNA, but I hesitated. It suddenly occurred to me that one major transgression affects every small indiscretion you might contemplate and makes it seem less important and too little to challenge your conscience. It's not a license to steal exactly, but everything, no matter how contradictory to who and what you were before, suddenly becomes insignificant. If you're a murderer, you don't have pangs of conscience when you defraud someone or commit some other non-capital crime. It's as if you've already crossed over; the devil has won your soul. Additional stains don't matter.

And yet this wasn't true for me. The idea of fudging my time and squeezing out more money for the work I had done hadn't even occurred to me. Did that mean I had successfully rationalized my adultery, that somehow what I was doing was not immoral and therefore I still had a lily-white soul to protect? Even now, even after all I had done, if I was Catholic and stepped into a confession booth, I'd look for a telephone to use or a magazine to read instead of a priest to hear my about my adulterous peccadillos.

Before I could respond, Ronnie provided his own answer.

'Of course, you're not like that. I remember that time you actually returned to Target to show them they had made a mistake on your bill and forgotten to charge for something,' he said.

His voice had some light disdain, but it was also clear that he would bring up the incident to brag about my honesty when he was with friends. Unfortunately, most of the people he revealed that to would think me a fool. They would actually be embarrassed for him as well.

The truth was that I wasn't only this overly honest person; I was worried that the cashier, who was probably living hand to mouth, would be penalized for the mistake. Not only would that be damaging to her weekly budget, but it would put her up as top candidate for being let go if cutbacks hit.

I stood there awash with guilt for a moment because of what he was saying. I always felt foolish when he said it in front of other people, too. I wanted to snap back at him and tell him to stop making me sound like some saint just because I had compassion for another person. If anything, that was an area he should improve. But I always swallowed back the words then and did so now. I just turned away. I had planned our dinner and wanted to get to it. He went to play in the echo chamber on his computer, but surprised me by returning to the kitchen after only ten minutes or so. He stood there in the doorway, watching me. Kelly hadn't come down to set

the table yet. At any moment she would pause in her texting
and remember she had some responsibilities.

'What?' I asked, seeing the odd look on his face. I felt a
chill, a shudder. Did he just realize something? Had someone
seen me with Lancaster and called him to ask who that was?
Did I leave some clue around? Maybe he had overheard a
phone call. I could feel paranoia hovering and looking for an
opportunity to slip into my psyche, like Satan waiting for a
priest to have doubt.

'I get the feeling you're not really crazy about returning
to work and that's really why you did everything so fast. You
wanted to get it over with,' he said, nodding, happy at the
conclusion he had reached.

I didn't respond. His insight actually took me by surprise.
What else would he soon realize? I returned to the stove for
a moment to finish the sauce I was making for the chicken
dish I was inventing as I went along.

'I feel . . .'

'What?' he asked when I paused too long.

I turned back to him.

'Confused. I was thinking that I might take a few days,
go to Palm Springs.'

'Palm Springs! You hate staying in your parents' complex.
You always say it's like God's waiting room, the lobby of
impending death.'

'I can ignore it, go for a hike in the Indian Canyons, meditate.
I did it when you went on that insurance retreat a few years
ago.'

'You took Kelly.'

'She hated it; she'd hate it now. She needs a little more
concentrated time with you, anyway,' I added. It was a perfect
codicil, a nice tag to divert the attention from me to him. His
eyes widened with surprise.

'Why?'

'Why? Why? She's your daughter, your only child. She
spends most of her free time only with me, Ronnie. These are
important years. So many her age are drifting away, floating
out there like pieces of satellites in weakening orbits, destined
to fall back to earth.'

'Satellites?'

'Whatever. She looks like an adult; she wants to be treated like one, but she's really still your little girl, Ronnie. She's really afraid of what's ahead. We were just like her. At least I was. I needed my father as well as my mother. I'm sure you did, too. My father was never there enough for me. You know how I felt, how I still feel about that. I don't want to see Kelly feeling like me years from now.'

'Oh. I hadn't thought of all that,' he said, the guilt washing over him.

'Well, think of it,' I ordered. 'Start right now by letting her know it's time to set the table. Show her you know she's part of what we are. If she doesn't learn responsibility here, where will she learn it?' I said, sounding like a lecturer in parenting. 'It's your responsibility as much as it is mine. This is a partnership when it comes to raising our daughter.'

'Sure,' he said and left to do it.

Talk about a murder case that had at the heart of the defense the concept of psychological manipulation . . . *I'm a helluva manipulator*, I thought. *Am I better at it now or was I always this good?* Shouldn't I feel guilty about it, about how dishonest it was? Considering what I was doing, how could I sound so sanctimonious?

But really everyone is a manipulator in one way or another. Granted, it is for much smaller and less significant consequences, but men tell their wives things they want to hear just to get them to agree to something, don't they? And wives do the same to their husbands. Children manipulate their parents to get their parents to give them permission to do something. *Everyone else is doing it. You're treating me like a child. I'll get something educational out of it. I need to be given more responsibility.* There are so many subtle ways family members manipulated each other.

And what about salesmen manipulating customers into buying their products, their cars? Or politicians who hire consultants just to figure out ways to manipulate the voters? Of course, there was a limit to what you could or should get an intelligent, moral person to do, but sometimes it's not because they're not intelligent or moral enough to resist. Sometimes the manipulator can see there are other weak spots, self-image problems, dependencies, and if he or she is good at it, they can get their subjects to do what they want them to do.

Othello was insecure because he was black. Macbeth was driven by ambition. Both were competent, even superior, in what they did, and they did suffer pangs of conscience, but they were susceptible.

I knew that Ronnie was susceptible to feeling guilty about his neglect of Kelly and I took advantage of that. It wasn't my fault that he was too driven in his work and too distracted with his other nonsense. The truth was that he was never as close to her as he should have been and should be now, and I knew that he knew that, too. Kelly had to drum up a school assignment to get him to sit down with her for an intense hour or so. I could bring him to tears about it if I wanted to. Getting him to ignore and not question my little getaway was a slam dunk.

I could imagine Lancaster sitting there at the kitchen table, smiling at me.

'I knew you had it in you,' he would say.

'Shut up,' I would tell him playfully, and he would laugh.

This was a short conversation we were destined to have once I left and met him.

I imagined him putting up his hand, so I would stop talking and listen to what was going on outside the kitchen right now.

I heard the banter between Kelly and Ronnie after he called her down to set the table. He wasn't exactly establishing rapport with his 'Chop, chop. Why do we have to remind you to do your part? Can't you think of these things on your own?'

Mr Sledgehammer.

He was inserting himself in her life, letting her know he wasn't oblivious to her comings and goings. I'll grant that. The irony is young people like that. They'll complain about being nagged, but, deep inside, they like the fact that their parents care enough to complain and show how they're interested in what they do, how they mature and what they feel.

Of course, she marched in like an errant but abused child, her lips so tight, her cheeks puffed. She looked as if she was holding back the regurgitation of a stream of profanities. Ronnie's involvement was sudden, unexpected and a little over the top. I made a mental note to tell him how to tone it down but still sound authoritative, but authoritative with real concern for her.

'Easy,' I said when she nearly broke a dish. She glared at me, saw there was no sympathy and then calmed and set the table. Ronnie didn't ease the situation by putting on dinner music she hated. I wasn't that fond of it myself. If any two had to get to know each other better, it was my husband and daughter, I thought, strengthening my rationalization by telling myself that I was doing a good thing, leaving them in each other's company.

Surprisingly, as if she had witnessed my conversation with Ronnie, Kelly started our dinner conversation by asking me how I liked working again. She had given me the opening I was looking for.

'I'm not sure,' I said. 'I think I have to think about it a little more without any distractions.'

'How do you do that?'

'Well . . .' I looked at Ronnie, who seemed genuinely interested in what I would say, as if this was a question he had been asking himself.

'Well, first you have to clear your mind, set the table for a new dinner of thoughts.'

'What's that mean?' Kelly asked, grimacing the way she did when she didn't grasp something quickly enough.

'I've told you many times, Kelly, that when you make that face after you ask a question, you not only annoy and offend the person, but you look ugly and mean. Just ask your question calmly. Don't be so condescending.'

'Am I still in an English-speaking home?' Ronnie joked.

I glanced at him sternly, and he dropped his smile as if it had begun to burn away his face.

'You will come to realize,' I began, directing myself only to Kelly and in a much calmer voice, 'that your day-to-day life is more complicated than you would think. The majority of your time is consumed by what I call the business of life, especially for a wife and mother.'

She didn't say, 'Huh? Please. Give me a break.' But her eyes and her mouth were resonating with it.

'There are responsibilities to keep up the house, to look after everyone's needs, including your own. Schedules, appointments I set for all of us with doctors and dentists, even your hairdresser, as well as your father's barber,' I added, shooting him a look they made him glance down, 'repairs when appliances break down, shopping for your clothing needs as well as my own, maintaining friendships, sometimes just to be social, all of it. Getting my car serviced and then house cleaning, preparing meals . . . exhausting.

'If we pro-rated what a wife and mother gets an hour, even if she gets half of the husband's net worth in a divorce, we'd see how underpaid she is.'

'We had a maid. You decided to fire her,' Kelly said.

'This isn't just about vacuuming and polishing furniture,' I replied sharply. 'The problem in most homes is the children never think about what it takes to keep them safe and happy.'

She rolled her eyes.

'You'll see,' I said. 'Someday you'll be in my shoes.'

'I'm never getting married, and don't worry, I'll never get pregnant so I have to or anything.'

'What?' Ronnie exclaimed, as if it just had occurred to him that Kelly could have sex. To this day, he didn't know exactly when she'd had her menarche, not that a father had to know that exactly, but when it came to being the father of a teenage girl these days, being oblivious to her sexual development was like driving with blinders on.

'Anyway, getting back to your question,' I said, returning to my softer tone of voice, 'to clear your mind, you need to pause, take a breath, maybe go out into nature. Alone.'

'You mean like meditate or something?'

'Yes, exactly. It doesn't have to be a long pause, but enough to help you find perspective,' I said.

She looked sufficiently bored now.

Ronnie still had his mouth slightly open. I gave him one of my stinging glares.

'Yeah, your mother's right,' he said. 'I'm guilty of not pausing enough myself. I'm Mr Workaholic.'

'Please,' Kelly said. 'Spare me, Dad. You golf, you go out with your friends, you—'

'Golf's a killer,' he interrupted, picking up on one of his favorite subjects. 'Everyone thinks people talk business and relax, but you're out there constantly competing and criticizing your own performance. In what other sport can a man thirty pounds overweight, wearing ridiculous-looking shorts revealing his stick legs, hit a ball farther than you and kick your ass over eighteen holes? I can beat him in most anything else!'

Blood actually rushed into his face to highlight his indignation.

'So why do you play?' she fired back. *She's more my daughter than his*, I thought.

'I play. Everyone plays,' he replied calmly, which brought back her now famous smirk. 'Everyone complains about themselves, but everyone plays,' he added, sounding now like someone who had been defeated, made to face the truth.

Kelly turned back to me. 'How do you intend to clear your mind this time?' she asked.

'I think I'll spend two days with my parents in Palm Springs, take walks in the Indian Canyons, do some reading, listen to music, classical music. In short, I won't think about any responsibilities. You'll be on your own and so will your father.'

'Oh.'

'You can order in or go out for dinner.'

'Oh, we'll go out,' Ronnie said quickly and turned to her. 'Right?'

'Whatever,' Kelly said. Then, out of the blue, she asked, 'Are you looking for a mystical experience?'

'What?'

'I was just reading something about that.'

'I hope it didn't involve drugs.'

'Like no, Ma,' she said. 'It's an assignment we were given in literature class. We have a collection of mystical experience descriptions and we have to write about the one we believe the most and why. Maybe when you come home, you'll tell me about yours,' she said.

I looked at Ronnie.

He had a big idiotic smile on his face.

'Maybe,' I said. 'One thing is for sure: I wouldn't get one here.'

Ronnie lost his smile. Kelly went back to eating. Silence fell like an iron curtain, but something came of it. Kelly was at the dishes beside me and Ronnie didn't rush off to his computer. He went into the living room and read the *LA Times*.

'When are you going to Palm Springs?' Kelly asked me.

'I was thinking of going tomorrow.'

'I could be sick and go with you.'

'You hated being there last time, Kelly, and I thought I explained how it was important for someone to be alone when she wants to clear her mind. I'm not blaming you for anything,' I added quickly, 'nor am I saying I don't like being with you. This is different.'

'Whatever,' she said.

'Just take care of your father. Go into the living room now and plan on some things to do over the next few days.'

'Now?'

'I'll finish up here. Go on,' I said.

She shrugged and left.

Manipulator, I thought I heard Lancaster whisper. I actually turned around to see if he had snuck into our home and listened to it all. Of course, he wasn't there. Sometimes, when you're involved with someone as quickly and as intensely as I was with him, you feel as if he's always with you, hearing your very thoughts. It's easy to imagine how he would react and what he would say. I wouldn't call it love, exactly. It's more. There is something more. In spite of what I told Kelly, I did believe that people could fall or grow into love, but they don't always take each other so deeply into themselves that they truly do become like one. That's special.

I slipped by Ronnie and Kelly and went upstairs to our bedroom to call Lancaster on my cell phone. I didn't want either Kelly or Ronnie to see the house phone was being used and then start asking me who I had called. Lancaster picked up almost before it rang. He saw the call was coming from me. Otherwise, he would have said hello first.

'Where and when?' he asked instead.

'There's this place I know in Idyllwild. It's a nice little

village in the San Jacinto mountains, the whole enchilada
. . . pine trees, cedar . . . great rock formations and ideal for
hikes. It's the middle of the week, colder there, so it won't
be touristy. The place has cabins. I'm familiar with one cabin
resort and I'll make arrangements. It won't take us that long
to get there. I'll pick up groceries. We'll eat in every night,
sit by the fireplace and tell each other ghost stories or
something.'

'Something,' he said and laughed. 'Sounds perfect. A real
escape for you.'

'For us both.'

'What makes you think I need an escape?'

'You do or you wouldn't be here. Maybe I'll get you to tell
me what it is that's after you.'

He laughed, but I thought he laughed nervously.

'So, where and when?'

'I'll need a few hours in the morning to pack up what I'll
need and we'll need. Let's do ten at the same place we first
met, corner of Western and Parker.'

'OK.'

'Bring warm things to wear. Do you have any?'

'I have everything I need to go anywhere. That's how you
travel when you don't know where you're going,' he replied,
and I laughed.

I heard Kelly coming up, so I said goodbye and began to
change into something comfortable.

'We planned two dinners,' she told me from the doorway.

'Oh. Great.'

'I'm bringing Lexi with me the second night.'

'The purpose of all this is for you to spend quality time
with your father. Bringing along a girlfriend will detract from
that,' I warned.

'Really, Mom, we'll run out of things to say after one dinner.
And he likes Lexi.'

Lexi, I thought.

'Lexi. She's the buxom one?'

'She hates when anyone points that out, Mom.'

'She'll get over it,' I said. 'And do more to point it out
herself.'

Kelly raised her eyebrows and gave me a half-smile.

'You're weird. You need that clearing of the mind, all right.'

I looked at her, wondering again just how sensitive my daughter was to what was going on inside me. When I looked back, she was gone. I changed and went down, expecting to find Ronnie still in the living room, maybe moving on now to television, but he was in his office as usual, diddling on his computer. I stood in his doorway, watching him mesmerized by what he was seeing and reading.

Of course, it often occurred to me that there was a time before family radios and television when people had nothing but themselves for entertainment. The point I thought we missed about all that was that in those days – the 'olden days', as Ronnie puts it – there was little to take you out of your home. Television did more because there was little left to the imagination. You were captured totally in someone else's imagination, whether it was the set designs, the settings chosen or the lighting and sound to accompany the actors.

Computers wired you to the outside world in a much more complete way. It was something you did alone. Ronnie tried to get me to go into his office to witness what he was seeing, but for the most part he was oblivious to everything and everyone else around him. He was truly gone for those hours he spent reading emails, sending them, copying and pasting in quotes and jokes, and reading the blogs he favored.

Did he ever love me as much as he loved all this? I didn't suspect him of going to porn on his computer. I never saw any evidence of that. It didn't take away his sexual energy exactly; it took away his attention and the energy to conduct any family socializing. It certainly dampened down romance. Maybe, ironically, marriages lasted longer because people who really weren't made for each other could put off that realization for years with the distraction. Maybe that was a bad thing because prolonging a bad marriage was worse than cutting it off at the knees.

I left him and went back upstairs to pack a small bag I would take tomorrow. I sorted out the sundries I would need. I wouldn't bring any makeup, just lipstick; we weren't going out in the evening. I packed my best hiking shoes. Then I sorted out my warmest jacket and some sweaters. Ronnie was at his computer longer than usual. I was packed and prepared for bed before he came up, and when he did, he was quiet this time. I heard him smother a laugh, probably recalling an image he had seen on the computer, and then turn away and go to sleep.

This time I was up quite a bit before both him and Kelly. I brought my bag and jacket down and put it all in my car. Out of habit more than anything else, I put the cereals Kelly and Ronnie liked for breakfast out on the table. I squeezed some oranges for their juice and made coffee, both to get my first cup and to be there for them. Then I wrote a note and told them to have a good time together and that I would call tonight. I told them if they wanted to talk to me for any reason to call my mobile phone.

I didn't call my parents until I was finished getting groceries for the cabin. There was no problem getting one reserved. In fact, the place I was going to had none reserved for the next two days. It wouldn't have mattered anyway, because I had no intention of even striking up a short conversation with anyone else up there. We'd only leave the cabin to go for our hikes. I had other plans for the rest of the day and night.

As usual, my mother was surprised to hear from me. She always made it sound as if I hadn't called for months. My purpose in calling my parents was to give them updates on all of us so they wouldn't be calling me and have Ronnie realize I wasn't with them. I would do the same with his parents. When I was finished, I congratulated myself on how clever a conniver I was. I was sure Lancaster would be amused by it all.

Feeling more energized than I had in quite a while, I headed for our rendezvous point. He was practically standing on the exact spot he had been standing on the first time. He was wearing a tight, light blue cotton sweater with a V-neck collar, similar to one I had bought Ronnie years ago. It made both of them look more muscular. Lancaster's straight-leg jeans had to have been tailored. I thought he looked younger than he did the last time I saw him. He was any girl's fantasy lover come to life. Did my being with him make me look younger? I was not only excited but proud I had captured his interest. I pulled up to the curb and he got in quickly, throwing his bag over on to the rear seat.

'What took you so long?' he kidded.

'Puberty, adolescence, eighteen years of waiting for you and speed limits, in that order.'

I started away.

'You know, when people are happier, they're wittier, don't you think?'

'I think when they're happier, they're everything-er,' I said, and he laughed. He had those perfect white teeth you see in smiles advertising dentists.

'Watch the road,' he said when the driver of an oncoming vehicle sounded his horn because I had drifted a little too close to the center line.

'Then don't be so handsome,' I told him. He sat back, now looking thoughtful.

I drove on, describing all I had done to cover up for our little adventure. I thought he would smile and laugh and congratulate me on all my planning, but he looked troubled instead.

'What's wrong? I thought you'd be pleased.'

'I'm pleased you're so smart about it, but I fear all this subterfuge will eventually become troubling for you, troubling enough to take away significantly from your joy. Conscience is king, you know.'

'Don't start getting all moral on me,' I warned.

'I'm not. I'm thinking how much happier you would be if you had nothing to scratch at your conscience.'

He wasn't wrong, but it put me into a darker mood.

For the next twenty minutes or so, neither of us spoke.

Were we catching our breath, or were we opening a valve to let all the trapped regrets and warnings come pouring out?

I don't think either of us could say.

More important, I don't think either of us wanted to.

NINE

I followed the sunlight up the mountain. More like a spotlight, it seemed to be leading the way after every turn, glimmering on the large rocks and the road, threading through clumps of trees to bathe us in a welcoming embrace. To me, it was as if Nature herself approved of us, as if we were a natural phenomenon only Nature could understand.

Then again, all of us read the tea leaves to see what we want them to say. I'm no exception. It doesn't mean that we read them wrong necessarily, which is why I can live with that sort of dishonesty.

'I didn't mean to throw water on our fire back there,' he said suddenly, as if he saw the same warm welcome in the world we were entering and was just as encouraged. 'Sometimes, I think we shouldn't say anything serious to each other. Serious comments take you out of the moment. They chip away at your self-confidence. Neither of us wants to end up like Romeo and Juliet. Forbidden love affairs tend to crash and burn eventually.'

'Yes, even accepted ones often do. I think I'm on the verge.'

'It's easier for me to say all this. I know that.'

'You really have ties to nothing, not even some religious chains that could constrict you?'

'When I'm with you, I am tied to you,' he said, 'and nothing else – certainly not anything in my past. I'm not handing you some line. It's how I live. I give my all to the present. I have no old voices haunting me.'

'You don't think about the future?'

'Why should I? It'll come. And before you ask, no, I never dwell on the past and count my regrets the way some people count their blessings. The past just weighs you down. It's baggage. For me, it's as if the world rolls up behind me as I go. If I look back, I'll see nothing,' he said and turned, and did so just to illustrate. 'Nothing.'

'I envy you. Probably most people would, even though they might not admit it.'

'I've heard that said.' He smiled.

'That's a perfect shit-eating grin,' I told him, and he laughed.

'What I like about you is there is no subterfuge with me. What I see is what I get. Thank you for your sincerity.'

'I don't know why, but hearing you say that frightens me. It's like being out there, naked, without a single rationalization or false face. It terrifies me to know I've dropped all pretense.'

'Don't be afraid. You're not this way with anyone else, and you can trust me.'

'I never trust anyone who has less to lose,' I said.

He nodded, holding his smile. 'What can I say to counter such wisdom?'

I looked at him with my eyebrows raised. He couldn't see my eyes behind my sunglasses, but he didn't have to.

'I'm serious,' he protested. 'I wouldn't be with you if I didn't respect you.'

He was convincing. I didn't want to look at him through rose-colored glasses, knowing all along that what I was seeing could very well be untrue, and yet when I was with him, I welcomed my refusal to search for and find flaws. The irony was I was often sickened by the way my girlfriends made excuses for their husbands, even the way I sometimes made excuses for Ronnie. Of course, we were really making excuses for ourselves, finding ways not to look like fools. If one found ways to explain her husband's infidelity or disrespect for her, all the others would give her a pass, knowing full well they were either in similar circumstances or anticipating that they would soon be.

Lancaster is right. Stop analyzing, I told myself. *Go naked. Enjoy. At least for these two days.*

'Have you ever been here?' I asked, when a sign announced that we had entered Idyllwild.

'Never to stay, but I did pass through it one time or another.'

'You sound like you've been everywhere.'

'Well, so many places are so similar that when you've seen one, you seen them all. One way to avoid that is to drive cross-country. Have you ever done it?'

'No. Four hours in a car is my absolute limit.'

'Pity. You'd then see how many countries make up the United States. The people are different from one geographical area to the next. It's actually fascinating.'

'Ronnie has been after me to do that. He's practically used the same words.'

'Is that the only way I remind you of him?'

'The only way now,' I replied. 'And don't say "pity" again,' I warned. 'I blame myself for who I am and where I am, and that includes friends and family.'

He laughed. 'Maybe you are too hard on yourself. You can't underestimate the power of coincidence and fate. They have a lot to do with who and what you are. Look at us. If I hadn't been standing in that spot in the supermarket and you weren't distracted, we might never have met.'

'How do I know you didn't deliberately move in front of me when I wasn't looking?'

'Same thing as far as you're concerned. It would still be something you didn't control.'

'So I'm trapped, no matter what I think or do. Is that it?'

'For now,' he said. 'All life's a maze. You'll figure a way out.'

He looked at everything as we meandered down the main street of the mountain village.

'Yes, I did pass through here,' he said.

I knew where the specific cabins I wanted to go to were because I had thought about Ronnie, Kelly and me coming up here in the summer. We never did. If we did half the things we talked about doing, would our lives be different, better or worse?

'Sounds like that describes most of what you do in your life,' I said. 'Pass through it.'

'Do I hear a little disapproval in your voice?' he asked. 'Even a note of bitterness?'

'No,' I said quickly, too quickly.

'Once you start analyzing and judging—'

'OK, OK. You can't expect me to shed all my bad habits overnight,' I said, and he laughed.

The little note of tension died away, and I turned to look at the village, too, and the few people I saw walking slowly, pausing to talk to each other and glancing our way with some curiosity. I looked at the trees, especially the pine because they held on to their green. There was something elegant about how alive and proud they appeared to me, especially against the trees that had lost their leaves, trees that were defeated by the late fall and winter.

I lowered the window to let the cool, really fresh air wash around us. The sun was high and because of the altitude made us feel a lot warmer than it was. It was an umbrella of light protecting us against any falling shadows or depression. Our smiles sparkled and glittered. I could feel myself opening up, pushing away the tension that usually lined my insides. It was like being reborn.

Perhaps my elaborate excuse for getting away wasn't as false as it first seemed. I really was clearing my mind. I felt as if I would be able to make many important decisions while I was up here with Lancaster. There would be time to meditate. I would cleanse my soul. I would see again.

'Looks authentic,' Lancaster said. 'Like the people who live here really belong here and want to be here. In too many places I've been, people seem cast in a temporary role. Everyone's trying out a new persona. The whole country's got attention deficit disorder. That's why the moving van business is booming. I have no doubt that once the average lifespan becomes one hundred, marriage will disappear entirely as an institution. Or else marriage licenses will be good for only twenty years.'

'It's practically like that now.'

'For you?'

'Maybe,' I said.

'Good. You strike me as someone who needs to be completely free.'

'To pass through places with you?'

He shook his head. 'That would be marriage with a different name, but a rose by any other name . . .'

'Is still a rose,' I finished, and he laughed. I did, too, even though I was half-serious. It's always better to run away with someone rather than be alone, even if only for a little while.

I turned off the main street and headed for the cabins. They were set back a few thousand yards from the road. There were about fifteen of them evenly spaced over the property, interspersed by towering pine trees. All the cabins were cedar with brown trim. Each had an outside barbeque and a front deck with logwood chairs and a small bench. Most were two- or three-bedroom, but when I had called for a reservation, the owner, a stern-sounding woman named Betty Lester, said she had two one-bedroom cabins and that one of them had been recently upgraded with new carpeting and appliances. As if she had been negotiating with customers all morning, she added firmly that the price at Lester's Cabin Retreat was non-negotiable, despite the time of the year.

Betty had a log-cabin home with an office to the right on entry.

'What do you think?' I asked when we passed through the main gate built out of wood that had turned gray.

'Quaint,' he said. 'Peaceful.'

'Exactly.'

I pulled up to the office and got out. Lancaster waited in the car. I saw an African American man out in front of the farthest cabin. He was painting some siding. He looked our way, watched us for a few moments and then returned to his work; either the sight of us was too common and uninteresting, or he had more interest in work than people.

I paused for a moment to take some deep breaths. I felt my lungs clean out. The air was so much clearer at this altitude. When I looked back at the car, I saw Lancaster laughing at me. He seemed to take some pleasure in almost anything I did or said. Would he still be this way if he was married to me as long as Ronnie was? Didn't Ronnie smile and laugh at little things I had said and done when we were first together? I supposed love, like most anything, could grow stale. Passion could wither like grapes left on the vine if it wasn't nurtured and attended to regularly. But why think about it? Lancaster was right. Live in the present.

I hurried into the cabin office.

It was barely bigger than my bedroom's en-suite bathroom. There was a small counter, but no furniture in front of it. It wasn't a lobby so much as a drive-through, a place to register and do little else. The walls were mahogany-stained logs with framed photographs of wildlife – birds, a black bear, geese on a pond, and a close shot of a coyote. It resembled a dog, but the wildness was in its eyes. A well-worn greyish-brown area rug was laid over the hardwood floor. On the counter was a lamp made out of what looked like deer antlers. Behind the counter was a fixture for mail for each cabin and beside it were keys on a mat woven out of what appeared to be straw, but I was sure was something else. Next to it was a miniature dark-cherrywood grandfather clock. The owner appeared in the doorway behind the counter, coming from what looked like a small den or living room.

Betty Lester was a woman easily in her sixties with gray-brown hair cut sharply to frame her long, lean face, featuring large, almost vacant, round dull-brown eyes, the eyes of someone who believed she had seen everything that was worth seeing. There was no element of surprise or even the slightest sign of interest in them at the sight of me. There was just a short pause as if she was taking a picture. Maybe she was, with her brain. I took one of her as well.

She had pale orange lips, with the lower looking a little thicker than the upper. Small patches of tiny brown spots were at the corners of her mouth. Her skin was almost made of cellophane, the veins in her jawline and neck practically embossed. She looked about five feet seven, with long, thin spidery arms but small hands, the tops of which were blotched with age spots. The jeans she was wearing looked as if they had belonged to her husband. They hung like an afterthought off her hips and were fastened with what looked like a rope rather than a belt. She wore a flannel shirt under a thick, dull gray cable-knit sweater that was bunched in a roll just under her small breasts.

'I turned on the heat in your cabin,' she said after I introduced myself. 'Should be cozy. Colder this year, but we've had less rain and snow. Woods are dry. Be careful out there. No campfires and there is absolutely no smoking on my property, period,' she said sternly. She looked as if she would kill if her point was challenged.

'Good to hear,' I said, which almost brought a smile. It was more like a small collapse in her drumskin-tight cheeks. I looked at some of the giveaways on the counter. One sheet outlined suggested hikes. I studied them a moment. 'This trail starts at the far end of your property?'

'Exactly. If you do the circle, it will take you about an hour and a half at a steady pace. There's a spring and a creek about midway, and over here,' she said, pointing to the map outlined, 'you'll find a scenic view.'

'Thank you.'

I opened my purse and put the money on the counter. She looked at it as if it was foreign currency.

'Ninety-eight percent of the people I get use credit cards,' she said and looked up at me without touching it. Were her suspicions aroused? Did it matter?

'Money still good?'

'Of course. Just sayin'.' She picked it up and counted it carefully. From the way she touched them, I had the impression she was looking for counterfeit bills. She grimaced after a grunt to indicate she was satisfied and then showed me where to sign in. As soon as I did, she gave me the key which was on what looked like a coffee-white toy rabbit's foot. 'It's the fourth one on the right when you drive in.'

'Thank you.'

'Right now, my girl is on holiday. Best time of year to let help take off,' she said. 'However, there are plenty of towels and wash cloths to last you two days. I put in bottles of fresh spring water. Better than any water you buy in the supermarket. Our tap water's good, too. We don't have telephone landlines for outside calls. Most everyone uses cell phones anyway and I have no switchboard. We're not a hotel or motel. My husband was always talking about doing that, but it was another one of those things he never got around to doin'. He died two years ago.'

'Oh. Sorry,' I said, because everyone does. She didn't even hear me.

'I don't know what I'm going to do with this place. Our son moved to the East Coast. Works on Wall Street and couldn't care less about running a family business back here, not that it would be worth his while,' she added. 'He makes more in a week than we make all season. You wonder why you work so hard on something all your lives, especially today. Kids can't wait to get away.'

I nodded. This was one of those conversations you have with people where you just agree to avoid further conversation. I knew that what would please her about life here would not please her son, and there was nothing in the world that would change either of their minds or feelings.

She was obviously waiting for me to say something more, so I told her how I had admired her property every time I had come up here and had made a mental note to stay here someday. And here I was.

She drew her lips back, which made the bridge of her nose even more prominent. If she tightened her face just a little more, it looked as if the skin would break and she'd begin to bleed.

'Let me know if you need anything else,' she offered, but not with any real interest. It was more like what she had memorized years ago to say. She turned away and waved her right hand over her head to dismiss me like she might some annoying fly or mosquito.

I left quickly and got into the car. For a moment I just sat there, staring ahead. Suddenly, I was trembling.

'What?' Lancaster said.

'I think I just met Mrs Bates.'

'Mrs Bates?'

'*Psycho*,' I said.

'Oh boy. Is there a Norman?'

'No. Her son left for more exciting pastures. No Oedipus complex at work here. Husband died two years ago.'

I took a deep breath and drove down the gravel road that ran past the cabins until I reached ours. We got our bags out and entered the cabin. I set mine down quickly in the living room. While Lancaster went to the bathroom, I went back out and brought in the groceries.

The African American man was no longer painting. He had probably gone to lunch. With the breeze stronger, lifting and twisting and turning dried leaves, the place suddenly had the desolate look of a property that had been deserted. Other than the sound of the wind rushing through the forest and the whisper of car tires as an automobile went by, it was silent.

What of it? This was why I had come up here, wasn't it?

I inhaled the scent of the cedar and returned to the cabin. It was a quaint little place with a small well-decorated living room. There was no television set, which pleased me. The furniture consisted of one small settee with light brown cushions and two matching easy chairs, all set around a cedar-wood table upon which was a vase with a handful of fake pussy willow.

The kitchen had a wall oven, a range, a refrigerator and two porcelain sinks. On the recently installed white tile counter stood a microwave. There was an oval dark-cherrywood table and chairs that looked new, too. The floor consisted of large tiles matching the counter top. I put my groceries down on the counter and started to put things away.

Lancaster stepped into the doorway.

'Comfy,' he said. 'The mattress on the queen-size bed feels new. I like the comforter. Reminds me of the one I had on my bed in Carmel. I stayed in a cabin not much bigger than this one.'

'Ronnie and I spent a week in Carmel when Kelly was five and able to stay with our parents. She liked jumping from one to the other. She can treat people like television stations. Like Ronnie, Kelly won't ride in my car with me unless I change from NPR to some rock or pop station.'

'First time you mentioned your daughter's name,' he said.

'Is it?'

I looked away and continued organizing the food.

'Need any help?'

'No. It's nothing,' I said. I finished, picked up my bag and walked out to look at the bedroom. The large pillows were fluffy. There was a fresh scent, too. 'She keeps it nice.'

'Probably thinks of it all as an extension of her own home. It makes her feel significant, especially after what you told me about her son leaving and her husband dying. The place is probably her family now.'

'Talk about analyzing too much . . .'

He laughed.

I started to put my things away, hang up my shirts and an extra pair of jeans. He did the same with his things.

'I can't wait to get out there,' I said. 'How about I make us some sandwiches and we just walk until we find a nice place for lunch?'

'OK.' He smiled widely at me.

'What?'

'You're like a little girl again, aren't you?' he asked. He touched my cheek as if he wanted to be sure I was really standing there and wasn't part of his imagination. I brought my hand to his and then brought his to my lips. His smile weakened into a more intense look. I could feel the energy building between us. 'That's what coming up here is doing for you.'

'Yes.'

'You know what makes me even hungrier than a walk in the woods on a brisk fall day like this?' he asked.

'Yes,' I said. 'I know.' I knew because it made me hungrier, too.

Ever so slowly, moving as though the world itself had nearly stopped spinning on its axis, he brought his lips to mine. At first it seemed as light as air, his lips touching mine so gently that I wasn't sure we had touched. It was as if we were feeling the static electricity emanating from each other's passion, and that nudged and unfolded the sexual energy balled up inside us.

'We should christen this place before we do anything else,' he said.

Before we took another step, our clothes literally seemed to fall away and land in a pile at our feet. He put his arm around my waist and turned me toward the bedroom. I lay my head against his shoulder as we walked slowly into it. I pulled away the comforter and the cover sheet and then we both got in. He seemed to feast on my breasts, taunting my nipples with the tip of his tongue, his leg gently moving in between mine. I brought my building sexual excitement to him, moving slowly, firmly, rhythmically, while he lifted my breasts with his mouth and then kissed me, drawing hot breath from my lungs. I felt as if he wanted to devour me, force me into him, to be forever a part of him, to disappear entirely inside him.

He held back patiently as I worked myself higher and higher, closer and closer to that vivid trembling that came at the firing of my first orgasm. I was gasping and he was holding me as if I might somehow fall off the bed. He was so strong, so confident and so unselfish. He put his satisfaction on hold, driving me to feel more, go into another orgasm and another. I had never had sex like this. It seemed it could go on forever. My heart pounded, but joyfully. I wanted to lose my breath. I chased after every gasp. I was turning and twisting, on the throes of a convulsion, and the only thing that calmed me down was feeling him finally slip softly, gracefully into me.

I fell back and he moved over me, his hands at my side so he could push himself up and look down at me. I lifted my head to reach his lips, but he teased me by pulling back. He said nothing. There were no accompanying words of love or pledges and exclamations of his joy. He was steadfast, silent, his eyes penetrating mine. I felt my body weaken. Every part of me that even suggested resistance or control retreated. He was moving with strong, steady strokes, subduing me completely. I closed my eyes and felt a rumbling begin in my loins and travel up my spine. Did I cry out? I can't remember. He continued, pursuing me inside until I felt him exploding as if he had brought his entire body to my one warm place and entered me completely if only for a few moments. My lips were salty wet with the taste of his. I kept my eyes closed, and when he lifted himself away, I drifted, refusing to see an ending, even though my body had settled and my sex had balled up again to wait for another nudge.

When I opened my eyes, he was standing there naked at the side of the bed. He had his hands on his hips and looked as if he had just won a marathon.

'Don't be so proud of yourself,' I said, and he smiled.

'We should always make love as if we're afraid it might be for the last time. That's nothing to be ashamed of. I must say that you make love as though you haven't for some time.'

'Sometimes Ronnie accuses me of not wanting it as much as he does.'

'And?'

'I haven't initiated it for some time.'

'Not good.' He sat on the bed. 'How's that song go? *You've lost that loving feeling* . . .'

'The thing is, until you came along, I wasn't looking for it elsewhere. The very thought of adultery didn't occur to me, maybe because most of the men I know through my friends and his look the same to me. Oh, one might have nicer eyes or a nicer mouth, be in better shape, have a more pleasing voice, but each has so much more *not* to recommend him.'

'Maybe you're just too choosy.'

'You should be pleased about that.'

'What about that attorney you've started working for?'

'He's good-looking, even a little flirtatious, but he lacks soul,' I said, and Lancaster laughed. 'Stop trying to find me another lover anyway. Are you planning on going?'

'Someday. I'm afraid about what you'll be like then.'

'I might come after you.'

He smiled. 'You might do just that. Then *I'll* be stalked.' He slapped his leg. 'Well, what about those sandwiches and a walk in the woods?'

'Right.'

I rose. We both went to retrieve our clothes, and then I went into the kitchen and prepared some sandwiches quickly. Twenty minutes or so later, we left the cabin. We didn't hold hands until we reached the beginning of the trail as outlined on the sheet of paper I had taken from the office.

When I looked back, the African American man was looking our way. He wore a curious expression on his face. He looked worried, as if he was about to shout, 'Be careful,' or something. I smiled back at him, but he didn't smile back at me. He shook his head and turned back to his work.

We made a turn and the world of cars, people and electricity disappeared.

We were like Adam and Eve, only, unlike them, we weren't leaving Paradise. We were entering it.

At least, I thought so.

But I had been wrong before.

TEN

I remember there weren't enough birds to please me. Spring had so much more to offer than fall, despite the short-lived beautiful leaf colors, which was probably why everywhere in the world where there were seasons, everyone looked forward to one or the other so much. Now leafless, the trees looked lonely to me. They had been turned into sentinels of the dead, guarding memories and heritage. There were no smiles in trees that had lost their leaves. Beside the absence of birds, there weren't even insects to visit their limbs. In fact, what struck me about our trail was the deep stillness. The loudest sound was the crunch of our feet on the tiny branches and dried leaves.

I wasn't walking so much as lumbering along, inhaling the sweet pungent scent of the pine needles and the aroma of fresh earth. It was mesmerizing. I felt new energy in my legs, little electric explosions in my thighs and calves and even my feet. Lancaster reached out to touch my arm so I would stop walking. I was annoyed at the interruption.

However, glancing in the direction he was looking, I saw a stag mule deer. It was standing statue-still and looking our way. Its antlers were forked and it had the characteristic large ears. I didn't know how many human beings it had seen or how often, but from the way it was standing there, apparently unafraid, it seemed we were just as much a curiosity to him as he was to us.

'Hey,' Lancaster shouted. He didn't move.

'Deer,' I cried, and his ears flickered and he started away quickly, disappearing deeper into the forest.

'Well, that's something,' Lancaster said. 'You can see squirrels and coyotes everywhere, but mule deer are a treat. Maybe we'll see a mountain lion.'

'No, thanks,' I said. 'I'll skip that treat, thank you.'

We walked on. Maybe it was the stillness of the forest, the cool air, the absence of any real distraction, but we both seemed to fall deeper and deeper into our own thoughts, which was what was supposed to happen. Neither of us spoke for nearly half an hour or more, until we came to that scenic view Betty Lester had mentioned. There were some nice-size rocks to sit on and look out over the valley below.

We sat and gaped. There was something unique about being high up and looking down. Yes, maybe it made you feel more God-like. You were above the din, superior to all below who were still caught in the bedlam of their everyday lives. The vastness filled you with an exhilarating feeling. You were untouchable, unreachable, and as close to immortality as you'd ever be. This was where dreams rested before leaping off to find a proper home. They were swarming around me like angels exploring all they could outside of heaven.

After a few moments during which we sat absorbing the scene before us, I turned to him. He looked younger somehow, his face reddened by the rush of blood that rose to face the cold sting of the wind. Strands of his hair danced over his forehead. His eyes seemed brighter, his lips fuller and the breadth of his shoulders wider, stronger. I saw the anticipation in his soft smile. What amazing thing would I say to fit this incredible experience?

'This is that moment when we tell each other things we would never tell anyone else, even people close to us. Nature has a way of unwrapping secrets of the heart,' I added. I was challenging him.

He was thoughtful a moment, his smile flying off like a kite caught in the wind. Could he pull it back?

'Your expectations are too great. That might be your overall problem,' he said.

'I have an overall problem?'

'You've stepped out of your life to find another life. I'd say that's a symptom of something that can be safely called a problem.'

I stared at the magnificent, crystal-clear view before us and resisted digesting his words, even though I knew they rang with the certainty of Big Ben sounding the hour.

'Right from the start, we're guilty of over-expectations,' he continued. 'We expect far too much of our parents, and yes, they always expect far too much of us, whether it be to become as successful as they are or more successful than they are. It's the same thing – imposing goals and achievements on us that might not even be on our list of desirable aims.

'You know your teachers always expect more effort, more results, and then you start romancing the dream and experience one disappointment after another until someone says, "Why do you have to be so passionately in love? Why can't you just settle for someone who seems to have the same goals in life, enjoys most of what you enjoy, and keeps you from being depressed about yourself?" Those seem to be attainable expectations.'

'And then you realize you want more,' I said.

'We all want more. Settling for enough seems too much like . . .'

'Dying,' I said.

'I guess so. Sad, because no one is ever fully satisfied. The real curse of Original Sin was the creation of too much ambition. Disappointment leads to depression, and depression leads to trouble or finally embracing the exit.'

'So you'll never be happy either?'

'I've made a wise decision. I'm satisfied with the pursuit of happiness and not the attainment of it,' he replied. He looked at me. 'I don't think you can be.'

'You think you know me well enough to come to that conclusion?'

He shrugged. 'I'd like to be wrong. Prove me wrong. Be happy.'

'With or without you?'

'Has to be without me. I'm not eternal. Besides, once you discover everything about me, warts and all, you'll regret and that will lead to unhappiness again. Why do you have to replace everything? If your marriage isn't working for you, maybe marriage itself doesn't work for you, and therefore no new one will suffice.'

'I thought you said we were going to avoid being serious,' I snapped back, now angry at how well he knew me, saw inside me and unwrapped me.

He put up his hands. 'Sorry, sorry. You pushed me into it. Shall we continue the walk?' he asked, standing.

A little sullen now, I got up and walked faster, remaining a few steps ahead of him. He didn't try to catch up. At one point when I looked back, I didn't see him, but I didn't panic, nor did I stop to wait for him. Either he was deliberately hiding from me to tease me or something off the trail had captured his interest. I walked on. In fact, I walked on even faster and completed the remainder of the circuit without looking back or pausing once for him to catch up to me. I stepped into the cabin and immediately went to take a hot shower.

When I emerged, I put on the bathrobe hanging on the bathroom door and stepped back into the living room, expecting to see him. He wasn't there. Shrugging to myself, I went into the kitchen and began to prepare our dinner. It had just begun to get dark outside when he returned. I had set the table.

'You've been a busy little bee, I see,' he said. I knew he was standing there, waiting for me to ask him where he had been and what he had been doing. Perhaps he expected me to voice some complaint, to emphasize that we didn't come up here to be alone, but to be together. I didn't say a word. When I was with him, I prided myself on doing and saying what was unexpected. I smiled instead and returned to the kitchen.

He went to take a shower as well. When he came out, wearing his robe, I was sitting in the living room, sipping some of the red wine I had just opened. He looked at the fire I had started in the fireplace and then smiled. I watched him walk over to the fire and rub his hands in the heat. Then he turned to me.

'You're not leaving much for me to do,' he said.

'Feeling like a kept man or something?'

'Something.'

'I was once told that Europeans approach a fireplace first with their back to it. Is that true?'

'I think it's a mistake to stereotype people. You can miss out on someone quite wonderful.'

'I read that line and I used it on my husband, but he didn't understand how anyone could be quite wonderful.'

'Even you?'

'I didn't pursue it,' I replied.

'Maybe you should have. Maybe you're not giving him the benefit of the doubt.'

'I don't like to hear you defend him,' I said. 'It's as if you're trying to drive me away.'

'Insecure? You?'

'Do I contradict myself? Very well then I contradict myself. I am large, I contain multitudes.'

'Quoting Walt Whitman. I'm impressed.'

He poured himself some wine and sat on the settee. 'Something smells very good.'

'I prepared some chicken marsala.'

'I thought you were a good cook from the moment I laid eyes on you in the supermarket.'

'Aha! So you *were* watching me before I bumped into you?'

'You caught my attention, yes.'

'And maneuvered to be in my way in that aisle after all?'

'As I have said, maybe I did.'

'You did. What was it that told you I was vulnerable?' I asked, now very interested in myself – more so than usual, in fact.

'Little things, like the way you chose your groceries. You stabbed at boxes, flung vegetables and fruits into your cart, even looked like you were mumbling angrily to yourself as you went along. I thought, there's a woman who is not comfortable in her own skin right now. Most of the women I see shopping, especially in supermarkets, seem pleased or to have accepted themselves where they are and what they're doing. It's like this is what their mothers had done or it was always their intention.'

'To do what?'

'To accept being a mother and a housewife. They weren't at war with themselves.'

'And I am?'

'Practically nuclear,' he said. 'That's what I saw.'

'And you prey on such women?'

'Only those as beautiful as you,' he replied. He sipped his wine and gave me that teasing smile.

'You're so pleased with yourself.'

'Am I?'

'Are you the best thing that's happened to me or the worst?' I asked.

He shrugged. 'Why put any label on it at all? I'm what's happened to you right now. Period.'

'OK,' I said. 'I'll accept that. For now.' I rose.

'Need any help?'

'The definition of a man,' I said. 'Asking when it's all been done.'

He laughed, his laughter trickling behind me like a spring over a rock.

I brought out the food and we had our dinner. Like Ronnie, he raved about my cooking. There were moments when he even sounded like Ronnie. I don't mean the words; I mean his voice became indistinguishable with its cadence and the way he complimented me on something. I knew he was being sincere, but it still sounded rehearsed, expected.

It suddenly occurred to me that this escape to a mountain cabin might, ironically, damage our passionate romance. It was one thing to come up here and take a romantic walk in the woods enjoying nature, but another to permit it to take on some domestic qualities. Domesticity stifled spontaneity. There were responsibilities, roles to play. There I was, clearing the table and cleaning up the kitchen. Unlike Ronnie, he offered to help, but I didn't want us to become a cute little couple doing the most mundane things together.

I wanted us to remain characters in an exciting, heart-pounding, passionate romance movie or novel. Domesticity strips away mystery. I didn't want to know or to learn his eccentricities, nor did I want him to learn all mine either. I wasn't interested in how he usually went to bed or usually rose in the morning. I didn't want to watch him brush his teeth or tell me how important this food or that was to his nutritional health. I didn't want to know his opinion about any of that or have him suggest things I could do to enhance my health, the way husbands and wives advise each other. I didn't want to hear the latest news about coffee or vitamins, and I certainly didn't want to discuss politics. I didn't even want to discuss the latest bestselling books. I wasn't looking for a husband. I wasn't even looking for a companion. I wanted only a lover.

And a lover to me meant not doing things that had to be done. I didn't want to look at clocks and follow schedules. The day and the night had to flow into each other without any hands on any clock.

But it occurred to me that what I had done was create a two-day husband. If there was a television set in the cabin, we'd surely be sitting beside each other, watching either his or my favorite program. Then we'd yawn, suggest bed and maybe go to sleep without making love. He saw all this in my face.

'We could go for a brisk walk,' he said.

'It's brisk out there all right. Temperature dropped at least thirty degrees since this afternoon.'

'Then let's just lie here together, hold each other and not speak at all,' he suggested. 'I think you need to be held, to feel cherished.'

I didn't disagree. At first we sat beside each other on the settee, and then he put his arm around me and I lay against him. I felt his breath on my hair and then the back of my neck. He moved his hand inside my robe and stroked my breasts as if he thought it might mellow me instead of arousing me. His lips were on my cheek and then my neck. The fire crackled. I thought I could hear the pounding of my heart, echoing through my arteries and veins, my blood warming and my skin beginning to tingle.

I moaned softly, so softly that I wasn't sure I had. Maybe it was only a thought.

'If I were a cat, I'd be purring,' I said. 'Can you need too much love and attention?' I asked in a whisper. 'Need more than anyone can give you?'

'Yes, perhaps.'

'Then you can never be truly happy?'

'I told you. Happiness is the one thing you don't want completely satisfied. It would be like reaching the end of the universe and realizing there is no place to go but back.'

'You make tragedy sound inviting,' I said.

He laughed, stroked my hair and turned me toward him. His robe was opened as much as mine. Our bodies touched, his chest to my breasts, his stomach to mine, and his hardened penis nudging its way, parting me softly. When he entered me, we just lay there, neither moving. It was almost a contest to see who would have to move first. We surrendered to each other simultaneously and began a slow but hard drive at each other, demanding more and more until I reached my climax and he rushed to catch up to me.

Afterward, I fell asleep in his arms, or at least I thought I had, because when I awoke in the morning, he wasn't beside me. I rose slowly, for a moment confused about where I was. Then I recalled everything and went to the bedroom, expecting to see him lying there, perhaps. He wasn't and he wasn't in the bathroom either, nor was he in the kitchen preparing our coffee. The emptiness in the cabin gave me a chill. I went to the front door and looked out at the immediate area. There was no one there.

Maybe he took a walk for a newspaper or something, I thought. I went to wash up and prepare the coffee. I had bought some of my favorite Danish, too, and eggs, but I didn't feel as hungry as I had imagined I might be. I sat sipping my coffee and looking out the front window of the cabin. It was like staring at a large photograph. No one was out there.

Something else unexpected occurred. Time was passing dreadfully slowly. This was how it passed below the mountains, at home, in my world. When you were having fun, enjoying everything you were doing, or were absorbed in work as I had been when I worked for Sebastian Pullman, time always passed too quickly. I had already made up my mind that the moment we had left this place, we'd feel we had spent too little time here. We'd regret leaving. What if that wasn't going to happen? I felt a terrible sense of anxiety, something I hadn't felt for a while.

When I looked at my watch, I saw that only fifteen minutes had gone by. It had felt like hours. Where was he? Why wasn't he eager to have breakfast with me? Why didn't he want to wake up to my waking up? That initial moment was very important for lovers. Where had I read it? There was a line . . .

The first thing I want to see every morning is your face and the last thing I want to see every night is your face.

'Hey!' he said.

I spun around.

'Where did you come from?'

'I've been standing here watching you for ten minutes, expecting you to realize it.'

'I didn't hear or see you come in. Where were you?'

'I just took a short walk. When I awoke, you were sleeping so soundly, I didn't want to wake you. I did anticipate your waking up as I got dressed, but you didn't stir, so I thought I would just let you be a while.'

'There's coffee,' I said.

'I can smell it. Wonderful. Thanks.'

He went into the kitchen and returned with a cup.

'You all right?' he asked.

'Yes . . . I don't know,' I added.

'What's wrong? You think this was a mistake?'

'No . . . I don't know,' I added again.

He nodded and sat. I watched him watch me as he sipped his coffee.

'Maybe you're better off being busy after all,' he suggested. 'Remember your *Julius Caesar*? *Yon Cassius has a lean and hungry look. He thinks too much. Such men are dangerous.*'

'Thanks for comparing me to an assassin.'

He laughed.

'Well, isn't that what you're about to be, at least symbolically? You're killing off the old Clea Howard, aren't you? Maybe not abruptly, but in little ways that will have the same fatal result.'

'So if I had no mind and I didn't think too much, I'd be in a satisfying marriage and life?'

'Can you be unhappy if you're incapable of knowing it?'

'And you're suggesting that's a preferable way to be?'

'No. I'm just pointing out what you know to be true as well. I suppose the trick is to learn how to live with disappointment if you are capable of feeling disappointed.'

'Tolerate, compromise, sell out, stifle yourself or leap into a yawning grave. Thanks for the choice.'

He laughed. 'Somehow, I think you'll manage to find another way.'

I spun completely around on him.

'You're really an optimist, aren't you? You pretend to rush about, move constantly to avoid being bored or depressed, but the very act of moving about means you're optimistic. You think there's hope or you wouldn't bother.'

'So? Is there something wrong with that? Does it disappoint you?'

'No . . . I don't know,' I added.

'You're afraid to be optimistic, Clea. It's a leap of faith. Ronnie's optimistic, isn't he?'

'Sometimes sickeningly so, but most of the time he likes wallowing in potential disaster.'

'Does he? Maybe it's just amusing to him. Maybe it means little more than that.'

'I told you that I don't like you defending him. It gives me the feeling you're driving me away.'

He shrugged. 'I'm here as long as you want me to be.'

'Do you want to be?'

'As long as you want me to be, I want to be,' he replied. He slapped down on his knees. 'No more of this dull intro-spection. Let's have something to eat and maybe go on a longer walk this time. Let's come back exhausted and fall into each other's arms, maybe too tired even to make love.'

I laughed. 'I doubt you'll ever be that tired.'

'We'll play it by—'

'Penis,' I said, and he threw his head back and laughed harder than ever.

It was amazing how quickly and effectively he could change my mood. He was better than any drug. I prided myself on the way I had avoided drugs. Some of my girlfriends and their husbands were into cocaine occasionally, but Ronnie was just as determined to avoid that scene as I was. Actually, Ronnie even hated getting too drunk. He didn't mind a buzz, but he hated not being in control of himself. I had to admire him for that, as much as I admired myself for it. If I wanted to think about it, I suppose there were many things we had in common. Of course, there had to be. We didn't come together solely for the sex.

When Lancaster and I had eaten breakfast, I dressed and we went out for that longer walk. The weather had changed quickly.

It was mostly cloudy with a stiff, cold breeze that turned into gusts from time to time, scattering leaves, riling up dust and whistling through trees. If anything, though, that made us walk faster, harder. I glanced at him and saw he was as determined as I was not to be defeated by the drop in temperature.

After a while, it felt like a race, a contest to see who would cry uncle first and ask for a rest. Neither of us was giving in.

'You're in great shape,' he said, sounding breathless. 'You exercise.'

'Not regularly and not nearly enough,' I replied.

We were taking a harder route, going up and down small hills, rougher ground, twisting past branches to avoid being scratched, going over rocks and occasionally crossing a muddier area. I had my hands clenched as well as my teeth. I felt as if I was on a death march. Soon, every step felt like I was pounding the earth more out of anger than pleasure. We had left pleasure far behind us now.

Suddenly, I heard the sound of a chainsaw. That made me pause, and when I paused, I realized he wasn't beside or behind me again. How far back had I left him? I waited, debating whether to go back or continue. If something had happened to him, I certainly would have heard him cry out. He was just resting and now he was too embarrassed about it. I smiled to myself and walked on, more slowly. When I came around a turn, I saw that African American worker cutting up firewood. He didn't hear me, but when he turned his head a little, he saw me and stopped his saw.

'Whoa,' he said. 'You done a walk.'

'Yes, I have.'

'Well, you just make the turn down here and you'll be back on the cabin property,' he said, nodding in the right direction.

'Please tell my friend when he arrives,' I asked.

'Friend?'

'He's a little behind me,' I explained. 'Women have more endurance.'

'That so?'

He looked behind me, shrugged his left shoulder and started his chainsaw again.

I continued on. I was feeling it now. Walking a few miles

on a straight road was one thing, but hiking through a forest, over boulders and up and down rough ground was another. I didn't want Lancaster to see me practically collapse on the bed when I got into the cabin, but that was what I did. I lay there for a good fifteen or so minutes before I heard him enter.

He came to the bedroom doorway. I turned on my back and looked at him.

'If there was ever a case of someone being chased by demons . . .'

'That's what you need – some demons,' I said.

He smiled. 'I think I'll try that Jacuzzi. Some of these muscles in my legs and rear, I haven't used since I was eight.'

'Sounds like a plan. I'll get it warm and bubbly for us both,' I said and went to it.

It was deep enough and wide enough for the two of us. I remembered the last time Ronnie and I had done this. It was at a resort in Cabo, Mexico, at least ten years ago. Back then, we could have a second, even a third honeymoon, but that idea seemed to drift away with so many others.

'You should be this content all the time or most of it, Clea,' Lancaster said. 'You wear it well.'

'You were right,' I decided instantly. 'I'm not returning full-time to work, not even part-time. That's just filling hours with sand when I should be filling them with wine.'

'Your husband wanted you to work?'

'Yes, actually, he did.'

'He was afraid of your having idle time. He was casting another chain over you.'

'Yes.'

'That's what husbands and children do, cast chains over you. A woman like you can't survive like that.'

'No.'

'Maybe you should go with me,' he said.

'Maybe I should.'

He lay back in the warm water and then I started the pumps and both our bodies shook with pleasure. I wondered who had the bigger smile on their face.

ELEVEN

The ride down from Idyllwild felt just like that – a ride down, a descent from the clouds, from something heavenly to something mundane. With every turn, I felt my body harden and my nerves grow tense. It didn't surprise me that he sensed how I was feeling. By now he had developed a remarkable insight, a sharp awareness of all my feelings and moods. It had taken Ronnie years to do that, and I didn't think he had ever achieved it to the extent Lancaster had in a matter of days.

'You're worrying about returning or not returning to work, aren't you?' he suddenly asked, perhaps because I had been so quiet after we left the cabin.

'I don't want to return to work at the law firm. You were right about how unsatisfying it would be, but I'm stubborn about admitting defeat or failure. If something like the coffee pot, juicer or vacuum cleaner breaks, and I'm frustrated with fixing it, I still won't let Ronnie do it, even if he's home at the time. He'll hear me cursing and complaining and come running to my aid, but I'll keep trying until I discover the problem. He hates that.'

'He wants to be the man in the family. Is that wrong?'

'You just can't stop defending him, can you? You males are incapable of any sort of independent review of your actions, just like cops and doctors – and lawyers.'

'I'd add politicians.'

'They're mostly lawyers.'

He laughed. 'You're a challenge, all right. You're lucky your parents never became suicidal.'

'After they saw it was too late, they saved themselves with indifference.'

'Aren't you doing the same thing now when it comes to your relationships with your husband and your daughter – even your friends?'

'Stop analyzing me. I thought we weren't going to do that to each other. It was practically a promise.'

He shrugged. 'It's in our nature to make promises we know we can't keep.'

'Rationalizing,' I accused.

'Also in our nature,' he replied.

We drove on in silence nearly the remainder of the journey. I was working on how I would do just what he had said: rationalize why I had decided not to return to work for Carlton Saunders, especially after starting successfully and anticipating his call to return. I supposed I could fall back on a typically safe excuse. I thought I would tell both Carlton and Ronnie that I had decided that my daughter needed me now after all. She was at a vulnerable age. I wasn't going to be one of those mothers who were oblivious and then suddenly shocked at what or who her children had become right under her eyes, not that there's a guarantee you'd have any real influence on what your children did or didn't do. Competing with the power of peer pressure was like attempting to block Niagara Falls with cardboard boxes.

As if he was party to my thoughts, Lancaster suddenly said, 'You're not someone who is comfortable lying to herself. Otherwise, you wouldn't be with me.'

'But I'm comfortable lying to others? Is that it?'

'Indifference, rationalization. Without both, Adam and Eve couldn't have survived leaving Paradise.'

'You are so . . .'

'What?'

'Fucking self-confident,' I said.

His laughter carried us both more relaxed the rest of the way.

At his request, I dropped him off where I had picked him up. If I ever told any of my girlfriends that, she would be sure to say he probably didn't want me to know where he was staying or with whom. Maybe he was married. Maybe he had a girlfriend and I was simply another amusement. Maybe that's true, I thought, but right now that wasn't something about which I had any concern.

After he got out, he leaned to look back in at me.

'Work things out. I'll be here for you whenever you want me to be.'

'No matter what?'

'No matter what,' he said. He closed the door and I drove off. When I looked back through my rearview mirror, he was already gone. For a moment I felt as if the umbilical cord for my spacewalk had snapped and I was about to float into oblivion.

However, as I drove on, despite all the tension and conflict in my mind, I realized that the ride back hadn't drained me of my optimism. My excuse for leaving turned out to be true. I did feel renewed. Nature had done its job. My brain felt less cluttered. I could feel the restored energy pulsing through my body. I was actually looking forward to seeing both Ronnie and Kelly. I started planning on what I would make for dinner and imagined us being light and playful with each other, just as we were during the earlier years. I would be very interested in how they had gotten along in my absence. I even felt a little jealous about it, which I considered a good thing to feel at this point. I wasn't as indifferent as Lancaster had made me out to be.

Perhaps absence does make the heart fonder. It wasn't a cure. It was simply a way to address symptoms, like taking an aspirin to reduce your fever but not to destroy what causes your fever. Maybe that was all we could expect, some temporary moments of happiness and contentment along the convoluted path of struggle we called life.

I thought about some of those happier moments in my marriage. I certainly had them. How could I deny the day Kelly was born and the way that had strengthened my relationship with Ronnie, for example? Of course, it did feel as if we were different people then. Time, experiences, events, even other people change us, and if we don't change together, we grow into strangers. Maybe that was all it was; it was no one's fault. Guilt has no place in evolution. It's beside the point.

There were birthdays, vacations and major events like our buying our house – all moments that stood out. I could trace our lives with them the way someone might connect the dots to form a picture. One might even use the connecting dots to claim there was a pattern to his or her life, a logic, some cause and effect. I think what had happened was I'd become afraid of connecting the dots, afraid of the new picture that would be created.

I turned into our driveway and opened the garage door with that magic button above the visor. Ronnie's car was there. I had half expected him to be golfing, having lunch with his friends, and I expected Kelly probably would be at the home of one of her girlfriends. Now I was hoping to see them happily waiting for me, both of them racing to catch me up on what had occurred during my absence, but the moment I got out of my car, I had a heavy sense of dread fall over me. I think it was the silence that I hadn't anticipated. It was Sunday. If Ronnie was home, he'd have the television on to watch some sporting event. And if Kelly was there, she would have music streaming too loudly out of her room.

I closed the door softly behind me, put my purse on the counter in the kitchen and walked slowly into the living room, my overnight bag in hand. They were both sitting there on the sofa, Ronnie on one end, Kelly on the other. They had identical dour expressions. The duplication was almost comical. Were they this far apart because they'd been fighting, arguing? Was I walking into another annoying and silly father–daughter confrontation? Couldn't they get along with each other for at least two days without my being a constant referee?

'What's happening?' I asked, deliberately evincing little interest.

'Do you have your mobile phone on you?' Ronnie asked.

'My mobile phone? Yes,' I said. 'Why?'

'Look at it,' he ordered. In my mind's eye, I could see rage seeping out of the corners of his tight-lipped mouth.

I opened my purse and took out my phone.

'So?'

'Is it on?'

'On?' I looked at it again and realized it wasn't. I pressed to turn it on, but nothing happened. 'The battery must have died,' I said. 'What about it?'

'Late yesterday afternoon, your mother was rushed to the hospital in Rancho Mirage. She had a serious heart attack.

I've been calling you every hour on the hour ever since. I haven't slept.'

Kelly's lips began to tremble. Her eyes were so fixed on me that I felt she was burning a hole in my chest with her laser-like intensity.

'Is she dead?' I asked.

'No, but it's not looking very good,' Ronnie said. 'We didn't go to the desert because we wanted to get in touch with you and all of us go there together,' he added.

'Where were you, Mom?' Kelly demanded. 'Why didn't you call to see how we were?'

'I'll go up and put some things together in case I have to stay with my father,' I said instead of responding.

'Jack seems pretty much in control and handling it well. Your father always struck me as someone who could command a nuclear submarine,' Ronnie offered.

I supposed in some way that was meant to make me feel better, but pointing out that my father could hold a steady course even in the midst of losing the woman he had been married to for more than forty years gave me little comfort.

'Where were you?' Kelly asked. 'You told us you were going to Palm Springs and would be with them.'

It was amusing to me that Kelly was the one asking. Did they decide before I arrived how they would conduct their interrogation? Perhaps Ronnie believed I would be honest if Kelly was the one demanding answers.

'I changed my mind,' I said.

'So where did you go?' Ronnie followed.

I think it was my father who, when balling me out for lying to my parents blatantly, advised me I'd be more successful deceiving someone if I worked in some truth and simply excluded the untrue parts instead of trying to get by with a complete bald-faced lie. I had the impression it was a technique he used when he wanted to sell a client a particular stock or mutual fund that would garner him a bigger commission. Not very Eisenhower of him, I thought later on, when I was able to understand more about all adults, not just my parents.

'I went to Idyllwild,' I said.

'Idyllwild? Why did you go there instead of to Palm Springs?'

'I said I wanted to be out in nature. I thought the desert would be busier this time of the year, and, to be honest, I didn't want my parents cross-examining me. I'll be right down,' I added and hurried up the stairs.

It occurred to me that I should have told them I was going up to Idyllwild from the start, but it really was impossible to anticipate every possible complication, especially something like my mother having a heart attack. I had spoken to her before I left and heard nothing in her voice to even suggest she wasn't feeling well. She cracked her syllables, vowels and consonants with that Vassar College elegance of which she was always proud. She had met my father at a sorority mixer. She told me she never had her mind set on any specific career. She dabbled with the idea of getting into publishing because she was such a good reader, but my father, who is two years older, was already being courted by Wells Fargo for an opening on the West Coast. The publishing world is really centered on the East Coast, and it didn't break her heart to sacrifice the goal in order to marry Dad and move to California.

I think, in most families, we're brought up to believe that our fathers will die before our mothers. Of course, that generality is losing validity in a world in which women take on more stressful lives, employment and responsibilities, not to mention smoking and drinking more. Despite the high intensity of his work, my father was exactly how Ronnie depicted him, always calm and centered, no matter what he was doing or what came up unexpectedly. He was Obama cool, barely blinking faster or breathing harder when confronted by something unpleasant or challenging. I believe I inherited some of that. Look how well I had handled my husband and daughter just now, I thought.

I emptied my overnight bag on the bed and quickly replaced everything with clean clothes and different shoes. Knowing my father, he wouldn't ask me to stay with him for his sake. He would assure me he was fine, but he would accept that I had to remain to be with my mother.

I glanced at myself in the mirror to check my hair and

lipstick with the concern a single-engine pilot would have inspecting his airplane before flying, and then I scooped up my bag and hurried down the stairs. They were both in the kitchen, dressed to leave, waiting, Kelly looking more impatient than Ronnie.

'My parents are with your dad,' Ronnie said. 'They've been with him right from the get-go.'

I nodded.

Kelly had her book bag. Probably more out of nervousness than anything now, she wanted to address the homework she had left for the last minute. She knew she would need distraction. Teenagers, despite how tough they want you to think they are, have far more difficulty confronting tragedy, especially when it's imminent.

We all got into Ronnie's car and headed off, no one speaking until we reached the freeway. I had not asked for any details, but whenever we are facing or hearing about death, we cling to the details for some support, a way to distract ourselves. How did it happen? Why did it happen? Who was there? When did you hear? None of it really mattered at this point, but what else would you discuss if you didn't ask these questions? Arrangements for funerals?

'Grandma Lydia isn't that old,' Kelly said, opening the door to take us out of dark thoughts.

'No, she's not,' Ronnie said. 'Statistically, women live longer than men, even now.'

'She hasn't been sick,' Kelly pointed out.

I knew she wanted to add, 'This is unfair. This is unusual. This is a violation of some rules.' When you're young, no matter what you learn in school or reading, you somehow cling to the idea that the abnormal and the unordinary happen to someone else. You get a cold. You'll get better. You break a leg. You'll have it mended. You get good grades. You'll get a good job. And then you go out in the world and find just how capricious life really is. Colds turn into pneumonia, broken limbs can cripple you for life, and people get jobs not always because of what they know, but whom they know.

When you're a parent, you want to smother your child or children in fantasy. You want to keep them from seeing the cold, hard things in life for as long as possible. Of course, some parents don't believe in that. They raise little realists and as soon as possible point out that Santa Claus and tooth fairies are silly fictions. I suppose I've been a little of both kinds of mother. Ronnie's never been anything but typical. He likes make-believe, even now.

'She never smoked, did she?' Kelly asked me.

'She smoked Virginia Slims when she was younger, yes, but not for the last twenty odd years. What did my father tell you?' I asked Ronnie.

'He said something about throwing an embolism, whatever that means. I didn't want to ask lots of questions and keep him on the phone.'

'He asked for you,' Kelly inserted, 'every time we called.'

'What did you tell him?' I asked Ronnie, flicking off her comment like I would a fly.

'I was—'

'Dad didn't know what to say because you lied about where you were going,' Kelly said, her voice bitter now.

'Why didn't you call to tell us you had changed your plans at least?' Ronnie followed quickly.

They hadn't really rehearsed everything, but they had been asking each other the questions they would ask me.

'I wasn't thinking about any of that,' I said. 'I wasn't thinking about anything I ordinarily would. That was why I went away.'

'What's wrong with you?' Kelly demanded. 'Why did you have to go away to do that?'

'I don't think this is the time to talk about me,' I snapped back at her. 'My mother is dying or is already dead.'

She wilted quickly, snuggling tighter in the corner of the seat. Ronnie sped up as soon as the traffic opened up. He shot into a car pool lane and we were lost in the whir of wheels and the liquefaction of the scenery as we rushed head-on into our own thoughts and anticipation about the scene that lay ahead, a scene that always lay ahead, but one we ignored for as long as we could.

When we arrived at the hospital, we found my father and Ronnie's parents in the hallway outside of ICU. My father looked about as rumpled as it was possible for him to look.

His ash-gray hair wasn't neatly brushed; his ice-blue eyes were a little bloodshot and the circles under them were darker than usual. There was a slight slump in his shoulders. He always prided himself on his good posture. My father was a handsome man, just under six feet tall, meticulous about his clothes and his coiffure, his fingernails manicured, his face closely shaven, and he was always intolerant of lint.

Ronnie's mother looked as if she had been crying steadily for at least twenty-four hours. Her face seemed as crumpled as a cellophane bag. She was the shortest of the foursome at just a little over five feet two. More than my father, Ronnie's father resembled a man whose wife was clinging by a thread to life: his clothing more disheveled, his face unshaven, the gray stubble making his suntan complexion look as if it was bubbling in places. Ronnie looked more like him than he did his mother, which was something I always thought lucky for him. Her features weren't as feminine as my mother's. Her nose looked a little too big for her small mouth and thin lips. Her hair was teased into a gray-blue helmet.

I hugged my father. He was always stiff when it came to demonstrating affection, especially in public. I wasn't sure he even realized I had kissed him.

'What are they saying?' I asked.

'She's ticking down,' he replied.

What a strange way to put it, I thought. He made my mother sound like a bomb.

'They say we all have a finite number of heartbeats determined at conception,' Ronnie offered. His mother's eyes widened. His father shook his head as though he pitied him for being so stupid. He was simply trying to find something to say, but no matter what anyone said right now, I thought, it wouldn't satisfy anyone else.

Kelly stepped out from behind him and my father showed more emotion. Parents always give their grandchildren more affection, I thought. It's as if when their children reach a certain age, that display has to be constricted and put into storage until the grandchildren come along and it can be revived. He hugged her tighter and kissed her and smiled. Then he looked at me.

'Where were you?' he asked.

'I had to do something,' I said, hoping that would suffice for now. He grimaced and shook his head.

'You can go in to see her,' he said. 'She goes in and out. If there weren't the machines, she would have been down for the count.'

First she was a bomb and now she's a prize fighter, I thought and started for the ICU. I paused and looked back at Kelly. My eyes asked. She hurried to catch up with me and we entered together.

Ronnie liked to joke and tell our friends, 'Look at your mother-in-law and that's what your wife will be like in thirty years or so.'

Whenever he cracked that line, everyone laughed on cue as if there was a built-in laugh track like the ones they use on television comedy series. But when I saw my mother hooked up to oxygen and the monitors, looking as if she was shrinking in the bed, I did think of myself and what it would be like for me. I thought there was no way I could end up like that. I'm not going to die. I'm going to evaporate.

'You don't think about Death,' Lancaster had told me during one of our deeper conversations. 'Death thinks about you and you are like a voyeur listening and looking in on the discussion.'

'What's the difference?' I had asked.

'The difference is that if you could avoid the word itself, you would; we all would. Death doesn't like to be ignored.'

Death wasn't being ignored here. The entire complex was dedicated to dueling with him. Some would hold him off for a while, but from the looks of it, most would succumb. Certainly, my mother would.

Kelly started to cry. I embraced her and she embraced me. My mother didn't look conscious. I moved softly away from Kelly and kissed my mother's cheek. Then I took her hand and looked at Kelly. She kissed her, too.

'Mom,' I said. 'We're here. Kelly and I are here. Can you hear us?'

I thought her eyelids fluttered, but maybe it was my wishful thinking. She didn't open them. We stood there. A nurse came and looked at the monitor and at us, but quickly moved away before she had to deal with questions or sorrow.

Kelly looked as if she was about to get hysterical. I saw she was trying hard to swallow back the tears. She was trembling, too.

'I'm just going to sit here, Kelly. You can go out with Dad. Maybe go to the hospital cafeteria with him and get something to eat or drink.'

Kelly nodded, glanced at her grandmother. Obviously she was hesitant about kissing her again, about getting too close to death. She was probably terrified that she would feel cold to her lips. I nodded, excusing her, and she hurried out. Fleeing, I thought. I envied her.

I sat and held on to my mother's hand. She had smaller hands than I had. I always thought her fingers were more feminine than mine. She was so attentive to her skin, religiously applying her favorite creams and lotions. Her nails looked as if they had been manicured an hour ago. Just like her to be perfectly prepared. She told me often, as repetitiously as someone sniffing around memory loss in fact, that her mother always insisted she have on clean undergarments whenever she went out. 'Just in case.'

Just in case? For whom? If you're dead, you can't be embarrassed, so it had to be for those you left behind so they wouldn't be embarrassed. How selfish was that?

I was sure that somehow she had clean panties on. I drew closer to her.

'I'm so sorry this is happening now, Mom, so soon, too soon. I needed you. I wanted to talk to you about my life. You always said you couldn't even imagine being with someone else but my father, but I'm sure you fantasized about it sometimes. Dad's good-looking, strong and reliable, but he's not Mr Perfect. I know daughters are supposed to think of their fathers as being perfect, but you know I never did. He wasn't around enough.

'Anyway, I met someone and I can't seem to stay away from him, and even though he pretends to be so independent, I'm sure he can't stand to be away from me.'

I looked at the door and then I leaned in closer.

'The truth is he haunts me. *Stalks* is not the right word. *Stalks* is too impersonal, and if there's one thing he's not, it's impersonal. He gets so into me that I think he hears my thoughts. He anticipates everything I do almost before I intend to do it. Although neither of us has said the word, I think we love each other. Love leads to all that I have described, don't you think?'

I waited and then sat back.

Was this the conversation I wanted to leave with her, the last conversation between us? What else should I be talking about? Should I tell her things I liked about her? Should I sit here reminiscing about the good times we had with each other? Should I laugh about things we had laughed about together, things about my father? Should I ask her to repeat that recipe for chicken paprikash her grandmother gave her? I would have to confess that I didn't pay enough attention to her when she told it to me, every time she told it to me.

Should I talk about Kelly and reassure her that she is going to be all right in life? Should I talk about what life would be like for my father without her and what I intended to do about it, if anything?

It was horrible, I'm sure, but none of that trumped my desire to talk about Lancaster. I suddenly had this comforting and confident feeling that somehow he would find out about this. He wouldn't insert himself, but he would get here just so I could see him and he could give me a sympathetic and supportive look. He would want to do that.

I don't know how much longer I sat there talking softly to my mother, who probably did not hear a word. I think she was already gone, despite the report from the machinery tracking blood pressure and heartbeats and oxygen levels. Eventually, my father came in and stood beside me, and then Ronnie came in with Kelly, and somewhere during that traffic I went out to the bathroom.

I felt my cell phone vibrate while I was still in there. I smiled and said hello.

'How is she?' he asked.

'Not good. How did you find out?'

'Good news hobbles along; bad news has wings.'

'I'll be down here until . . .'

'Look for me,' he said.

'I will,' I promised.

Afterward, we all ate in the hospital cafeteria, even Ronnie's parents. We were nearly finished when my father spotted the cardiologist in the doorway.

'Well,' he said, rising slowly. 'I'll go speak to him,' he added, nodding at the doctor in the doorway.

We all froze. Kelly started to cry.

Please, I thought. Please don't come back and say, 'She expired.'

Then she would have gone from a bomb to a prize fighter to a parking meter in a matter of hours.

TWELVE

After every one of our relatives died and the deaths of some of our closer friends occurred, my father used to annoy my mother when he would inevitably say, 'I envy the Jews. Traditionally, they don't wait more than twenty-four hours to bury their dead, as long as it's not on the Sabbath.'

I knew why he said that. He hated all the anticipation and he hated to be stuck in the groove of one emotion or another too long. For him, it was like being on cruise control on the freeway, eventually too monotonous. He had a desperate need for choice and eventually would slow down even though he didn't have to reduce his speed, which was something that also drove my mother bonkers. And me, too, for that matter.

I understand that it is in most everyone's nature to want to spend the least amount of time being sad, but my father even believed that being happy too long brought you close to idiotic. He was especially relentless about his objection to mourning, to wearing the clothes and the face of the bereaved for a moment longer than he absolutely had to. In these clothes and under those scrutinizing eyes of fellow mourners looking for a sign of deep emotional loss, he resembled someone whose entire body itched.

'By the time the man or the woman gets buried, everyone else feels like jumping in after them,' he muttered once. That brought a blast from my mother about his selfishness which sent him fleeing to the ninth hole on the golf course. Golf was the modern man's substitute for a monastery, except for those who exploited it for a business meeting. 'Get them when they're frustrated with their putt,' was my father's motto.

When I looked at him now, I knew he was thinking he was already cruising too long at grief speed on the freeway. Despite the cousins and my mother's brother and his sister, and the friends they had made who were all attending the funeral, and despite the comfort they all tried to bring, he obviously longed for a chance to mourn alone and bring this all to a quicker end.

As did I.

Only Ronnie seemed really to enjoy the fellowship. He fished for and hooked into as many different conversations as he could. Unlike most who were timid about showing interest in anything on such a depressing occasion, he rushed about like a kid in a candy store with a limitless budget. I knew it was his way of handling the sadness, but anyone watching him would think he was starved for companionship. It was as if he had been in solitary confinement for years. Seeing him in action was the only thing that brought any sort of smile to my face. When he caught me looking at him and laughing to myself, he rushed over.

'What?' he asked.

I just shook my head.

'What?'

'Nothing, Ronnie. Don't make a scene,' I said, and he shrugged and turned to Wade Barry, a cousin on my mother's side who was recently elected to the state assembly. Wade was a short, stout man with ears too big, suggesting he was built to hear more, especially complaints. In minutes, Ronnie was lecturing him on what taxes to eliminate.

Fortunately for Kelly, my cousin Amy had brought her teenage daughter Ellen with her and they could go off to compare life in their schools and cities, as well as the unreasonable rules parents seemed to pull out of pure air. I saw them smiling discreetly at what each other was saying, and I recalled some of the cousins I had met infrequently and only at funerals.

I thought of the old adage that nothing brings families together more than weddings and funerals with little in between. Memories of weddings weren't bad, but having to refer to funerals to recall the last time you had seen some relative had to be gloomy. After all, the smiles had to be quick and the laughter suppressed. You fled the images, the scent of candles and the sounds of quiet sobbing. You promised to stay in touch with those you met there, but rarely did. We don't realize how attached we are to moments, and how we are remembered or avoided because of them. A friend you were with in New York City when you and she were rushing not to be late to a show or an uncle who had burned himself on a hot pan in the kitchen were bells that rang the resurrection of faces and voices more vividly. You could know someone for years or a lifetime, and if he or she did one thing that really upset you, that would be the sole doorway to envisioning.

Three of my girlfriends – Rosalie Okun, Brondi Spector and Toby Ludlow – drove to Palm Springs together to give me support, but I suspected they were going to make a day of it, shopping at the outlet mall off the 10 Freeway as well. They each made the point that they were sorry it took my mother's funeral finally to see me. I had been so aloof lately. The questions were smeared like hot fudge over their faces. Where had I been? Why hadn't I answered their calls? My silence in response rushed them out faster than they had intended, which was something I welcomed as much as I would taking off a heavy sweater on a warm summer day.

I was so prepared for the loneliness of sorrow. It was as if I had been practicing with an undertaker for days. Dark corners and empty rooms brought sufficient comfort for now. People avoided me as if I was the one looking up at them from an opened coffin.

I didn't see Lancaster until we were at the cemetery the following morning.

I wasn't looking for him especially, but while the minister recited the prayers, I raised my eyes and looked across the row of tombstones and monuments. It was a remarkably beautiful day, with not a cloud in the sky – a day too beautiful for funerals. People should be able to wait for the weather report before dying. Every color was vibrant. Even black looked more like an elegant tuxedo black than a funeral black. I had the funny image of my mother pounding on the inside of the coffin, having it opened, sitting up and declaring it was a better day for a picnic.

Lancaster was standing by one of the larger tombs, leaning against it actually, and looking toward us, looking at me. He was in a dark blue suit and tie, glowing like some sort of angel. He was smiling, but it wasn't out of place or disrespectful; it was a smile full of warmth and affection, a smile meant to give me strength. I was holding Kelly's hand with my right hand and Ronnie was holding my left. Ronnie was shifting his weight from leg to leg periodically like some little boy who had to pee. He wasn't as sad as he was just plain uncomfortable.

Afterward, we returned to my father's condo on the golf course. Having mourners there seemed totally out of place. While we gathered, just outside the rear patio doors we could witness men and women in colorful golf clothes intently addressing their little white balls on the plush carpet of green, as if what they did with it would determine how they would spend eternity. Occasionally, one or more of them looked our way, saw or knew what it was and instantly returned to their safe, insulated world of putts and drives. Ronnie stood outside with some of the other men, watching the golfers and criticizing their approach to the ball or their follow-through.

His mother, rather than I, supervised the food and drink, along with a caterer my father had hired. The way he referred to him made it sound as if he was part of the funeral preparations package or had to give the undertaker a kickback.

Kelly spent the most time looking at my mother's things. My father gave her some of her jewelry. I saw the conflict in her eyes. She wanted it, but hated taking it.

'It's all right,' I told her. 'Someone would probably steal it right out from under him eventually.'

'Why didn't he want to give it to you?' she asked. A clever question.

'I don't wear what I have,' I replied. A poor answer. She knew it, too.

We didn't wait for the last mourner to leave before we did. My father looked so envious. I had the feeling he would leave with us and desert the funeral, even his condo if he could. Our hugs and kisses weren't much different from what they always were: short, as official as government protocol.

Ronnie waited for a little more than eight hours afterward, a deadline he had obviously established for himself, before he asked me any more about my *disappearance*, as he put it. It didn't happen until we were home and were getting ready for bed. We had a pair of French Charles X antique Fauteuil chairs with velvet upholstery in our bedroom. They were an anniversary gift my parents had given us, mainly, I thought, because they had too much furniture when they were moving from a house to a condo in Palm Springs. Ronnie claimed they were very uncomfortable chairs and rarely sat in them unless he was putting on socks and shoes. I told him they were really meant to be works of art and there to add style and beauty to our room.

'Furniture that isn't meant to be used is a waste,' he replied. He always thought we would be better off selling them and using the money for something sensible, like a new wireless sound system.

Tonight, he was seated in one of the chairs, sitting back with the tips of his fingers pressed against each other in the shape of a cathedral. He wore only his briefs. The sight of him dressed like that and sitting in one of these antique chairs, probably originally owned by some nobleman who would never have tolerated anyone sitting in them practically naked, brought a broad smile to my face. I couldn't help it, even though I knew from his demeanor that he wanted this to be a very serious moment.

'What is it, Ronnie?' I asked, seeing that was what he wanted me to do: speak first.

'I still don't understand why you didn't call us to tell us about your change of plans? What if something had happened to me or to Kelly? How would anyone have gotten in touch with you?'

'I wasn't thinking about any of that,' I said. 'I've already explained it. I wanted to get away from any interruptions.'

'Even something happening to one of us?'

'I told you. I didn't think about that,' I said firmly.

He still kept his fingertips pressed against each other, his back straight, his eyes fixed on me like some high court judge in the Middle Ages deciding on life or death for heretics.

'You're different, Clea,' he said. 'I can see that now.'

'I'm tired. It has been quite a stressful few days for all of us, not any less for me.'

'No, I don't mean because of what's happened to your mother or any of that. You were different before all this.'

'That's why I wanted some time alone,' I replied and pulled back the blanket and top sheet.

'Where did you stay up in Idyllwild?'

I got into bed.

'I don't know if you'll remember it, but there were these cabins we both thought were quite nice one time when we were up there. We were right about them, and I was right about going to Idyllwild, especially this time of year. It was pretty laid-back up there.'

I closed my eyes, expecting that would be it. I had said more than I had wanted, but when I opened my eyes again, I saw he hadn't moved, not even moved his fingers, the sight of which was beginning to irritate me. Cathedrals, crosses, the Star of David, whatever, religious symbols or icons disturbed me. It was too much like having magic wands. I was happy that my parents weren't particularly religious, despite how they were raised. They never threatened me with God or hell. Restricting freedom was more effective.

'Aren't you coming to bed?'

'When you met that old college friend for dinner at Gianni's in Fullerton, who paid?'

'What?'

'Who paid for the dinner?'

'Why?'

'It's not on our credit card account – any of them, in fact. I review those accounts weekly,' he said. 'Charges are recorded instantly.'

'She paid. She ate the most,' I added, 'and I wasn't going to argue with her about it.'

'Did you pay for the cabin up at Idyllwild with a credit card?' he quickly followed, 'because I have yet to see any evidence of that. I checked on my smartphone today at your father's condo. Those things are instantly posted.'

'My father's condo,' I muttered. 'How quickly property is transferred in your mind.'

He turned a little red. 'I just meant—'

'Why did you do that during the funeral? You're beginning

to annoy me, Ronnie. I don't like feeling you're watching everything I spend and where I spend it.'

'I'm only—'

'Annoying me,' I said and turned my back to him. 'Put out the light and sit in the dark if you have to,' I added. 'I'm going to sleep.'

I didn't like how I was feeling. I went from fear to anger, angry at him for bringing on the fear, and all this just before I was going to sleep. He still hadn't moved. In a fury, I spun around, opened the bedside table drawer, took out a sleeping pill and practically gulped it down with a half-glass of water. I didn't look at him while I did it, and then turned over again so my back would be to him. Finally, I heard him get up.

When you're married to someone as long as I've been married to Ronnie, you can feel his moods in the air between you, especially his anger. I was tempted to turn on him and get hysterical the way any one of my girlfriends would, because it would be an easy way to take advantage. At this time, with my mother's funeral food still warm, as Hamlet exaggerated about his father's, Ronnie chose to interrogate me about spending money. I could make him feel terrible. The thing was that wouldn't be why I would get hysterical. He might sense there was another reason, which would only bring on more questions, more suspicions – if not now, eventually.

I just kept my body tight, my eyes closed, and said nothing. He turned off the light and slipped into bed. I thought he whispered, 'Sorry,' but it might have been wishful thinking. I turned away from him and concentrated on my sleeping pill, urging it to work faster and get me out of here.

Thankfully, the image of Lancaster smiling at me at the cemetery returned and remained under my closed eyelids until I drifted into sleep on the raft of the sleeping pill. When I awoke in the morning, Ronnie was already dressed and gone. I looked at the miniature walnut grandfather clock on my dresser and realized Kelly would be gone by now as well. After I sat up, I suddenly had the sense that I wasn't alone, however. My radar circle of awareness reached farther than the house. Slowly, I rose and went to the window.

He was out there, standing by his car, his arms folded across his chest, and looking up at me, that smile glittering around his lips. Dressed in those tight, straight-leg black jeans I loved on him and wearing a short-sleeve shirt in turquoise, my favorite color on him, he was radiating with the self-confidence of someone who knew he was where I wanted him to be, needed him to be. I stared down at him, rushing my body to wake up. I couldn't restrain myself.

The idea of actually doing this had never occurred to me. I had fantasized him in my bed; before, though, it always frightened me even to think about inviting him into my house. It all felt different now. Some other door had been opened. I was drowning in a flood of conflicting emotions. He was right. I needed him, desperately, before I disappeared.

I nearly tripped rushing down the stairs. When I opened the front door, he was standing there. He anticipated my every thought, I realized. I had the sense to look out to see if any of our neighbors were passing by. No one was. The world was on pause just for me, for us. I stepped back and he entered the house. A line was crossed. I closed the door. Neither of us spoke. I just took his hand and started for the stairway.

'Are you sure?' he asked as we began to ascend.

'Very,' I said.

'I don't know.'

'I do.'

'I like your house. It's big but has a cozy feel.'

I had heard that said many times. Unlike most of my girl-friends who had homes as big and as expensive as ours, I did my own decorating, even when I was working full-time. It was important to me to keep the house warm, to steer away from what would give it more of a museum feel. This was a house where people truly lived, not visited by its inhabitants on a daily basis.

'It's not cozy for me anymore,' I replied. 'It's become more of a dungeon. I see darkness where I never did before. Sometimes, I even imagine chains on the walls.'

He laughed.

'Thank God for hyperbole,' he said. 'How dull our conversations would be without it.'

'Amen to that. Great minds think alike.'

He paused outside of my bedroom. I still held on to his hand, but our arms extended like a rope fully protracted. I could feel his resistance.

'Do I have to pull you in? I told you that I was sure.'

'Are you really fully aware of the danger? You will no longer see your husband beside you in that bed. His warmth won't feel the same. The way he moves will irritate you. You'll recoil when he touches you. Even your dreams could be different.'

'That's all already true,' I said.

'For most marriages, the bed the couple share becomes their life raft. Their sex, the way they comfort each other, their softer conversations, merely the sound of each other breathing keeps them together, safe. You're casting all that away.'

'It's already gone. There's nothing left to throw overboard to keep us floating.'

His resistance dwindled and disappeared. He followed me to the bed. I pulled back the blanket and he began to undress. I was naked in an instant, but he was moving slowly, still tentative and still anticipating me changing my mind. When he was down to his briefs, he said, 'There's no turning back, no escape hatch, no way to be rescued.'

'Contrary to what you think, that thought helps me move forward.'

He smiled the smile I wanted, slipped off his briefs and gracefully moved beside me and then over me. I felt his warm breath on my closed eyes, and when I opened them, he seemed to be liquefying and dripping his body on to me. Perhaps the most complete act of love was literally two people becoming one, and we were in the process of doing just that.

'In the name of fairness, I must tell you not to start making comparisons,' he warned, 'not unless you vividly recall the way it was with your husband in the beginning and not the way it is now.'

'It wasn't any different,' I insisted. 'I was just too naive to realize it.'

'You're a hard case.'

'Soften me,' I challenged.

He began with short, sweet kisses on my face, my hair, my breasts, pausing to look at me often, scanning my face for the slightest indication of regret. Was he really expecting me to change my mind, even now? I relaxed my legs and opened the pathway to assure him I would not turn back. He settled between them as softly as a balloon floating back to earth. My moan was more like a prayer, a chant, a way of bargaining for ecstasy. I was Hemingway's Old Man of the Sea, making promises to God if He would just let me bring back the big fish, only I wanted an orgasm that would make all previous ones pale in comparison.

Before either of us could continue and successfully create the consummate love experience, the phone rang. I looked at it. It seemed to ring louder each time, like someone screaming more and more desperately.

'Not answering might bring more attention,' he suggested. 'It might even be your father.'

'I doubt it.'

Nevertheless, after the next ring, I picked up the receiver, but I didn't say hello quickly enough for him.

'Clea?' Ronnie asked, as if he wanted to be sure he had called the right number. 'Are you all right?'

'I'm all right,' I said, unable to disguise my disappointment.

'You didn't say anything when you picked up, so I—'

'You didn't give me a chance. Actually, you woke me.'

'You're still in bed?'

'I'm getting up now. Unfortunately.'

'I was worried about you sleeping so late, but you were sleeping soundly so I didn't try to wake you.'

'It's all right,' I said. 'Check it off your list.'

'Look, I'm sorry I asked you all those questions last night, but they were on my mind and—'

'I've forgotten all about them,' I said. His silence told me he didn't like that response. 'I've got to take a shower,' I added.

'What are you going to do today?'

'Why?'

'If you're going out, perhaps we can meet for lunch. I found this new health food restaurant with the best veggie burgers ever, and I thought, knowing how much you like those, that you might want to meet me. I can adjust my time to—'

'I don't know. Don't wait. If I feel like it, I'll call you ahead of time. This house wasn't kept as clean as I had hoped while I was gone. I have a lot to do.'

'We can still talk about the maid returning.'

'Later,' I said. 'I'm still in the fog of sleep. You might remember that I had taken a pill.'

My tone made it clear that I was blaming him.

'OK. Call me if you want to do something. They have called for rain today, but it's supposed to clear out by late afternoon. Maybe we could all go out to dinner tonight. Any place you want,' he added.

His tone of desperation released guilt inside me and up my throat like a surge of acid reflux. It was the one feeling I wanted to avoid right now, mainly because of Lancaster's prescient warnings.

'I'm getting up. I'll see how the day goes,' I said with just an iota of warmth and hung up.

Lancaster had gotten off the bed while I spoke to Ronnie and was now standing by the window, looking down the way I had stood looking down at him.

'What's wrong?'

'I think we'll do better somewhere else,' he said. He looked around the bedroom. 'This lacks . . .'

'What?'

'Newness, originality, adventure.'

'I thought you said it was dangerous to be here.'

'That's a different kind of danger, an internal danger.'

'Are you trying to be my conscience?'

'I'm everything else. Why not that?'

I threw off the blanket.

'I'm taking a shower,' I said. 'You can join me if you want.'

'That's what Ronnie does,' he said. 'Do with me what you don't do with him; go with me where you don't go with him. Otherwise . . .'

'Otherwise?'

'Otherwise, I'm just a stand-in, an understudy on the same

stage. You know where to find me when you want me,' he added and went for his clothes.

'Where?'

'Anywhere else,' he said. 'Maybe the motel.'

'I don't want anything to become routine. That's what I'm fleeing now.'

He smiled.

'Believe me, it won't be. I'll give you a call later to see what sort of mood you're in.'

I watched him continue dressing a moment and then I went into the bathroom to take my shower – or more like sulk under a stream of warm water. Any frustrating of my craving for pleasure, for freedom and for a solution to boredom turned me into a petulant child. Perhaps I was always spoiled; maybe there was never a time when I didn't get my own way.

Maybe I was full of flaws – Miss Imperfect who had no right to condemn anyone for anything, least of all my husband and daughter, and certainly not my parents. Maybe I had turned to Lancaster because he was someone who didn't care, someone who wouldn't mind or fault me for it.

I knew there were many who would blame me for that, of course – rows and rows of hypocritical friends as well as clergy of all faiths – but I had gone beyond caring about the morality of it all.

I suppose that was an additional flaw for me to swallow and digest and absorb into myself as I constructed my new identity.

It was the most exciting thing in my life now – being reborn – but unlike the first time, the first birth, I could be God and reconstruct myself according to my own design.

Who wouldn't want to be able to do that?

As if he was still here, I could hear Lancaster's answer.

'Anyone who didn't want the burden of the responsibility and the dangers inherent when you begin to worship yourself.'

THIRTEEN

I did start to clean the house. It was my form of penance, at least for the moment. I suppose it was more correct to say I attacked it with a vengeance, repeatedly running the vacuum cleaner over the same spot as if I wanted to suck the life out of it. Suddenly, it was clear to me. The house was indeed my enemy, something I never dreamed I would come to believe, especially when I recalled how excited I was about our buying it and redoing the landscaping as well as the interior decorating.

I recalled the first time we looked at it, wondering if we could really afford it. Ronnie was so proud that we could and, in my mind, overpaid just to prove it to the real estate agent. Kelly was almost five years old and was just as amazed at the size, especially the size of her room. I remember thinking, *Maybe we do need more children if we're going to have a house like this. It's too big for only the three of us.* Eventually, I realized, however, that having all this space between us kept us satisfied, especially Kelly and Ronnie. Perhaps that was a clue about what was to come.

Somehow, now, it had become a heavy weight on my conscience, an anchor I did not want. It kept me from sailing on. It was so demanding with its appliances breaking down, its light bulbs dying and needing replacement, and the dust tormenting me by sneaking in and around daily to coat the furniture, furniture that moaned and cried for polishing. There was the making of beds and washing of clothes, sheets and pillow cases. Of course, there was all the maintenance, the pool man and the gardener, and servicing the air conditioners. With Ronnie at work and me now the at-home housewife, who do you think was left seeing after all this?

Burdens. Everything I once enjoyed had become a burden. The obvious solution from the beginning was to have a maid. All my friends did. But eventually a maid had come to symbolize how distant you became from the life you had chosen. Sometimes, when she was younger, Kelly would even act as if the maid owned the furniture, as well as most every-thing else. She wasn't afraid to say things like, 'Marta won't like you putting a glass on that table without a coaster.' Or, 'Marta gets the clothes softer.' Or, 'Don't tell Marta I spilled that on the floor.'

Marta had been with us even before I began to work for Sebastian Pullman. She was a forty-year-old mother herself, with three children and a husband who seemed to be constantly out of work as a plumber, which Ronnie couldn't understand. He bought into the stereotype of a plumber being one of the richest tradesmen in our world. He was probably right about him being lazy, though. I tried to get him to do some work for us, but he was always otherwise occupied. One thing good about Marta, she never looked for sympathy. She was very independent, and, though at least twenty pounds overweight, had a very pretty face and clearly had been very attractive when she was younger. I had no trouble deciding on hiring her rather than the others who were recommended.

Ronnie's mother had always had a maid, even before she had him and his younger sister, Tami. More than my mother, from the beginning his mother was on me to hire a maid as soon as possible.

'Men expect you to carry ninety percent of the load without complaint. They hate looking after the children and think the wife has it easy. Don't let Ronnie treat you that way. I never let his father,' she told me.

Maybe it was in the nature of a mother-in-law to try to ally herself with her daughter-in-law, first by emphasizing the need for 'us women' to band together for our own self-defense. In those days, she was like my attorney, negotiating with the management. I didn't complain. I appreciated Ronnie's mother taking the brunt of any argument, and I was certainly happy to have someone else do the housework.

Nevertheless, it got so I anticipated Marta's criticism of me as well. She hadn't reached the point where she would dare say to me something she would say to Kelly, but I had a hair trigger by now, and just an offbeat comment about how someone had been dropping crumbs of cookies constantly behind the sofa pillows in the living room brought on a snappy reply.

'That's why we hired you,' I said. 'If we didn't have things to clean, we wouldn't need you.'

She looked at me with pain in her eyes. I had never said anything like that to her. If anything, I was her major supporter here, going after Kelly for not looking after her things, criticizing Ronnie for being too messy in the kitchen or leaving his office untidy and making more work for Marta. Usually, I would agree with her comments and move on, but not this time. This was also about the time Sebastian was thinking of retiring and therefore it was probably another reason for my not wanting to continue working outside the house. Now, all that had changed. I wasn't exaggerating when I had told Lancaster the house too often felt like a dungeon.

After just under an hour of house chores, I stopped, wondering if meeting Ronnie for lunch was any sort of option to take seriously. I saw the raindrops on the windows, zigzagging down. The house is crying, I thought. It's upset with how I think of it now. I started to smile at the idea when I heard my mobile phone ringing. I went out to the kitchen, opened my purse and answered it. I knew it couldn't be Ronnie. He would have called on our landline first.

'Sorry about leaving you like that this morning,' Lancaster said. 'I can't concentrate on anything but you.'

'Is it guilt or desire?'

'After you see the result, you tell me,' he replied.

I smiled. It felt as if the smile radiated throughout my body. The heavy depression and sense of rage dissipated. The energy that replaced it was the energy of youth, fresh, full and driven by the kind of excitement that turned your nerves into electric probes searching for pleasure. You wanted speed and movement, you wanted laughter, and you wanted to feel more alive, a feeling you could reach only by courting danger. I was Hemingway's bullfighter in *Death in the Afternoon*, never feeling more alive than when he was looking into the eyes of the charging bull.

All the morality and sin, the condemnation and criticism were wrapped up in my charging bull. I would snap my red cape and send it in another direction, and the applause I would hear would carry me off on the shoulders of my own selfish pleasure. It didn't matter. There was no regret, not now, maybe not ever.

'I'm on my way,' I said. 'Despite my shower, your kisses still linger on my breasts. They tingle.'

'When I'm with you, I feel like we're writing poetry together,' Lancaster said

'Let me count the ways,' I said. 'My private Casanova.' I hung up and hurried to change. It was almost like the first time. I was in my car and backing out of the garage, with everything I had done to prepare a vague memory, an uncertainty. Had I done any of it? I shot out of the driveway like an ambulance chaser. NPR was suddenly not good enough. I wanted Kelly's music. I wanted the car to vibrate with the rhythm. I wanted to sing along.

'I'm coming, my love,' I said. 'I'm coming,' I screamed and laughed. 'I've made up my mind. I cannot tolerate what my life has become any longer. We're going to plan this change, this escape for me together. I'm going off with you. I don't care about the end game. I want to travel, to see the world the way you see it, to feel the way you feel about anything and everything. I want to take the risk. I'm a kite whose string has broken. Let the wind carry me. I won't even ask where. I'll never complain.'

How easy this is going to be, I thought. Why did it take me so long to realize it? I had cut that string long ago. My husband and my daughter lived in their own worlds and really didn't want me intruding in them. Ronnie and I had a paint-by-numbers marriage now, and I had a paint-by-numbers relationship with my daughter. We moved from one thing to another like the hands of a clock, ticking to do this, ticking to do that, all of it programed and expected. If I threatened or even thought to make any changes, it set off alarms. What would happen to our family clock? It would stop. Could you live with that?

You can't live here and be anything more than an obedient wife and a reliable mother. Oh, pardon me if I don't break down feeling so sorry for you. 'What's wrong with you?' I heard Ronnie and Kelly ask simultaneously. 'How could you want to be an individual now? How could you be so selfish as to challenge our selfishness?'

I heard laughing and realized it was my laughter, which only brought on more. That was all the answer I needed to give them.

I made a turn and accelerated toward the highway that would take me out to our motel. I was thinking of it as *our motel* now, our rendezvous, a room with a rose on a pillow and with the windows and doors shut to keep out the rest of the world. Nothing or no one could stop us from reaching the ecstasy we were meant to enjoy. It was easy. Pay the ferryman to cross us from one world to another.

How delicious was my anticipation. I could hear his voice, feel his breath on my cheek. Yes, the sex was wonderful, but it wasn't only the sex. I liked being with him. I liked the way he challenged almost every thought, every idea and every hesitation I expressed. He enjoyed me as much if not more than I enjoyed him. He made me feel like the woman I wanted to be again. He was restoring me. How could I ever turn away from that? How could I lose him?

Lose him? What if he wasn't there? What if my behavior this morning was too much? What if, since he called me, he had rethought it all? He could have second, even third thoughts. Maybe I had become too much baggage. If he left, how would I know? Where could I find him? What would I return to?

Panic seized me. I sped up. The rain was falling faster, heavier. He was calling to me. I heard my name. The anticipation was getting intense. I felt my breathing quicken and then become even more difficult. My heart was pounding to the same rhythm of the windshield wipers. The drops were getting through and becoming tears on my cheeks.

Suddenly, I heard the sound of the horn, a desperate cry like the shrill, desperate cry of a horse, and then I heard the screech of tires and the explosion of metal and glass. I was in slow motion, turning and turning until the darkness came crashing down over me like a heavy iron lid. I heard it slam shut against my own desperate cry, a 'NOOOOO' that echoed and echoed until it died away.

*   *   *

I felt nothing, no pain. I floated in the darkness. I had no idea how long. Light returned first as a very thin silvery sliver and then widened and widened until I could see the white ceiling. Sounds were muffled. They began like a recording being played too slowly and gradually started to speed up until I heard someone say, 'Mrs Howard?'

I turned toward the voice and looked at a nurse smiling down at me. She had short, dark brown hair and a face that looked chiseled out of greyish white granite with brown spots along her temple that looked tapped on with a small felt pen. Her eyes were like polished pecans. My first thought was *How did she get into my dream?*

She took my left hand. I looked at it in hers and then up at her.

She spoke slowly, calmly.

'I know you're confused,' she began. 'You're in the intensive care unit of the hospital. You were in a car accident, an accident with a dump truck,' she added, smiling as though that was one big joke. 'You have a stable fracture of your tibia in your right leg, three cracked ribs and some neck and facial trauma. You had internal bleeding, but that's stopped.'

'I don't remember being in an accident,' I said. I wanted to get out of this dream as quickly as possible, but instinctively I knew she could keep me here.

My jaw ached and I raised my right arm to feel it.

'You have a slight fracture in your jaw bone, but it's not serious. We'll keep you on soft foods for a while, however.'

'I don't remember any accident,' I repeated with more emphasis.

The bed sheets felt real now and the machinery around me looked authentic. I realized this wasn't a dream. Nevertheless, I thought I should protest that I didn't belong here. This was all some terrible mistake. Hospitals were infamous for making mistakes, weren't they? People had the wrong leg or arm amputated, and people too often were given the wrong medication. I watched *60 Minutes*. I knew all the deeply held secrets.

'You've been in a coma for nearly five days. You had some swelling of your brain. I'll get the doctor who will explain it all to you, and we'll inform your husband that you've regained

consciousness. He's been here on and off the whole time with
your daughter. They left just a little more than a half-hour
ago, in fact,' she said, 'to get some dinner in the cafeteria.'

'Five days?'

She smiled. 'Under the circumstances, you did well. If you
saw your car, you'd agree that you're very lucky,' she added,
making it sound like a personal achievement, something I
could have controlled and did so well.

'Has anyone else come to see me?'

'Your father and your in-laws were here yesterday while I
was on duty.'

'Anyone else call?'

'I don't know. I'll check at the desk. Just relax. The doctor
will be here right away and give you more information.'

She raised me up a bit by pressing a button on the bed.
'That OK?'

I could see more of the room now and through the window I
could see that there was no longer any possible doubt. I really
was in a hospital intensive care unit. There was a lot of activity
going on, but I didn't see any windows to the outside. I
couldn't tell if it was day or night. Had I become my mother
as I had feared? Was I on my death bed? Was this the journey
from one world to another?

'Mrs Howard?'

'Yes, yes, I'm OK,' I said, even though I felt a little dizzy.
'What time is it?'

'It's nearly six p.m.'

'My throat feels like sandpaper.'

'I'll get you something to drink,' she said. And then to really
add some humor this time, she added, 'Don't go away.'

I closed my eyes. There was pain, but it was dull and almost
felt as if it was outside my body, but those parts of my body
that had no injury weren't behaving any better. The feelings
emanating from them were odd. It was as if a crust had
formed over all of me. There were tingles and itches, stinging
and aching, along with some numbness. I wanted to squirm and
work my way out of my own body, the way a snake might
slide out of its old skin. That's what I would do, I thought. I
would get into a new body and leave this shell on the bed,

still hooked up to the machinery and IV bags. My new body would have no broken bones, no fractures and no traumas. I would be fresh and vibrant again.

And Lancaster would be waiting for me right outside.

'What took you so long?' he would ask with that wry smile.

'It doesn't matter,' I would say. 'Just get me out of here, quickly.'

But nothing like that happened, of course. When I opened my eyes, I was still here, still a prisoner of pain, a wounded warrior of highway wars. Yes, I was in an automobile accident. I would get a Purple Heart from the Department of Motor Vehicles.

How did this happen? How did I get into an accident? I struggled to remember. Images were jumbled and distorted. I moaned with frustration. I had been on my way somewhere, but where? And when exactly was it? Trying to remember was actually painful. I closed my eyes.

'Mrs Howard?' I heard and opened my eyes again. 'I'm Doctor Temple,' he said. He looked like a man in his late twenties or early thirties with prematurely graying hair because his face was so soft, so wrinkle-free, and he had youthful ice-blue eyes that twinkled with amusement. The nurse who had spoken to me came up beside him and fiddled with a glass of water that had a cover and a straw protruding. She held it close enough to my lips for me to begin to sip.

'Mrs Dennis told me how much she has told you. It's protocol to explain as much as possible as quickly as possible to a patient who regains consciousness as fully as you've regained it after being in a coma for days. Nevertheless, I'm sure it's still all quite shocking for you.'

I stopped sucking on the straw. The water felt as if it was burning a little anyway.

'Was it deliberate?' I asked.

The idea was just bubbling up in my troubled brain.

'Deliberate?' Dr Temple asked. He looked at the nurse, Mrs Dennis, who shook her head slightly.

'The truck driver,' I said. 'Did he deliberately crash into me to stop me?'

'Stop you from what?' Dr Temple asked. He looked more confused than I felt.

How would he know anything anyway? I thought.

'Never mind,' I said. 'Why did I go into a coma for days?'

'You suffered a concussion and a contusion. You had some brain swelling, but, thankfully, almost immediately we saw signs of reduction, so we were confident you'd regain consciousness. The neurologist, Doctor Fernhoff, will be here to see you either later today or tomorrow morning and explain it all in more detail. While you were unconscious, we put you through all the scans and got started on mending all your injuries. You'll be uncomfortable for a while, but you won't be in any great pain. Now that you've regained consciousness, we'll look into getting you into your own room.'

'How long will I be in the hospital?'

'Oh, it will be a while,' Dr Temple said, smiling as if I had asked the dumbest question of all. 'Just concentrate on getting well again and don't fight the process that will help you to do so,' he added. Now I thought he sounded as if he was threatening me. *Don't resist or else.*

Ronnie and Kelly stepped through the doorway and stood just behind the doctor. He turned to them.

'Not too long,' he said.

They both looked so terrified that I nearly laughed. When the doctor stepped back, they inched their way toward me. Ronnie leaned over to kiss my forehead. Kelly stood back, studying me as if she suspected an alien might have entered my body during all this.

'I guess I look awful,' I said. Ronnie started to shake his head, but Kelly said, 'Yes.'

Dr Temple started out and Mrs Dennis followed him. Ronnie watched them leaving and then turned back to me.

'You went through a red light,' he said, his voice heavy with criticism. 'You were going pretty fast, too. Do you remember anything?'

'I don't remember any light, red or otherwise.'

'The truck driver had only minor injuries, but I'm sure some lawyer will get him complaining about pains and aches and work up a fat settlement. Don't worry. The insurance agency will take it out of our hide.'

If he was hoping to hear me apologize, he was in for a long wait. Anyway, it was unfair to blame me. I couldn't remember so I couldn't defend myself.

'Maybe he was the one who went through the red light,' I suggested.

'I wish,' he said, 'but there were witnesses.'

'How do you feel?' Kelly asked. 'Does your leg or your head hurt?'

'No,' I said. 'I feel some stinging on my side and on my face. My jaw aches a little, but I don't feel anything up here,' I said, raising my right hand to touch my head and realizing it was bandaged. Of course it would be.

'Do you remember where you were going?' Ronnie asked. His eyelids were nearly closed. I knew that face too well. He was asking for a reason, out of a suspicion.

'No,' I said. 'I don't remember anything about it.'

'Because I had called you that morning to invite you to lunch. Does that help your memory?'

'No,' I said.

'Why would you go out in the rain? You said you had house-work you had to get done.'

'I don't remember.'

'What could have been so important?'

Mrs Dennis had not really left us, apparently. She had lingered behind and came up very quickly.

'You don't want to pressure her about anything, Mr Howard,' she said softly. 'It's too early.'

Ronnie nodded and backed away from the bed, as if how close he was to me mattered, too.

'I've got everything under control at the house,' he said. 'You don't worry about anything. Just work on getting better. I'll call your father as soon as I leave you and give him an update.'

'How is he? He didn't miss his golf game, did he?' I asked.

Kelly actually smiled. 'She's feeling just fine,' she told Ronnie and finally stepped up close enough to lean over and kiss my cheek. 'I'm glad you're going to be OK,' she said. 'I'll come to see you after school tomorrow. Oh. All your friends have been calling.'

'Who?' I asked quickly. Ronnie's eyebrows rose. I caught his new interest.

Kelly rattled off the names of my girlfriends and then added that Carlton Saunders had called.

'Maybe he thinks you'll need a lawyer,' Ronnie said. His comment was full of implications. Even in my semi-dizzy state, I picked that up.

I stared at him. He shrugged, smiled and stepped back to kiss me.

'I'll be here in the morning,' he said. 'Before I go to work. Have a good night.'

'Maybe I'll go dancing,' I said. Suddenly, I felt so over-whelmingly tired that I couldn't keep my eyes from slamming shut. Their voices drifted away as they spoke to the nurse and then I was asleep again.

I don't know how long I actually slept, but I remembered another doctor, the neurologist, coming to see me. He was much older than Dr Temple. He said a lot, but all I recalled was his saying I had only a hairline fracture of my skull and there was nothing to do about that but let it heal. Fortunately, I had no need for any surgery.

His face drifted in and out of my memory as I slept and woke up, slept and woke up, greeted new nurses and watched all the action around my bed. I really did feel like an observer and not the actual patient. And then, when there was a lull and the entire place seemed to go into a semi-conscious state, he walked in and touched my hand. When I opened my eyes, he leaned down to kiss me, not on the cheek but on the lips. Why hadn't Ronnie done that?

'I was worried about you,' I said.

'You were worrying about me? That's a switch. I've been by a number of times over the past few days,' he said. 'I just learned you regained consciousness.' He looked back and then turned back to me and said, 'Don't worry. No one knows I've been here or knows I'm here now.'

'I know. You're good at slipping in and out of people's lives,' I said, and he laughed.

'Have no fear. I'm not slipping out of yours,' he said.

I smiled. My eyelids were heavy again. I fought hard to keep them from closing, but they wouldn't be denied.

'Don't worry,' I heard him whisper. 'I won't slip away from you.'

FOURTEEN

He wasn't there when I woke up again. There was so much activity around me that I couldn't have slept much longer anyway. Bandages were being changed and IV bags replaced. The blood pressure monitor was annoying. Maybe it was because of my head injury, but the beeps sounded louder. I wanted to rip everything off, bandages included, and detach anything I could. Despite my leg and other injuries, I thought I could hobble out. As my frustration grew, I could feel myself getting angrier.

When they were finished, a new nurse arrived, bringing me some soft-boiled eggs to eat. I saw her name was Lila Rubin. She was much younger than the first nurse, but she seemed quite capable and efficient. Maybe it was her youth or simply the positive energy I felt coming from her, but I thought I could trust her more. I calmed myself and then looked around as much of the area outside of mine as I could.

'Is the gentleman visiting me still here?' I asked. I didn't think I had slept that long and imagined he had to leave my bedside when they began to do their work on me.

'No,' she said. Then she smiled and asked, 'Do you mean your husband?'

'No,' I said.

'Oh, because he did stop by this morning.'

'This morning? It's morning?'

'It's morning,' she said, smiling. 'You were asleep and he didn't want to wake you. He said to tell you he would come by on his lunch hour. Maybe you were aware of his presence. You know, it's a kind of semi-conscious state. Nothing to be alarmed about,' she added. 'People can be that way even without a head injury.'

'No, I don't mean him. I meant someone else.'

She kept her smile, but I could see the wheels turning. I hadn't said brother or referred to Lancaster in any way that might suggest he was a relative. Without asking anything more, she helped me start to feed myself. I asked her for some bacon and toast. She said it was a good sign that my appetite had returned, but for now I was still on soft food. She offered some Jell-O. I took it because there was nothing else.

Now that I was awake and beginning to feel better, time seemed to drip minutes and hours at the rate the drops were coming out of the IV bag. I could almost time my heartbeats to it. The doctors returned, which was my only distraction. I hesitate to say amusement, even though they seemed so pleased with how I was reacting and laughed at some of my complaints. I was told the only reason I was being kept in ICU now was room availability. The moment one was free, I would be moved.

On his lunch hour, Ronnie arrived. He looked like someone who had just wandered in off the street. His face had that vague, distracted-by-something-else kind of look he could take on in the middle of a conversation I might be having with him. The sight of me pitched up in the bed a bit more had the effect of someone snapping fingers right in front of his face. His eyes brightened and he hurried over to kiss my cheek and to pull a chair close to the bed.

'They're getting ready to move you in a little while,' he said. 'You'll have a television and a phone. Let me know what magazines you'd like me to bring after work.'

'I don't want any magazines and don't let anyone know I have a phone,' I warned.

'No one?'

'My father, your parents and Kelly, of course, but no one else. I don't want to entertain my vapid friends with details I can't remember.'

He nodded.

'Maybe you should try to remember.'

'Maybe I should try?'

'I mean really make an effort. One of the guys at the company, Tony Woods, had a cousin who suffered temporary amnesia after falling off a roof. He remembered nothing about falling; he didn't even remember being on the roof. His psychiatrist had him go back in time and begin recalling earlier things as a way to bring him to the present. He said it worked.'

'Psychiatrist? He needed a psychiatrist for that?'

'It was a complicated situation. I had the impression that Tony's cousin tried to kill himself, so after he was made to recall what had happened, they could go after the causes of his depression.'

'You think that was what I did – try to kill myself by deliberately getting hit by a truck?'

He raised his hands. 'Why should I? Although there are plenty of stories out there about people who missed some signals and didn't see someone they were close to slipping away.'

'Slipping away?' The words were resonating in my mind. Did I just say something similar to someone or did someone say it to me?

'Yeah,' Ronnie said, nodding. He had his legs crossed and was sitting back. There was something about his demeanor now that annoyed me. He was taking too long between sentences. It was as if he was watching for some sort of reaction in me to whatever he had said.

My eyes went to a figure moving just outside my area. It looked like Lancaster. He glanced in and walked quickly away. Ronnie turned to look in the direction I was looking and then turned back to me.

'Anyway, why don't we try that technique?'

'You think you're a psychiatrist now?' I asked.

'I'm only trying to help you get better. So let's see if you can recall something relatively recent.'

'I'm really not in the mood for games, Ronnie.'

'It's not a game,' he said, really trying to sound casual about it. Trying too hard, I thought. 'It's a technique. I only want to help you, Clea. If you don't make an effort to help yourself, you could be like this for quite a while. At least, that's what I was told.'

We stared at each other a moment. I was half listening to him. I was really wondering what Lancaster would do now. Would he wait outside the ICU for Ronnie to leave and then come in? Or would he leave the hospital and return perhaps when I was moved into a room?

'So let's start.' He leaned toward me. 'Flora Anthony,' he said.

'Who?'

'Your old dorm mate, Flora Anthony, the one you met for dinner at Gianni's not long ago. Any memory of that?'

'No,' I said quickly. Why bring up that memory? He was really annoying me now.

He widened his eyes. 'That's an amazing coincidence.'

'What is?' ·

'Not remembering dinner with Flora Anthony.'

'How is that an amazing coincidence?'

'She has no memory of having dinner with you,' he said. 'In fact, she hasn't seen you since college.'

My first reaction was, *Why in hell did I use a real person?* Why didn't I invent someone from the past? It was my father's fault. He was the one who convinced me always to use some truth when telling a lie. My second reaction was outrage. Why was he behaving like some trial attorney, cross-examining me and trying to trap me?

'When did you see or speak to Flora Anthony?' I asked.

'A few days ago. I spoke to her on the phone. It wasn't difficult to find her. You've got a great alumni association. She lives in upstate New York, by the way, a small village called Centerville. She married not long after we married, and she has two children a few years younger than Kelly. Her husband's family has a big residential gas company so they moved there because he's in line to take it over. They have a twenty-five-acre property, and because I mentioned I was in commercial real estate insurance, she had to tell me how many times they were offered millions for it. Once I got her on the phone, I couldn't get her to shut up. She seemed starved for conversation. Was she always like that?

'Oh,' he added before I could respond, 'she wishes she *had* met you for dinner. Apparently, she always admired you and thought you would end up a fashion model or a Hollywood movie star. So, does that help any with your memory? Do you remember the restaurant?'

'I was there, at Gianni's. I needed to get away and be by myself.'

'I know you were there. You weren't waiting for anyone else?' he asked, sounding and looking more and more like an

Agatha Christie detective. Ronnie did love imitating movie characters. He looked as if he was enjoying himself, and at my expense.

'No,' I said sharply.

'Are you sure? You told the waitress you were. She remembers you almost as well as Flora Anthony remembers you. You must have looked terrific that night. She, too, thought you were possibly a Hollywood movie star. Oh, and remember Kelly saying something about a friend whose parents had stopped there and saw you in the bar?'

'How could the waitress remember me? I didn't tell her my name. What, did you bring a picture of me to the restaurant like some detective?'

'Insurance investigators are really detectives.'

'You're not an insurance investigator and you're not a detective, Ronnie. We're not in one of your movies. Anyway, why did you start investigating me?'

'It's like I said. I'm trying to see if I might have missed some signals,' he said. 'You know . . . like Tony's cousin's family might have missed. I did tell you that you seemed different to me lately. Remember my saying that?'

'So?'

'I felt you slipping away.'

'Stop saying that. Stop saying *slipping*. I'm not walking on ice.'

'We're all set,' we heard and turned to see Lila Rubin and an African American male hospital escort arrive with a stretcher. Another attendant arrived behind them. 'We've got her room set up,' Lila told Ronnie.

She looked suspiciously at my blood pressure monitor and then at Ronnie.

'Oh good,' he said.

'Yes. Just let us get her organized and you can visit with her in her room.'

'Sure,' Ronnie said, standing quickly. 'I'll wait in the hall.'

'We're going to four-o-one,' Lila told him. 'Give us about twenty minutes to get her comfortably settled in. Maybe get yourself a cup of coffee or something,' she added with a professional smile. She clearly wanted him out of their way and knew how to do it politely, just like a good flight attendant directing passengers to get to their seats. I did feel as if I was on a journey now.

He nodded and took my hand for a few seconds.

'See you there,' he said and left. I thought he almost had added, 'Don't slip away,' but choked it back when he looked into my eyes.

It irked me, but all I could think about was his running into Lancaster either in the hallway or in the cafeteria. Right now he looked like a paranoid husband, suspicious of anyone with an abundance of testosterone. Lancaster was too smart for that, though. He wouldn't strike up a conversation with him or encourage one if Ronnie began to speak to him.

Ironically, however, Ronnie was right about jarring my memory with talk about some recent event. As I was wheeled out of the ICU, I began to resurrect visions of Lancaster in my bedroom, and then I remembered he had called me and I was on my way to see him. It was raining. Something had put me into a panic so I had begun to speed.

After the elevator doors opened, I looked up and down the halls. I was confident that Lancaster would find out my room number. He might already know it and be close by, I thought. There was a strong possibility he and Ronnie could very well confront each other up here. It made me nervous and then, as I was taken into my room and they shifted me comfortably on to my bed, I thought, *Let it happen. Let the games begin*. I was on my way to start this anyway. The accident interrupted us, but it didn't end us. It was only a matter of finding the way to confess and make a clean break of it, I thought. *Lancaster will help me. He'll know just how I should do this.*

Ronnie was there moments after the new nurse had shown me how to raise and lower the bed and how to call for assistance. She had asked if I wanted the television on, but I didn't. I didn't want anything to prevent me from thinking. I even was annoyed that Ronnie had come back so soon. I needed more time. He thanked the nurse as she left.

'Well, this is a lot nicer,' he said. He turned on the television, more for himself than for me.

'Don't put on the news and sit here yelling at the television set,' I said before he turned away from it.

He shrugged. 'You don't like soap operas or those courtroom shows?'

'Just turn it off. When I get the urge for babble, I'll have the nurse turn it back on.'

'Whatever,' he said and turned it off. Then he took a chair again and brought it close to the bed.

'Don't you have to get back to the office?' I asked.

'Everyone understands. I've got people covering for me.' He smiled. 'You look more comfortable.'

'I'm not comfortable. I don't want to be here.'

'Of course not. Which reminds me,' he added and took a photo out of his pocket to show me. 'That's your car. Looks like it was hit by a bulldozer and not a dump truck. No one can believe you survived. Totaled. Lucky you were hit on the passenger side and lucky no one was sitting there. Anyone who would have been would be dead for sure.'

I stared at the picture a moment more and then pushed it away. Ronnie took it and looked at it.

'You know this corner. Looks like you were headed southeast. There are no stores close by. Where were you headed? Seeing the picture doesn't help?'

'No,' I said. He put the picture back in his pocket.

'So let's get back to it. Why did you want to go so far to be alone that night? Gianni's. That was a trip. You didn't have anything to eat either. Why did you make up that story about the food?'

'I already told you. I wanted to be alone and I didn't want to be interrogated about it then and I don't want to be now. Don't aggravate me, Ronnie. I have enough of a headache as it is.'

'Just trying to understand and help you regain your memory, that's all,' he said. He waited a moment and then, after what was obviously some serious thinking, he added, 'The doctors asked me about you.'

'What do you mean? Asked what about me?'

'Personal stuff.'

'Why?'

'Some medical protocol, I guess. Apparently, you said some things to the neurologist that rang bells. Once you get into places like this, your private life is fair game. You know, psychological things can affect you physically, your recuperation – whatever the excuse for them to take a microscope to your daily life. Lawyers, doctors and priests, they all enjoy that client confidentiality clause. Frankly, I think it's because their own lives are too boring. What do you think?'

I looked away. I didn't want to start down this road with him. Was he teasing me? Taunting me? There was something very different about him. I had trouble looking at him. It was as if I was afraid he would be able to read my thoughts.

'I guess I gotta be honest,' he said. I turned back to him.

'Meaning what?'

'I thought something wasn't right with you and me for a long time. I was hoping you'd get over it, whatever it was, especially after I had gotten my promotion and the future looked rosier. I was even happy you went back to work, but surprised you decided not to pursue it. It probably would have been good for you.'

'So what you're saying is something was wrong with me, not you and me?'

'I don't know.'

He sat back and watched when the nurse's assistant brought in my lunch – again, just some liquid food. I voiced a complaint and she said she would tell the nurse and the nurse would speak to the doctor. The oatmeal was so loose it was unappetizing. And if I saw another Jell-O, I would really puke, I thought. I just drank some coffee.

'Once you're back on solids, I'll bring you some deli, maybe. I know you like that turkey breast with honey mustard on rye.'

'Thanks for putting it in my head,' I said, and he smiled.

'Anyway, I wanted to explain why I was worried about you before all this,' he continued. 'And why I behaved like some detective.'

The way he looked at me now told me he knew a lot more, but he didn't look terribly angry. In fact, he didn't look angry at all. I couldn't say he looked very hurt about it either, which really surprised me. Ronnie could put on that abused look at

the drop of a dime. He had used it on his parents his whole
life, and pretty successfully, too. Even though I was the one in
this marriage who had been an only child, he had been far
more spoiled growing up. If anything, right now he looked
unusually concerned for me, not for himself.

I had to admit that it threw me off. I struggled with choices.
Should I just look guilty like the perennial child caught with
his or her hand in the cookie jar and confess immediately, or
should I feign innocence and even take on an angry, offended
look? Now I was the one who was being abused – and look at
when he decided to do this to me, when I'm so physically and
mentally vulnerable. What kind of a man would do such a
thing to his wife? A selfish bastard, that's who. I could easily
get away with it and make him feel sorry for me. He would
apologize until I was sick of it.

The thing was, however, I wanted to be the one to reveal
my affair – not have him unravel it and reveal it to me first.
When and if he reveals it before I do, I'm at a big disadvan-
tage, I thought. I'm put on the defensive immediately. He
becomes the accuser and the victim, and I become the suspect,
the villain. That's a distortion. I'm the victim here, not him.
I was the one who was suffering. I was the one who had found
a solution and an escape, a way to heal.

I was sure this was the advice Lancaster would give me.
''Fess up,' he would say. 'Put all your cards on the table. You
can't stand dishonesty anyway and it's eating at you. Don't
worry about him. Eventually, he'll just change the channel.'

I really wanted to do that, but Ronnie was the one spilling
his guts now. He looked as if he couldn't stop regurgitating
the truth as if he had stepped into the ultimate confessional
and would keep the priest there for hours, maybe even until
he had to retire from the clergy.

'I want you to understand and appreciate that what I did, I
did for Kelly as much as for me,' he said.

'What are you talking about? What did you do?'

The nurse stopped in again to tell me that I had been
approved for a solid diet.

'I can have some toast with jam brought to you right now
if you like.'

'Please do,' I said.

She looked at Ronnie and then at me and then looked at the monitor.

'It might be a good idea for us to let her take a little rest right now, Mr Howard. Her blood pressure is up. We don't want to have to give her any more medication. The doctor would be upset if I didn't see to it that she takes a bit of a rest. Just a simple thing like moving her from ICU to here could make her tired in her condition.'

'Sure,' Ronnie said, standing. 'I gotta get back to work anyway. I'll come by with a sandwich or something for myself and have dinner with you.'

'We serve dinner early here,' the nurse said. 'About five o'clock.'

'No problem. I'll be here,' he told her. He approached me and gave me a soft, brotherly kiss on the cheek and then headed out.

'Sorry,' the nurse said.

'No problem. You're right. I am tired. I'll take a rest after my toast, but if a gentleman stops in to see me later, please let him.'

She nodded. 'Let's take it a step at a time,' she said.

I leaned back. I had no worries about her turning him away. Lancaster could get past the Secret Service if he wanted to see me. Even after I had my toast and jam, I tried desperately to stay awake just in case he did come. He wouldn't wake me, and I might not be able to see him until much later tonight or tomorrow. I was desperate to talk to him now. Nevertheless, the nurse had been right. I was very tired and I did fall asleep. I slept until nearly five, and when I opened my eyes, Kelly and Ronnie were sitting there.

'Hey, Mom,' Kelly said. She rose quickly to kiss me. Ronnie held up a paper bag.

'Turkey on rye,' he said. 'As soon as they bring in your tray, I'll take it out.'

'How do you feel?' Kelly asked.

'Like I could soak in a bathtub for days and still not feel any cleaner,' I replied.

'Nothing's changed. No one takes as many baths as your mother,' Ronnie told her.

She nodded.

'All my friends heard about your accident,' she said. 'It was in the paper, too, you know. Everyone wishes you get well quickly.'

'Pass on my thanks,' I said.

'Don't worry about the house or anything,' she continued. 'We're not messing up the kitchen. Dad's called Marta anyway.'

'Oh?'

'No matter what, you couldn't do any housework for quite a while,' he said. 'She'll be in tomorrow.'

'Almost as easy as replacing a flat tire,' I muttered.

'What?' Kelly asked.

'Nothing.'

They brought my dinner. Ironically, it was a slice of turkey, mashed potatoes and vegetables, with a small piece of chocolate cake. They gave me some ginger ale and a cup of coffee that was sure to be cold by the time I had gotten to it.

'Looks all right,' Ronnie said, smiling, 'but this is better.'

He put my sandwich on the tray. They both sat back to watch me eat.

'What are you two going to do for dinner?'

'Pizza,' Kelly said. 'At Dante's.'

'How could I guess that?' I said. 'You'd be half your weight if it wasn't for the invention of pizza.'

'Your memory isn't so bad,' Kelly quipped and looked at Ronnie as if she had spoken out of turn. I had the feeling he had told her something, but not everything. He was just staring at me now. I don't think I was paranoid, seeing accusations in those eyes. I had the sense that he didn't accept that I had forgotten anything.

Kelly did most of the talking during the remainder of the time they visited me. It was easy to see that she was very nervous and uncomfortable about being in a hospital and seeing me banged up and bandaged. Her face registered gratitude when I insisted they go have their dinner so that Kelly could get to her homework. And her text messages, I added.

She laughed, agreed, hugged me and then moved quickly to the door. Ronnie lingered.

'Maybe I'll stop by later,' he suggested. 'To say goodnight.'

'I'm OK.'

'Maybe I'm not,' he replied. He kissed me and joined Kelly.

I lay back, hating myself for still being so tired. The nurse's aide came in for my tray and muttered something or other about the remnants of my turkey sandwich. I think she was jealous. My nurse stopped in to give me some medication, check my pressure and temperature, and then asked me if I wanted the television on. She pointed out the remote, but I said I was fine.

Afterward, I lay there battling sleep again and keeping my eyes on my door. I know I drifted off for a while, but when I opened them this time, Lancaster was standing beside my bed. He had taken my hand into his and put his right hand over it.

He pulled the chair closer to the bed and held on to my hand.

'I figured something had happened to you,' he began. 'I waited for nearly an hour at the motel that day, calling you every fifteen or so minutes. Finally, I drove toward your house and saw your car being loaded on to a truck. I rushed over to the hospital. The emergency room was quite busy – chaotic, in fact – but I was able to find out about you.'

'You were in the ICU, weren't you?'

'A few times, but you were either asleep or otherwise occupied. And when I did find you somewhat awake and began talking to you, you drifted off.'

'I knew you were at my bedside.'

'It's not exactly high-security, even though they make it out to be. If you look like you know what you're doing, most people don't question you. You look as if something more than this,' he said, pointing to the monitor, 'is bothering you.'

'I have the strong feeling that Ronnie has found out about us,' I said. He nodded. 'In fact, I think he's been checking on me for some time.'

'Bound to have happened sooner or later.'

'I'm going to tell him the truth. You would have given me that advice anyway, wouldn't you?'

'At this stage, yes,' he said.

'I think he's coming back here tonight. I'll tell him if he does.'

'OK, if you feel up to it.'

'I do.'

'I'll check with you in the morning, and if you did tell him, I'll stop by less surreptitiously. What do they say – "The cat's out of the bag"?'

'Some cat.'

'What about your daughter?'

'She'll have more to text her friends. Many of them have divorced parents, too. It's like an epidemic.'

He smiled.

'Don't underestimate the effect it will have on her, despite how aloof she seems.'

'She'll be all right,' I insisted. I didn't like disagreeing with him, even slightly, and I was determined not to feel bad, even though that made me seem and sound selfish. Disagreeing with him made me feel as if I was wrestling with myself too much, and the tension that resulted from that brought more agony than this stupid accident.

He must have seen that in my face.

'All right. Concentrate more on getting better. When you're on your feet again, we'll talk about the future.'

'The immediate future, you mean. You don't talk about the future.'

'That's all the future there is really – immediate. But, as the Chinese say, a trip of a thousand miles begins with one step.'

'My worldly prophet.'

'My audience,' he said. He leaned in and kissed me the way a woman should be kissed, injured or not, and then he left gracefully, smiling in the doorway in such a way as to leave the image on my eyes for minutes afterward. Contented, I closed them and drifted off.

When you've been injured as I was, your sleep is short but deep. Every time you wake up, you think it's another day, but in actuality only ten or fifteen minutes might have gone by. I know the nurse had been in and out. The lights were dimmed in the hallway and then, just before ten, Ronnie returned as he had promised he would. I was more awake than I had expected to be. I had even turned on the television but kept the sound so low that it was more like silent movies.

I can do this, I thought. *I'm glad he came.*

'Hey,' he said. He gave me the obligatory husband kiss and pulled up the chair Lancaster had sat in. 'Everything's good with Kelly. I made sure she had a salad. She ate one of those everything pizzas. Never saw her so hungry. I think she skipped lunch or something. Teenagers. How are you doing?'

'Better,' I said.

'Good. I have an important meeting first thing in the morning tomorrow, so I won't be here until lunch. Your dad and my parents are coming to see you in the morning anyway, and I'm talking to your doctors all the time. As far as you're forgetting things . . . there's this doctor who I think can help.'

'I don't have memory issues, Ronnie,' I said quickly. 'I can remember everything I need to remember.'

'Oh. Even the day of the accident?'

'Yes. I'm sorry it has happened this way. It was my fault. I was speeding and not thinking about the rain or traffic lights enough.'

He sat back, his arms folded across his chest, looking like the dean or principal of some high school – at least the dean of the school I had attended, who took that posture whenever a student was trying to explain or defend his or her having done something against the rules.

'Why?' he asked.

'I was eager to see someone, someone I've been seeing for some time.'

'Seeing?'

'Romantically,' I said. He almost didn't blink; he didn't change expression.

'Tell me about it.'

'It just happened one night. We met in the supermarket and . . .'

'Fell in love at first sight?'

'Something like that. We began to see each other regularly.'

'Where?'

'We met at a motel. The Sky Top. It's off the freeway going south-east toward Los Angeles.'

'Yes, I know it. And this whole thing about having to be alone, needing time to meditate, think – that was all really to see this guy?'

'Yes.'

'Even when you went up to Idyllwild and stayed at the cabin. You stayed there with him?'

'Yes,' I said.

He looked away and then turned back to me, his expression unchanged.

'Who is he? What's he like? Is he from here?'

'No, he's not from here. He was just passing through.'

'What's his name?'

'What difference does it make? I'm not going to introduce you to him.'

'Yeah, I guess not. So how did you two stay in touch, make your dates?'

'He called me on my cell phone. When we met, we planned other dates, times. What difference does that make?'

'Did this happen because of something I did or said?'

'No, nothing specific. If I had to give an answer, it's everything.'

'Everything?'

'Everything about my life, Ronnie. Being with him makes me feel better about myself. I'm sorry. That's how it is.'

He nodded.

'You never told Kelly about any of this, did you?'

'Of course not.'

'And what do you plan to do now?'

'When I'm able to, I'm going away with him.'

'Anywhere in particular?'

'Why? Are you going to follow us?'

He shook his head. 'No, I just wanted to see how far along your plans were. So you were going to do this before the accident?'

'I was on my way to tell him, yes.'

'He must be quite a guy. I know how particular you are when it comes to people, especially men. Is he a doctor, a lawyer, what?'

'None of that matters, Ronnie. I'm not a gold-digger.'

'And you want me to just do what . . . accept it?'

'It would be best for both of us, for all of us, if we just act civilized about it.'

He thought a moment and, with a surprising lack of anger or outrage, nodded. Lancaster is right about him, I thought. He'll just change the channel.

'OK. I'll agree to all that if you'll agree to one thing,' he said.

'Which is?'

'Like I said, there's a doctor I want you to talk to tomorrow. He'll be here in the afternoon, just after you have your lunch.'

'What doctor?'

'His name is Pearson, Elliot Pearson. He comes highly recommended. He's been practicing for over thirty years. It took pulling some strings to get him on such short notice.'

I pushed myself up farther in the bed.

'What kind of a doctor is he? I have a neurologist. The doctors here are very good. I'm doing well. I don't have any serious injury, anything life-threatening. Are you telling me something else is going on? What? They found evidence of cancer somewhere? What?'

He put up his hands. 'Nothing like that,' he said. 'You're going to be just fine . . . physically.'

'Physically. He's a psychiatrist – is that it? Well?'

'Yes, he is.'

'I have no reason to see a psychiatrist, Ronnie. I just explained my accident to you. I was not attempting some vehicular suicide or anything.'

'Then there's nothing to worry about,' he said. 'He'll see you, talk to you a while and leave. And that will be that. You'll be on your way to do whatever it is you want to do. That's the deal.'

He sat back. *He's conniving*, I thought. *This is blackmail and vengeance all wrapped together. Ronnie has too big an ego to just accept this. How convenient this reason for our separation would be. I didn't walk out on him. Oh no. I'm suffering a psychological illness. He'll be the one to get all the sympathy. He could even be unfaithful and everyone would understand.*

'How much are you paying this psychiatrist, Ronnie?'

'It's all under our insurance policy. You know we have a gold-plated policy. I'd be some idiot to be in the insurance business and not have that for us.'

'I meant under the table. What do you plan on doing now? Have me committed?'

'You'll see that he's one of the most respected psychiatrists in this state. There's no way to corrupt such a man. What would I gain from that anyway?'

I smiled and nodded. 'You knew about my affair for some time, didn't you, Ronnie? That's why you knew about my not seeing Flora Anthony. You've been tracking me and my actions.'

'Let's not get into accusing each other of things right now, Clea. If you want me to accept what you want, then do the one thing I want for you.'

'It won't work, Ronnie. It won't stop me.'

'Then no harm's been done to your plans and wishes.' He looked at his watch. 'It's getting late. They'll come by to throw me out of here any minute, probably.'

'Maybe they didn't see you come in.'

'You might be right. I could kidnap you,' he joked. I thought that was a weird thing to say. Maybe not so weird. Maybe that was his intention, to have me kidnapped and taken to some psychiatric clinic.

He paused by my bed and looked at me.

'I'm not perfect by any means,' he said. 'Sometimes, I annoy myself. I'm the first to admit I've been oblivious to things I shouldn't have been oblivious to, and I'm probably as selfish and – what's your favorite word? – vapid. Vapid about a lot of things I shouldn't be. I get caught up in stuff, act stupid, immature, all of the man-boy stuff, but I've always had one goal since we got married and that was to make you happy, and after Kelly came, to keep us all safe. I don't think I've done badly at keeping us safe, but I've obviously done badly at keeping you happy. I'm sorry for that, and I'm not going to stand here and make all sorts of promises, take all sorts of oaths to be different. I am what I am. Sometime ago, you saw enough of what you liked in me to want to spend the rest of your life with me. I certainly saw everything I wanted in you.

'So maybe we lost it and it's gone, and if that's true and it can't be restored, retrieved, whatever, then I've got to learn to live with it. We all do, I guess. It doesn't matter if I say I'm sorry now, even though I am.

'What I want you to know as I leave tonight is that I'm going to sleep thinking about you, Clea. I'm going to reach for you in the bed and I'm going to feel my heart turn to stone when I realize you're not there.

'Goodnight,' he said. This time he kissed me on the lips, pulled back with his eyes closed, turned and walked out.

I wanted to cry, but I didn't. I swallowed back the urge and lay back and watched the doorway, waiting for Lancaster.

But he didn't come.

FIFTEEN

I fell asleep and slept through the night. I was very hungry in the morning and ate a full breakfast. Devoured it was more like it. My doctors arrived soon after. Neither stayed long. Both were very happy with my progress and even ventured a guesstimate about when I would leave. It was possible I would be discharged in two or three days.

I started thinking about my last conversation with Ronnie, and before my father and Ronnie's parents arrived, I called Carlton Saunders. Jackie told me he was on the phone with a client, but I guess as soon as he learned I was calling him, he got off because he picked up while she was still talking to me, telling me how shocked and upset she was when she learned about my accident.

'I've got it, Jackie, thanks,' he said. 'Clea, how are you? Thank God you're all right. I heard it was a horrendous accident.'

'They're putting my picture next to the word "lucky" in the dictionary,' I said, and he laughed. 'I have a question to ask in confidence.'

'Oh? Sure. Shoot.'

'Under what circumstances could a husband have a wife committed, or even vice versa for that matter?'

'Committed? To a psychiatric ward or hospital?'

'Yes.'

'Either would have to appeal to a judge first to establish the wife or husband was in danger of harming herself or himself and/or others, and then the individual would be what we call involuntarily committed and evaluated by a psychiatrist. There are many famous cases. Don't forget Fanny Farmer's mother had her committed. I just saw that film on the old movie channel. Any particular reason you're asking?'

'Not yet,' I said. I knew that was still quite cryptic and would only increase his curiosity.

'Well, what's the prognosis on your condition? When can I hope to chain you to a desk here again?' he asked, which I thought was a clever way to dig out the truth.

'I'm not sure,' I said. 'I'm not sure about too much right now.'

'Well, that's quite understandable.'

'I'll get back to you.'

'Anytime, Clea. Speedy recovery. And don't hesitate to call me . . . for anything,' he added. We both knew what he meant. It helped me to hear it.

'Thanks,' I said.

Not long after my call, Ronnie's parents and my father arrived. Of course, I wondered whether or not Ronnie had said something to them about us. It was difficult to tell. My accident and how I looked right now was enough in itself to dress them in funeral faces. Ronnie's mother was as upset at the sight of me as my mother would have been, but his father looked as if he might be the first one to break down in tears. My dad looked more disturbed than any of them, however, which surprised me. As we had just witnessed after my mother's death, he could control his emotions to the point where someone might wonder if he even had any. Right now, however, I could see he was fighting back tears himself. His lips quivered after he kissed me. He sat close enough to keep holding on to my hand.

'I can't even begin to imagine what kind of a blow it would have been to have lost both of you in so short a period of time,' he said.

For the first time during all this, I considered him and his feelings. As busy as he was when I was growing up, he still tried to be more of a father from time to time. Because of how distant he could be, I used to believe I was an accident, but not in the sense that my mother had become pregnant with me before they were married and therefore rushed or caused them to marry. It was more like he had never had the intention of having children. There were marriages like that. Each one realized and admitted they were too selfish to spare any of the energy they wanted to spend on themselves and spend it on a child instead. Maybe the wife didn't want to give up her drive to be famous or successful, and the husband didn't insist on it. They probably imagined they were always on a honeymoon that way or something, and whenever they witnessed the problems that their married friends had with their children, they went home congratulating themselves on not having any.

I guess I was wrong to think of my father along those lines. Was it his failing or mine that I really didn't know him? If you were brought up by them, how can you not know your parents well enough? On the other hand, I would be the first to say that Kelly didn't really know me. Just as I wondered about it in relation to my father, I had to question whether it was her fault or mine, or maybe both our faults.

'I'm going to be all right,' I said. 'According to the neurologist, I've already made significant progress.' Suddenly, it was more important to comfort him than for him to comfort me.

He looked at Ronnie's parents.

'She's going to be all right,' he said, as if I had just said one of the dumbest things ever. 'The agony of having children comes when you realize at some point that you can't always be there to protect them and that by giving birth to them, creating them, you have placed them in the path of indifferent Nature,' he said.

Both of Ronnie's parents widened their eyes with surprise.

'Well, that's a helluva thing to say,' Ronnie's father said, scratching his head.

'I don't even know what that means,' his mother added.

I smiled.

'I do,' I said. 'My father has always told me I was going to make him too old too fast.'

'Yeah, well, he still hits a pretty good drive on the first hole,' Ronnie's father said. Then he laughed and added, 'But maybe not on the ninth.'

'He's already got the epitaph for my monument,' my father followed, nodding at Ronnie's father. He wrote it in the air: 'Here lies Jack Remington. He finally got his hole in one.'

The two men laughed. Ronnie's mother shook her head. She had been dabbing her eyes the whole time, and mumbling things like, 'Thank God your mother didn't have to go through this.' To her, I guess, death was my mother's lucky break. I decided that maybe Ronnie is a lot more like his mother than his father after all.

When my father asked me what I remembered from the accident, I thought Ronnie had spoken to him for sure, but he and Ronnie's father went right into a discussion about the traffic lights in the desert and how, more often than not, the older drivers go through red lights. They talked about senior citizens as if they weren't members of that club.

'You've got to count to three after the light turns green for you,' Ronnie's father said, and my father agreed. Hadn't Ronnie made it clear that it was my fault? Was he protecting me or was he too embarrassed about it? I didn't feel like correcting them for fear they would start asking about the sort of details I really couldn't recall.

After another twenty minutes or so, the nurse came in to change some bandages, and they decided they'd go for lunch and return to the desert community where they lived behind walls and gates and let the outside world in only when they turned on their television sets. Retirement did mean retreat in one way or another, but I supposed retreat wasn't always bad. The alternative was more often not good. Right now, the only frustrations they suffered came from a bad game of golf. After all, what were retirement home developments if not a desperate attempt to return to Eden? Keep out the snakes and ignore the tree of knowledge. There were all those cherished answers designed to protect their indifference to world events now, questions like 'What difference can I make?' or 'They're all alike – why vote?'

Who was I to blame them? Wasn't I looking for and hoping for my own escape?

Before leaving, my father hugged me and kissed me more affectionately than he had at my mother's funeral.

I had to laugh about it.

'I guess I'll get into a car accident once a week.'

He had to laugh, too.

'Take care of yourself, Clea. Don't fight City Hall,' he added. Another retirement community expression, I thought. We said goodbye.

I was sad for a few moments afterward. I had thought more

about my mother in the last few minutes than I had for hours after her death. I couldn't help but wish I could pick up the phone and call her, and tell her all that was happening so I could get her words of comfort and advice. Why did death have to be so final? Why couldn't you at least make a long-distance call?

Ronnie called to tell me he would be here late afternoon when he would bring Kelly. He had something he had to do at a business lunch. It had just come up. He was very matter-of-fact and surprisingly didn't even ask me how the visit with his parents and my father went. He seemed to be in a hurry, under some pressure at the office. The truth was I never really took much interest in Ronnie's work. He brought home stories, but I only half listened and nodded when I knew I should, shook my head when that was required, and laughed when it looked as if he was hoping I would.

Maybe that was wrong.

I didn't fall into a long sleep again. I dozed on and off a little, but I was more aware of the time than I had been. A little before two o'clock, a man with curly graying brown hair knocked on my opened door and stepped into my room. He was easily six feet tall, svelte and quite impressive-looking in his three-piece light blue suit and silver tie. I liked his crystal navy blue cufflinks. He had gleefully happy eyes the color of fresh string beans, and a firm mouth with a cleft chin.

'Mrs Howard?' he said.

I lifted my left hand to show him my wrist band that had my name imprinted on it. He laughed.

'Of course, I could be impersonating her,' I said.

'Would you like to?'

'You're Doctor Pearson,' I said, or more like accused. I did have my left forefinger pointing at him.

'I don't have a wrist band, but I have a driver's license, if you want to see it.'

'No need. Your question was right out of Introduction to Psychology.'

He smiled and sat. He held a clipboard with a number of papers on it.

'Well, is it all right with you if we talk?'

'I was under the impression I had little choice.'

'No, no, no. Nothing like that,' he said. He glanced at the monitors and me. 'Looks like you've had quite an accident.'

'Surely he showed you the picture of my car to set the stage for you to believe I tried to kill myself?'

'Actually, no, but I bet it looks scary.'

'Let's cut right to the chase, Doctor Pearson. I admit I've been very unhappy lately. I might even be diagnosed as clinically depressed or something, but I've had no problem conducting myself well. I even did some part-time work for an attorney recently. He's trying to get me to come back to work, in fact.'

'That's good. Are you planning to do that?'

'No. Busy work is not going to be a substitute for what I need.'

'And what is it you think you need?'

'Rebirth,' I said dryly. 'I have given my husband and my daughter all the attention they needed up until now. They can be vampires, you know.'

He smiled. Perfect teeth, I thought, like Lancaster's.

'How so?'

'They drain you of ambition for yourself, excitement for yourself. They're too demanding. Despite all this quasi equating of the sexes we're experiencing, a mother sacrifices way more than a father, even if she's married to Mr Mom or something. There's more to it than changing diapers, taking baby for a stroll and cleaning up the house. That umbilical cord doesn't disappear so fast.'

'Wouldn't disagree with that when it comes to children. I have two boys and a girl, and my wife does tons more with them and for them than I do. What about your husband, though? What makes him Dracula?'

'Unless you married a nerd, there's an ego to constantly stroke. Men, like boys, have to be constantly praised. It's draining.'

'No mutual stroking?'

'Depends on the husband's ego, and there's all that expectation on the wife's shoulders. When we say, "I do," it's at least a seventy–thirty deal in the man's favor. Society, no matter what you read and see, expects it. Your own kids expect it.'

'And this is the way it's been for you?'

'I'm no different from every other wife and mother who signs the marriage certificate in blood.'

'Blood . . . You are fixated on vampires,' he said, smiling. Then he grew serious. 'Sounds as if you need – or your husband needs – marriage counseling.'

'It's too late.'

'Why?'

'Because . . . because I've found someone else. That's what I mean by being reborn. He sees like I do; he hears like I do; he feels, smells, tastes and thinks like I do. There's all that and there's the excitement. Despite how I look right now, I haven't felt this alive for a long time, maybe ever,' I said.

'I see. Sounds like your dream-come-true type of thing.'

'Exactly. In fact, I couldn't have dreamed it to be any better,' I said.

Perhaps if he saw and heard my determination, he would get up, apologize for stopping by and leave.

'Tell me something about him.'

'Why?'

'You can't blame me for being curious about a man who achieves so much for you.'

'He's extraordinarily good-looking, very clever and witty, has a terrific sense of humor, dresses to kill, and makes love with the affection and romance of a Cary Grant/George Clooney clone and the passion and hunger of a serial rapist,' I replied. 'Every woman's fantasy, by the way.'

He laughed. 'Well, I've never heard it put quite that way. What does he do?'

'He's independently wealthy, but he has the skill set of a lawyer, a doctor, a psychiatrist and an astronaut. There's a bit of the philosopher in him as well. In other words, I'm never bored for a moment with him.'

'You're right. He sounds like everything you could possibly dream of and more.'

'Exactly. So the very idea that I would prefer to kill myself is, as you can see, absurd.'

'I agree. I don't think you're suicidal at all.'

'Oh.' I smiled. I had convinced him so quickly. 'Well, Ronnie might not like hearing that.'

'Where did you meet this incredible man?'

'It was a chance meeting in a supermarket. And before you say it, yes, just like in a movie – electric, immediate mutual attraction, love at first sight.'

'It's nice to believe in it. And you've been seeing him often lately?'

'Very often. Every chance I had.'

He nodded, sat back, glanced at his clipboard and then looked at me.

'Almost sounds like you've invented him.'

'Invented? What the hell does that mean?'

'It's not unusual. When we're children, we often invent friends.'

'I'm not a child.'

'It's possible you wanted him so much, you created him,' he said.

'Created him? Oh . . . I see. This is a new approach. Ronnie put you up to this one, too? You can't show I'm suicidal, but maybe just a little schizophrenic?'

'Your husband's not putting me up to anything, Mrs Howard. He's concerned about you.'

'Are you sure he's not simply concerned about himself?'

'He's unhappy, if that's what you mean, but he's more concerned about you and your happiness.'

'He convinced you, huh? That's my Ronnie. He's a salesman of sorts, you see. He's always selling, even when he's not at work. How did he sell you? Or am I more correct in asking, how did he *buy* you?'

'I'm afraid it wasn't that devious. Nothing underhanded. He's presented me with some information and asked that I be the one to present it to you and then come to a conclusion, hopefully with you eventually reaching the same conclusion. Not immediately, of course, but over time. How much time will be mostly up to you.'

'What information?'

'Let's begin with where you met this man. Does he have a name, by the way?'

'His name is Lancaster.'

'What's his full name?'

I stared at him, then looked away.

I turned back to him. 'That's all I needed to know.'

'Not interested in his family?'

'We're interested in each other, period.'

'I see. Did he always live here?'

'I didn't say he lives here now. He's passing through.'

'Where did he come from? Where is he headed?'

'That's not important. What's important is that he is here now and he wants to be with me.'

'You were never curious?'

'I said it wasn't important.'

'OK. So where did you and Lancaster have your first rendez-vous after meeting at the supermarket?'

'I told Ronnie. I'm surprised he didn't tell you that first. The Sky Top Motel.'

'Oh, he told me. I wanted to confirm it. This was where you paid cash for a room reserved for a month?'

'I didn't pay for the room. Well, I did in the beginning because I went there to be by myself.'

'Room twenty-one,' he said, nodding, and pulled a sheet of paper from his clipboard. 'Reserved for a month, full payment, copy of the receipt,' he added and gave it to me. 'Signed by the manager, a Tom Arthur. He remembers you well. You paid him in cash and it was obviously quite a unique request.'

'So I forgot. Yes, yes, I paid for the room, but Lancaster had his own key and . . .'

I looked at the note on the bottom of the receipt and, for a moment, lost my train of thought. It read, *Have a fresh rose on the right pillow bed facing the wall whenever the room is made up.*

'You all right?' Dr Pearson asked.

'Yes, I'm all right. This is nothing,' I said, practically throwing it back at him.

'We'll talk about it, about why you went there in particular, why that specific room number.'

'Lancaster knew the place.'

'Another coincidence?'

'Call it serendipity. I do.'

'Yes,' he said. He held his smile, but it was different now. It was more inquisitive, more professional. 'What about asking specifically for room twenty-one? Anything special about that number for you?'

I could feel my eyes blinking rapidly.

'You and your husband had a good experience in a motel room twenty-one, perhaps?'

'No. It was when I was younger. I guess it just stayed in my head. Don't make it into a Freudian thing.'

'I promise,' he said, smiling again, 'I won't. Now, as I understand, you took a two-day holiday in Idyllwild recently, about the time your mother became seriously ill.'

'I'm not surprised he told you that. Ronnie loves bringing up my being unavailable.'

'And you stayed at Lester's Cabin Retreat?'

'So? Does that have to have some special significance, too?'

'You told your husband it was a place you both thought might be nice.'

'So? Yes, I was there.'

'By yourself?'

'No. Lancaster was with me.'

'Mrs Lester, the owner and manager, says you were by yourself.'

'She's a piece of work,' I said. 'He wasn't with me when I went into her office to rent the cabin, and I didn't think it was any of her business who I was with.'

'Apparently, she keeps pretty good tabs on the comings and goings at her place – a bit of a busybody, don't you think?'

'I didn't give her much thought.'

'I had an opportunity to speak with her.' He smiled in the way he had smiled at the beginning. 'She even got a little peeved at me when I repeated my question concerning anyone else being with you. As if I was accusing her of being a bad owner of the property or something.'

'Doesn't surprise me to hear that a psychiatrist sees paranoia everywhere,' I quipped. 'You probably use it like a flashlight.' He didn't laugh at that. 'Look. I met her for only a short while, but I wouldn't consider her a very reliable witness to anything.'

'Could be you're right. You went on hikes?'

'That's right.'

'And do you remember an African American man who worked there?'

'So?'

'His name is Henry Rice. He remembers you, of course. He also says you were alone at the cabin, and he says he was a little concerned about you going on the hikes alone. He claims you came upon him while he was cutting firewood and told him there was someone walking behind you. He watched for him, but no one appeared, and there was never anyone with you, even though you seemed to behave as if there was.'

'I don't know what he's talking about. I saw him briefly – twice maybe.'

'He claims he did see you move into the cabin . . . alone.'

'He wasn't paying attention. I remember now. He was painting something the first time I saw him.'

'You left a lot of food when you checked out, according to Mrs Lester.'

'She can consider it a tip,' I said.

He smiled.

'You're right. I had the feeling that whatever you left still in its packaging, she would keep. She said you used only as many towels and things as a single person would. She strikes me as the type that would count, don't you think?'

'She struck me as being a lonely, bitter old woman, nothing more.'

'OK. So, you told your husband that Lancaster's way of contacting you most of the time was to call you on your cell phone?'

'That was the number I gave him, yes. Obviously, I didn't want him calling my home.'

'Was he ever there?'

'I think this is getting too personal now,' I replied.

He pulled out another sheet of paper. It was a cell phone bill.

'As you can see,' he said, 'no calls were made or received on your phone for nearly a month, and very few before that. Your phone was retrieved with your things in the car. Your husband said the battery was still uncharged.'

'So I forgot. Most women forget to charge their batteries. Just take a poll. Big deal.'

'Apparently, you haven't charged it for some time. Just yesterday, he located the charger behind the dresser, on the floor in your bedroom.'

'It probably just fell there recently. I was in a rush and didn't notice whether the phone was charged or not.'

'What about that?' He nodded at the bill in my hand.

'It must be counterfeit or something, especially if Ronnie gave it to you.'

'Easy enough to get a copy directly from the phone company to confirm it one way or the other,' he said.

I gave him back the bill. My hand was shaking a little.

'You're a pretty intelligent woman, Mrs Howard. I'm sure you can help me help you. What's happened to you isn't as unusual as it might first seem.'

'Nothing's happened to me. I know what you're doing. I told you as soon as I realized it. You're calling me a schizophrenic,' I said.

'Let's avoid labels for now.'

'I'd like to avoid it all. I'm getting tired,' I said. 'I don't want to talk anymore.'

'Of course. I have a suggestion.'

'What?'

'When you're discharged from the hospital, you continue your recuperation at my facility. You're going to get top care. I can assure you of that.'

'What facility?'

'It's in a beautiful location – rustic, not that far. Your family can visit easily. However, I don't see you staying there very long. I'm confident you'll be well soon.'

'You're not just making a suggestion. You're making a diagnosis. Ronnie won't get away with this and neither will you. I've already contacted my attorney,' I warned.

He stood up.

'It's always better if you give it a chance because you want to, of course.'

'Forget about it. And tell Ronnie not to bother visiting me. I'll be by when I'm discharged to pick up the things I want.'

'Arrangements you'll make with Lancaster?'

'Exactly.'

'Well, let's leave it like that for the time being. I've enjoyed talking to you, by the way.'

'The feeling isn't mutual,' I said, and he laughed.

'Get some rest,' he advised.

I watched him leave and then I closed my eyes. I didn't want to think. Remember your *Hamlet*, I told myself: '*Nothing either good or bad, but thinking makes it so.*' That brought a smile to my face and a soft repose until I sensed he was there. It felt as if he had been there the whole time, watching over me, especially when Dr Pearson was questioning me. I sat up.

'I wish you were here sooner. Ronnie sent this psychiatrist.'

'I saw him. Nice-looking man. I bet some women feign insanity to get into his clinic.'

'It's not funny. Don't you see what they're doing?'

'Yes. I'll give you some advice. Don't fight them.'

'What?'

'Fighting them only validates them. Go along with them. Be cooperative. After a while, they'll see they can't change things and we'll be fine.'

'I wish I had your confidence.'

'You will,' he said. 'For now, I think it's better if I stay in the background a bit.'

'Not too far in the background and not too much of a bit,' I replied.

He smiled, rose, took my hand and said, 'I'll always be with you, Clea.'

He kissed me the way I wanted him to kiss me and then softly started out. He paused in the doorway to cast that smile into my eyes, where it would stay forever.

I settled back, contented and, despite all that had occurred, remarkably unafraid.

Kelly appeared.

She stood in the doorway as if she was uncertain she had come to the right room.

'You saw him leave?' I asked.

'Who?'

'Never mind. Where's your father?'

She came in and stood by the bed.

'He said it would be better if I came without him today.'

'Did he? So what else did he say?'

'He says you're not well, and he doesn't mean because of the accident.'

'Your father's good at convincing people of things. He should work for the State Department.'

'Did you tell him you were in love with someone else?' she asked, her eyes glassy with threatening tears. I didn't answer. 'And that you want to leave him – leave me, too?'

'Sometimes, we can't help what happens to us, Kelly. Someday, you'll understand.'

'But this man you're in love with . . . you're making him up.'

'That's what he wants to believe and wants you to believe, and why he sent that hired psychological gun here.'

'I don't want you to leave us, Mom. I'm sorry if you think I do. I know I don't spend enough time with you, but I want to. I really do. And I like talking to you very much. I don't want you to leave,' she emphasized.

'I won't leave forever,' I said. I looked away. When I heard her voice now, I didn't hear the voice of a sixteen-year-old. She sounded more like she had been when she was seven or eight, her voice smaller, more fragile. I could hear the fear and the need for reassurance.

'You're not a child anymore,' I said, more to convince myself than her.

'Maybe, but I'm not someone who doesn't want her mother around,' she said. I looked at her. Without her earphones and her distractions, she did look younger, more innocent. 'I don't have anyone else. You're supposed to be my sister, too,' she said.

She had never said anything like that, at least anything I could remember.

'I know you haven't been happy, Mom. I ignored it. I didn't know what to do, so I pretended you were just being you. It's my fault, too. I should have cared more. I'm sorry.'

'Stop it, Kelly.'

'I'm sorry,' she said and hugged me. She held me so tight I couldn't turn away if I wanted to, but I didn't want to. What I wanted to do finally was just cry.

Which was what I did.

What we did together.

EPILOGUE

D r Pearson's psychiatric retreat consisted of three Spanish-style structures with that familiar light tangerine stucco exterior. They were connected with Spanish-tiled walkways. As he had promised, the retreat did have beautiful grounds, set on a little over twenty acres, with great care taken in the design of the landscaping. There were hedge-bordered pathways that wove around ponds and fountains, flowers and an assortment of trees, including olive and jacaranda. Along the way there were dark-stained wooden benches evenly spaced.

The day I was brought there, I saw about a half-dozen gardeners at work and what looked like three residents enjoying the property. I never really knew exactly how many other clients, as he insisted on calling them, were being treated. Some refused to come out of their rooms.

Because of the fracture of the tibia in my right leg, I walked with a crutch or moved about in a wheelchair. Ronnie and Kelly brought me two suitcases of clothes and shoes, as well as my travel bag of makeup and toiletries. I had to say that Pearson's facility was quite comfortable. There was even a beautician to wash and cut and style your hair, if you wanted. There were six rotating nurses and at least ten aides, as well as two other psychiatrists and three interns.

I don't know whether it was his psychiatric technique or what, but the first day I arrived, he stopped by to see if I was comfortable and didn't talk about anything remotely associated with what he would eventually politely refer to as my *condition*. Instead, he talked about the facility, how he had come to buy the property, and how it had been one of his dreams to have a state-of-the-art facility – 'a place where people found their own way to stable mental health.'

'I'm one of those who believes in the healing power of nature,' he added.

All the rooms for clients, as far as I could tell, were designed to look like bedrooms in some house, rather than some facility. The furniture was upscale and warm, some rustic, some more on the modern side. Paintings, vases, all seemed well coordinated. I wasn't sure how he knew where to place each of his clients. Mine was contemporary with a sleigh bed. The dark brown finish was accented with a subtle golden-brown brushing. There were upholstered faux-leather panels adjoining the bed and mirror. I asked him about it and he revealed his wife was an interior decorator and responsible for everything at the clinic.

He asked about the work I had done on our house, and then he went on to talk about his coming from the East Coast and the differences in furniture styles, as well as lifestyles. Our conversation was so casual that I did feel myself relaxing and almost congratulated him on the way he had settled me into the situation. He mentioned some medication he was going to prescribe, almost as an afterthought.

It wasn't long after that the nurse, a Mrs Tyler, who looked old enough to be my mother, brought my dosage. She wasn't cold, but she was almost military in her demeanor. There was never an uncrossed T in her life, I thought. For now, I wasn't interested in her friendship anyway.

Moments after she left, I wheeled myself to the window to look out at the front of the property. All was quiet; in fact, it was if I was gazing at a large painting. There was hardly a breeze and for the moment there were no birds flitting about or signs of any life. I wondered if I had somehow put the world on hold.

I sensed he was standing behind me, but I didn't turn around. I thought he might have been there quite a while without speaking. I wondered why I didn't turn around quickly. Was I afraid to look at him now? Did I worry that he would see this as a betrayal? After all, that was really what it was.

'You have nothing to be embarrassed or ashamed about,' he said.

'It's not that. I think I'm a little afraid.'

'Don't be. I'll never be far away.'

'But you'll be away.'

'I told you from the beginning that I wasn't the type to make long-term commitments. You accepted that.'

'I will always wonder when you'll be passing through again.'

'Maybe not always,' he said.

'When will you leave now?'

'I'll leave softly. More like fade away. It started when you took that pill a little while ago. I think you knew that.'

I nodded, my eyes still on the world on pause.

'You told me to cooperate; you told me to come here,' I said.

'It's the easiest way. I hate long goodbyes with the smoke of regret trailing behind them. Neither of us needs to be that dramatic about it anyway.'

'So you think I'll be all right?'

'You'll be fine. Everything will be fine.'

'As it could be?'

'It's always as it could be. Don't look for perfection. Look for—'

'Survival with a touch of pleasure, a touch of happiness?'

'It's all anyone can expect.'

'Even you?'

'Especially me.'

I felt his hand on my shoulder and I closed my eyes. He kissed me lovingly on the top of my head and then grazed my right cheek with his lips. I kept my eyes closed. There was a heaviness around me. It was as if some curtain was slowly being dropped.

I took a deep breath and turned.

He was gone.

For now, maybe forever.

I looked back through the window.

The birds were flying about now, moving from tree limbs to tree limbs. I caught sight of a squirrel sprinting toward a hedge.

Through the entryway gate, I saw my husband and my daughter coming to visit.

Off in the distance, the clouds seemed to part to make way for a commercial jet. People on board were getting excited. They were probably coming home.

What feeling could match that? I thought.